A MISSING PLANE

ALSO BY SUSAN SHEEHAN

Ten Vietnamese

A Welfare Mother

A Prison and a Prisoner

Is There No Place on Earth for Me?

Kate Quinton's Days

A
MISSING
PLANE

Susan Sheehan

G. P. PUTNAM'S SONS / *New York*

G. P. Putnam's Sons
Publishers Since 1838
200 Madison Avenue
New York, NY 10016

Most of this work originally appeared
in slightly different form in *The New Yorker*.
Drawings by Tom Funk on pp. 7, 41, and 111
© 1986 The New Yorker Magazine, Inc.

Typeset by Fisher Composition, Inc.

Library of Congress Cataloging-in-Publication Data

Sheehan, Susan.
    A missing plane.

    1. World War, 1939–1945—Aerial operations, American.
2. World War, 1939–1945—Campaigns—Papua New Guinea.
3. Aeronautics—Accident investigation.   4. World War,
1939–1945—Missing in action—Papua New Guinea.
5. World War, 1939–1945—Missing in action—United
States.   I. Title.
D790.S46   1986   940.54′4973   86-17001
ISBN 0-399-13183-3

ONCE AGAIN
TO
NEIL

PART I

RECOVERY

tom funk

O NE DAY IN 1980, or perhaps it was 1981—the people who live in the villages of Papua New Guinea don't place a great deal of value on the precise measurement of time—two young men from Manumu set out to go bird hunting. Manumu is a village (population 121, elevation 1,700 feet) in a valley in the foothills of the Owen Stanley Range about 30 miles northeast of Port Moresby, the capital of Papua New Guinea. The men left Manumu carrying machetes, which they used to cut vines and small trees as they followed old trails and cleared new ones, gradually making their way up through dense undergrowth, climbing the rain-forested slopes into the mountains. When they reached a ridge leading to an 11,000-foot peak named Mt. Thumb, they came upon part of the wreckage of a large old plane. They didn't disturb the wreckage: the villagers of Papua New Guinea tend to be uninquisitive, and bird hunting was the object of their expedition. After about a week, the young men returned to Manumu with some parrots they had shot. They told a number of their fellow-villagers about the plane they had seen, but the knowledge of the plane and its whereabouts stayed within Manumu for a year or two.

The news might have stayed within the village indefinitely had it not been for the serendipitous combination of a man with an obsession and a small unit of the United States Army with unexpected time on its hands. The man is Bruce Hoy, a trim, bespectacled forty-one-year-old expatriate Australian Second World War enthusiast who in 1978 became the first curator of the Aviation, Maritime, and War Branch of the National Museum and Art Gallery of Papua New Guinea. His obsession is to try to find the approximately three hundred and fifty United States and Australian aircraft that disappeared while on flights in the eastern part of New Guinea between 1942 and 1945, when the island was the scene of extensive fighting between American and Australian forces and those of Imperial Japan. (In 1975, the eastern part of the island became the independent country of Papua New Guinea.)

The Army unit is the Central Identification Laboratory, which is based in Hawaii and is usually referred to as the CIL or CIL-HI. In 1982 it was a small Department of the Army field unit within the Adjutant General's office under the Directorate of Casualty and Memorial Affairs. Its personnel included a civilian physical anthropologist, civilian "identification specialists" (in private life most of them had been morticians, and most of them were alumni of mortuaries that the military had operated in Vietnam during the war years), an Army officer, and a number of Army enlisted men who were known as Fifty-seven Foxtrots, because their Military Occupation Specialty was numbered and lettered 57-F. After basic training, most men designated Fifty-seven Foxtrots went to Graves Registration School, where they were taught how to go into the field to recover casualties, how to recognize the thirty-two teeth and two hundred and six bones of the human body, and how to chart dental and skeletal remains. The CIL's primary mission is the recovery and identification of the remains of approximately 2500 Americans presumed killed during the Vietnam War whose bodies had not been recovered when the war ended in 1975. Because of poor relations between Vietnam and the United States since the war's end, the Vietnamese turned over only a few American remains, so conducting search-and-recovery (S-and-R) operations throughout the Pacific theater to find and identify Second World War dead was added to the CIL mission.

In January 1979 Bruce Hoy had received permission from the director of the National Museum to move out of the museum's main building, in Port Moresby, where he had worked in the busy midst of another department, into a two-story building the museum owned in Gordon, an industrial suburb of Port Moresby. The building had little to recommend it except that it offered Hoy privacy and a fair amount of empty space. After he had helped carry a desk, chair, and filing cabinet up a rickety spiral staircase to the second floor, which became his office, there was nothing else in it. There was little on the building's main floor, which he transformed into a combination library, relics room, and armory; an adjacent storage shed was also empty. Hoy abhors a vacuum. He installed the wreckage of a Second World War P-38 Lightning fighter plane in the yard outside his office, and began acquiring additional airplanes, and also guns, tanks, trucks, jeeps, and other relics associated with the war in New Guinea. Hoy preempts any undiplomatic comments from visitors to his museum branch by telling them it is "a junkyard."

The operating budget of the Aviation, Maritime, and War Branch has always been modest, but in 1979 and 1980 Hoy bought more than four hundred books for his reference library. He loaned the museum his own extensive collection of Second World War photographs acquired from the Australian War Memorial, in Canberra, and added numerous rolls of microfilm from the Albert F. Simpson Historical Research Center, at Maxwell Air Force Base, Alabama, which is the principal repository for United States Air Force records. He also acquired two almost complete sets of wartime maps of Papua and New Guinea. The branch had no typewriter, but he brought one from his house to his office and began to type letters to pilots, navigators, bombardiers, engineers, gunners, veterans' associations, and aerospace historians in Australia and America, and to anyone else who might have diaries, flight records, and memories or memorabilia of New Guinea's flying past. The National Museum soon bought Hoy a typewriter and additional filing cabinets to contain his correspondence and historical material. Hoy believes he is the only museum-branch curator in the world who types his own letters. He is a precise man and keeps count of the letters he dispatches: five hundred and three in 1981, six hundred and ten in 1982, six hundred and fourteen in 1983, and seven hundred and thirty-two in 1984—an average of two for each of the leap year's three hundred and sixty-six days. That statistical precision gives him satisfaction.

In 1982 Bruce Hoy was almost certainly the only curator who bought soft drinks wholesale and sold them to workers from a nearby joinery and steel-fabrication plant, mainly during their lunch hours. In its first four years, the branch rarely had more than two employees—a clerk and a laborer—and frequently had to make do with just a laborer. Hoy's wife, Lina, a Filipino whom he had met in Port Moresby, where she had come to work as a secretary, generally prepared his lunch—often sandwiches of peanut butter and Vegemite, a dark-brown, slick, salty spread made from yeast extract—before he left home in the morning, and he ate it at his desk. If his laborer was not around between noon and one o'clock, he would jump up to open the door to his office and the door to his small refrigerator any number of times to dispense a Coca-Cola or a Fanta. His yearly profit from the sale of about 4000 soft drinks was $200—enough, he says, "to balance my books."

Sometime in 1980, as Bruce Hoy was reading the American Fifth Air Force unit histories, he became fascinated by aircraft losses. He studied Australian aircraft-crash records and went through the microfilmed unit histories roll by roll, carefully taking notes. It was difficult for him to remember the losses and the plane serial numbers, so he typed up a separate aircraft-crash card for each plane. He supplemented the information he obtained from the unit histories in various ways: with written histories some units had published during or after the Second World War; with other rolls of microfilm, such as bomber- and fighter-squadron weekly status and operation reports; and with Fifth Air Force monthly casualty lists. In February 1981 Hoy first became aware of Missing Air Crew Reports. During the Second World War, a Missing Air Crew Report was supposed to be compiled for every plane that was lost. The report contained such information as the organization to which the aircraft belonged, the date, time, and point of departure, its intended course, its destination, and the number of persons aboard, with their names, ranks, and serial numbers. If a researcher knew the tail number of a missing plane, he could obtain the report from the National Archives, in Washington, D.C. Once he had the report, he could request the missing-in-action files of the men aboard, which are stored at the National Records Center, in Suitland, Maryland.

That fall, Hoy and his wife flew to the United States and visited the National Archives and the National Records Center, where he obtained the numbers of the Missing Air Crew Reports he needed for his work. On October 10, 1981, shortly after his return to Port Moresby, he wrote to the National Archives to request copies of two hundred and thirty-four Missing Air Crew Reports. In January 1982 he received five and was instructed to request another five. He figured that at that rate it would take him ten years to obtain the two hundred and thirty-four reports and presently recruited nine American veterans and four airplane enthusiasts to order reports on his behalf.

Only a man as driven as Hoy would have persevered with this sort of research. The Fifth Air Force had been nomadic. Its units had moved from bases in the United States or Australia to assorted bases in New Guinea (Port Moresby, Dobodura, Nadzab) and on to Owi, Leyte, Luzon, and Ie Shima as they chased the Japanese north toward home. Many of their records were lost or destroyed in transit. Many of the surviving records turned out to be unreliable. Missing Air Crew Reports were filled with errors; men who had hitched rides on transport flights were often not manifested; planes often fell to earth miles from where they were believed to have gone down. In 1980 Hoy had put up a large map of Papua New Guinea and the Solomons on the wall behind his desk. One of his semireliable research tools was a partial list, compiled over a number of years by the Royal Australian Air Force, of aircraft that had crashed during the war. On this list were the aircraft type and serial number, the presumed map coordinates of the crash, and a remark about the plane, such as "Believed missing this approximate area" or "Last contact from this position" or "Wreckage recovered in swamp." Using the RAAF's map coordinates—unless he already knew from other sources that they were incorrect—Hoy decided to use pins with colored plastic heads to mark on his map the possible locations of missing planes.

In March 1981 Hoy received a letter from Lieutenant Colonel David C. Rosenberg, who was then the commanding officer of the Central Identification Laboratory, explaining that the CIL was planning a trip to Papua New Guinea to look for planes in the Port Moresby area. Rosenberg sent Hoy a list of crash sites the CIL was thinking of visiting and suggested that Hoy might be able to check out some of these sites. Hoy was investigating some planes of his own and wrote to the CIL to request information about several of them. The CIL had much easier and quicker access to Air Force records than he did, and the CIL's first sergeant, John J. Hennessy, who was in charge of the CIL's records room, had developed an interest in researching the planes missing in Papua New Guinea.

There are more planes missing in Papua New Guinea than any other country on earth, many of them in the mountains, at sites never reached by the Australian and American Graves Registration teams that searched shortly after the Second World War. Papua New Guinea was thus the logical place for the CIL to seek employment, and by 1981 its members had realized that Bruce Hoy was uniquely qualified to help them. In December 1981 David E. Kelly, Jr., a sergeant assigned to the CIL, went to Guadalcanal to recover remains. He returned to Hawaii by way of Port Moresby and spent several days with Hoy. In Hoy's office and over dinner at his house, the two men held friendly conversations about how Hoy and the CIL could cooperate in the future to their mutual advantage. A month after Kelly's visit, Hoy and the CIL started communicating by telex. On January 29, 1982, the CIL transmitted a list of fourteen planes that it was interested in recovering, and asked Hoy for any information he had on them. One of them, an American B-24, was referred to as "Cox's aircraft" (its pilot had been Second Lieutenant William B. Cox), and, according to the RAAF register of lost planes, it was missing at map coordinates that put it 9 miles northwest of the village of Manumu. Cox's aircraft was of particular interest to Hoy because it had carried a flying officer from the RAAF in addition to its American crew of eleven.

At about the same time, Bruce Hoy studied two other pieces of information he had received from an RAAF historian in Canberra, which showed that the RAAF list was obviously wrong about the place where Cox's aircraft had gone down. He removed the pin he had had on his map for Cox's aircraft near Manumu and put it in its correct location. Something—Hoy has no explanation today except to say that it was a hunch—made him believe there was still a plane waiting to be found near Manumu, which was now marked by an empty pinhole on the map behind his desk. One day in mid-March, he acted on his hunch by asking an acquaintance who operated an airline if he could put Hoy's clerk, Charlie Obi, on one of the acquaintance's planes that were going to Manumu; Hoy was told he could. Papua New Guinea is a country of more than three million people, who speak over seven hundred tribal languages. The villagers of Manumu belong to a group called the Mountain Koiari. They speak their own regional language, and they also speak Melanesian Pidgin English, which is considered the lingua franca of Papua New Guinea. A few people in Manumu have learned English—the language used for conducting government and business affairs. Charlie Obi speaks four languages, including Pidgin and English. When he got off the plane at Manumu and asked the village counselor if there were any missing planes around there, the village counselor told him there was a *balus* (*balus*, the word in Melanesian Pidgin English for "pigeon," has also become the word for "plane") a three-hour walk from the village.

Obi flew back to Port Moresby and typed up a report for Hoy about his visit to Manumu. Its contents did not surprise Hoy. A few months earlier, he had written to Colonel Rosenberg, "Many of these missing aircraft are not really missing, as the people in the area may already know of them, but because nobody has asked them, they have not specifically offered the information. To them, the wreckage is 'something belong white man' or 'time before.'" In mid-March, Hoy also sent the CIL a telex asking for information on five B-24s he was researching. The last of the five was a B-24 numbered 42-41081. He requested its Missing Air Crew Report. The RAAF list had it missing at Rabaul, on the island of New Britain, a site that Hoy knew from other sources was incorrect. Hoy believed that the plane had gone down near Port Moresby, where he was still trying to come up with missing planes for the CIL to recover.

The CIL team that visited Papua New Guinea consisted of six men: Colonel Rosenberg, Sergeant Hennessy, Sergeant Kelly, Sergeant Jay Shawn Warner, Sergeant Richard B. Huston, and George Washington Gardner, a retired Marine gunnery sergeant who was working for the CIL as a Department of the Army civilian. Gardner was well liked at the CIL, but he occasionally irritated the sergeants by telling them "This is the way we did it in the Marines" when they wanted supplies procured the Army way. Kelly and Warner, who were the advance party for the trip, arrived with the team's equipment at Jackson's Airport, in Port Moresby, on the afternoon of April 11, 1982. The next day, they visited the Aviation, Maritime, and War Branch, and stored most of their equipment there. The two sergeants talked to Bruce Hoy about crash-site possibilities. He told them about Charlie Obi's trip to Manumu in mid-March. He said he believed it was worth flying to Manumu to learn more about the plane the villagers knew about. Hoy suggested that on Wednesday morning, April 14, Kelly and Obi go to Manumu.

On the morning of the fourteenth, a small plane carried Kelly and Obi from Jackson's Airport to Manumu. It was only a twenty-minute trip, but it would have taken two days to walk. Papua New Guinea's mountainous terrain presents extraordinary obstacles to would-be road builders. There are no roads linking Port Moresby with any other major city. The country has no railroads, either. It does have three hundred and sixteen registered airfields. Few other countries have such a dense network of airfields, and almost no other country is as dependent upon air transport. One out of five residents of Papua New Guinea takes a domestic airplane trip each year.

In Manumu, the village counselor was among a party of men, women, and children who walked out from the center of the village to its grassy airstrip. Kelly had brought along his rucksack, which contained food, overnight gear, and digging equipment, and Obi had borrowed a CIL rucksack. The village counselor escorted Kelly and Obi to a thatched guest hut at the end of the runway. Many villages had had rest houses for patrol officers in colonial times and still kept a guest hut for travelers. Obi started to query the villagers who had congregated around them about the airplane the village counselor had told him was three hours away.

Two men came forward and said they had actually seen the plane. They said they had found it while they were bird hunting in the mountains, a year or two earlier, and that it was eight hours away. Kelly expressed a willingness to "hump" to it with them. The more willing he said he was to walk to the plane, the farther away the plane got. The men finally admitted that it was a two-day walk to the crash site. Like most rural residents of Papua New Guinea, natives of Manumu are accustomed to long, arduous walks. The traditional activity of the country's villages is subsistence gardening. The island of New Guinea is geologically young, and most of its soil is poor, so gardens are planted in a different place almost every year to allow the soil to recover. The gardens are often far from the villages. The men frequently walk to other villages, and sometimes to Port Moresby: they cannot always afford to spend $45 for a round-trip flight. As a result of the villagers' going barefoot, the soles of their feet are incredibly thick, and their feet are wide. The men are fleet. Kelly guessed that what would be a two-day walk for them would be at least a four-day walk for an outsider—even one who exercised as regularly as he did and was in good physical condition.

Kelly questioned the two bird hunters intently. How many engines did the plane have? They didn't know—they had seen only part of the plane. Was the plane small or large? They had seen a wing, and it had seemed large to them. Kelly asked them to pace off the wing length as they remembered it. Their judgment was good: the wing had been part of a large plane. Had they seen any bones at the crash site? They hadn't. What had they seen besides the wing? They had seen some helmets and some expended rounds of ammunition. Kelly asked them if they would be willing to walk to the plane and bring back a helmet, some of the expended rounds of ammunition, some human bones, if they saw any, and a note of any big numbers they found on a large part of the plane. Kelly showed them with his hands the size of the numbers he wanted. He didn't want any of the small serial numbers that could be found on the engines, for example. The two men seemed glad to have a chance to earn some unforeseen money. They said they would get their machetes and food and leave that day. The next day, Kelly and Obi flew back to Port Moresby.

On Monday, April 19, a few days after the rest of the CIL team had arrived from Honolulu, Kelly returned to Manumu with Huston. Rick Huston, who in early 1982 was thirty-two years old, is a native of Montana. He has a baby face, a comely blond wife who is an officer in the Honolulu Police Department, and more beer-drinking experience than anyone else at the CIL. Dave Kelly, a year older than Huston, is a second-generation NCO, who grew up in Pennsylvania; like Huston, he has a beer belly and he has earned it. Kelly and his first wife had separated several years earlier and had subsequently divorced. Kelly had fallen in love with a Korean woman named Myong, whom he had met in Hawaii. He had married her three and a half weeks earlier. When Kelly and Huston landed, the two bird hunters gave Kelly a number they had written down with a felt pen on a piece of fabric they had torn off the plane; a helmet; some expended .50-caliber rounds; and a thick piece of cardboard with some operating instructions printed on it in English. They hadn't seen any bones. Kelly thanked them and paid them double the amount they had settled on—a procedure the team finds prudent in Papua New Guinea, where it often wants to hire the same people again. Kelly and Huston got back on the plane; twenty minutes later, they were at Jackson's Airport. As they approached their hotel, they saw John Hennessy emerging. They showed him the number the men from Manumu had written down for them—it was 180142. Presumably, the plane's actual serial number was 41-80142. The *41* would indicate that the plane had been ordered in fiscal year 1941. (The *4* was never actually painted on any plane tails.) When Hennessy looked at the number, he didn't recognize it. He went to his hotel room to consult a list of planes missing in Papua New Guinea. The number was not on the list. Kelly and Huston decided to go to Hoy's office to see if he could help them.

Hoy was outside in his junkyard when Huston and Kelly arrived with the items they had collected at Manumu. He stood under the wing of the P-38 looking at the number on the piece of fabric, trying to figure out what sort of aircraft the men from Manumu had seen. His first guess was that it was some sort of transport, perhaps a C-47, because of the presence of the rusty steel helmet. Hoy knew that steel helmets had often been worn by combat crews in the European theater, because of the high degree of antiaircraft fire there, but he had rarely heard of the practice in the Southwest Pacific. The photographs of Fifth Air Force crews he had run across showed the Pacific airmen wearing their service caps. Hoy knew without referring to any of the books in his library that the number wasn't that of a C-47: he had an almost complete list of the C-47s that had ever flown in New Guinea. He went upstairs to his office and picked up a book called *U.S. Military Aircraft Designations and Serials Since 1909*, compiled by John M. Andrade. The Andrade book spent more time on Hoy's desk than on a bookshelf; its cover was faded by the sun. He riffled through it, hoping to find another type of Second World War plane with the tail number 1-80142. He couldn't find any such number. He wasn't going through Andrade carefully, plane by plane, however, because his first thought was that the villagers had written down something other than the tail number—perhaps a number they had seen on an engine. After several minutes, he put the fabric and the piece of cardboard back inside the helmet and put the helmet on his "in" tray. He got up and started to leaf through some Missing Air Crew Reports, which sometimes had airplane-engine numbers on them. No sooner had he done that than another thought crossed his mind. What if the plane's tail fin had flipped over in the crash and the natives had looked at it and had written what they saw? They might have written some of the numbers upside down, and backwards. Hoy sat down, reached for the fabric, and reversed the numbers.

The number was 2-41081. It was the fifth of the five B-24s he had asked the CIL about in the last telex he sent before the team came to Papua New Guinea—the B-24 he knew was not in Rabaul, where the RAAF list had put it. As a result of the telex, the CIL had brought along the Missing Air Crew Report on that plane, and Hoy had read it. Although the plane with the serial number 42-41081 was a four-engine bomber, the report showed that when it had crashed it was being used as a transport. It had taken off from Jackson's Aerodrome on March 22, 1944, with twenty-two men aboard—a crew of three and nineteen passengers. That would account for the helmets, Hoy thought. It was bound for Nadzab, then the headquarters of Fifth Air Force Bomber Command. The plane had last been seen by the control tower at Jackson's. It had disappeared before it reached Nadzab, about 200 miles away. Hoy remembers the sense of triumph he had when he said to Huston and Kelly, who had grown discouraged after eight days in Papua New Guinea, "Well, I've got twenty-two for you," and the way they had looked at him—"as if they'd been struck by lightning." The CIL quickly made plans that would put the team on the site of B-24 42-41081 on Friday, April 23.

On Tuesday, the twentieth, Dave Kelly, Jay Warner, and Charlie Obi went to Manumu. Kelly hired the two bird hunters and two of their friends to walk back to the crash site and cut a landing zone for a helicopter on a flat place close to the site. He paced off the size of the helicopter pad he wanted them to build; it had to be about 9 feet square for the helicopter's skids. He explained—via Obi—that they would need to cut the trees around it so that the helicopter, a Hughes 500, could fly in and out and have sufficient clearance for its rotors. Kelly told the bird hunters when he and the other team members would arrive. He had only a vague idea of where the crash site was—the bird hunters had pointed up to a mountain. He instructed them to build a big fire that morning, with a lot of smoke, to guide the helicopter in. He then told them how much each man would be paid and that they would be provided with food. He mentioned bread, canned mackerel, biscuits, rice, and tea. One of the men added "lolly water"—a term that is used in Australia for sweet drinks like lemonade and soda and has made its way into Pidgin English. Kelly also said that when the team's work was done they would not have to walk out: they would be flown back to Manumu by helicopter. The men were to leave for the crash site that same morning. Kelly, Warner, and Obi returned to Port Moresby an hour later.

On Tuesday afternoon, the team began preparing the equipment it would need at the crash site. Bruce Hoy was invited to accompany the team on the mountain, but he would arrive a day later and planned to spend only one night there. In recent years, many poorly educated young men have migrated from their villages in the countryside to cities like Port Moresby to find work and to sample a more modern way of life. Many have taken to drinking and committing crimes. The Port Moresby police refer to robbers and burglars as "rascals." Crime is so commonplace in Port Moresby that many expatriates who work there keep guard dogs and live in houses surrounded by barbed wire. Even if they have air-conditioners in their bedrooms, some hesitate to use them because then they may not be able to hear their dogs barking or other signs of mischief. Hoy, who likes to describe himself as "a family man," would not have felt comfortable leaving Lina and their daughter alone for any length of time.

Several trips were required on Friday the twenty-third, to haul all the men and the slingloads of equipment to the crash site. As Huston approached the site, on the helicopter's last trip, he couldn't see any evidence of a plane crash from the air, but he could easily see the smoky fire the men from Manumu had built. When he landed, the helicopter's altimeter read 8400 feet. The entire team was safely on Mt. Thumb by eight-fifteen in the morning.

As soon as the team was on the ground and the helicopter had departed (arrangements had been made for it to swing by on Tuesday to check on the team), Dave Kelly complimented the four men from Manumu. The helicopter pad was a neat rectangle of small logs. The men had done a thorough job of clearing the trees from the landing zone; the pilot had requested that only one additional tree be topped off, to make his approaches and exits safer. The sufficiently smoky fire was left to burn itself out. Sergeant Kelly had Charlie Obi ask the men how they felt. They said they were cold and hungry. The natives of Manumu travel light. Although Mt. Thumb is only 8 miles northwest of Manumu as the crow flies, crows' flights are meaningless in reckoning distance in Papua New Guinea. The men had gone from an altitude of 1700 feet to an altitude of 8400 feet, making their way up into the mountains by following ridgelines—a longer but easier climb. They had left their village with the clothes on their backs, which appeared to be the only clothes they owned; one of the bird hunters Kelly had met in Manumu on April 14, and had seen again on the nineteenth and twentieth, had been wearing then what he was wearing now—a pair of blue shorts and a green T-shirt with yellow stripes and a hole in it. Just one of the four men had a sweater. They had carried axes and machetes, food for three days in a *bilum* (a handmade mesh bag), and a shotgun, which they had already put to good use: the CIL team saw a colorful parrot hanging from a tree. Sergeant Warner examined the men briefly—they looked healthy—and gave them some of the food, cigarettes, and lolly water (cans of Coca-Cola produced in Australia) he had bought for them in Port Moresby. At thirty, Warner was the youngest sergeant in the CIL. He regarded his Military Occupation Specialty with less reverence than his fellow Fifty-seven Foxtrots. He tried not to take life or himself too seriously, and succeeded. In Papua New Guinea, Warner was to be the team photographer and the team medic. (In civilian life, he had worked for an ambulance company as an Emergency Medical Technician, and he had taken the Army medic course.)

The helipad was on a flat area of a ridge on Mt. Thumb. Toward Port Moresby, to the southwest, the land dropped off precipitously. The first thing the team did was to choose a campsite, another fairly level area of the ridge, about 15 yards west of the helipad. It was one of the few suitable places for sleeping without rolling down a mountainside. The weather in Papua New Guinea is changeable, and it is sensible to set up camp before it changes for the worse, and to make the sleeping quarters as waterproof as possible. The villagers carried tents and boxes of C rations from the helipad to the camp, where they cleared the brush and trees from an area that measured about 20 by 30 feet. The Americans amicably selected spots for sleeping. They had brought along five mountain tents, each big enough for two if the two liked crowds. Colonel Rosenberg had a tent to himself, as did Gardner and Obi. Sergeant Kelly and Sergeant Huston shared a tent. Sergeant Hennessy shared a tent with file folders of records he had brought with him. Jay Warner preferred to sleep in a hammock. The men from Manumu were given a large sheet of clear plastic. They put posts in the ground, draped the plastic over the posts, enclosing their shelter on all four sides, and built a small fire under the plastic. Their plastic kingdom, which was near Warner's hammock, was soon warm. The villagers also built a fire for the CIL team in the midst of the encampment and dug a latrine and a trash pit at a respectable distance.

Warner and Huston went for a walk around the crash site. Huston was the team's official sketcher. It was also his assignment to find all of the wreckage, to mark its outer boundaries with white engineers' tape, and to determine "crash-site center." In addition, he was to keep his eyes open for remains and for personal effects—such as clothes that the plane's passengers had worn and B-4 flight bags they might have carried with them. Warner went along with Huston in his role as team photographer—he was supposed to take photographs of every stage of the S-and-R mission—and because it was easier for two men to lay the tape. From the campsite, the men could see a moss-covered propeller. The team surmised that the bird hunters had discovered the plane while walking the ridgeline. Warner and Huston headed down the slope from the campsite. As they made their way through thick brush, tangled vines, and tree branches, they came upon a second propeller, a wingtip, three .50-caliber machine guns, and various parts of the B-24's twin tail assembly, including its left and right vertical fins and the tail turret. At first, they solidly encircled each of the plane parts, laying the tape on the bushes and on the ground. The crash site appeared to be vast, and they realized that if they kept that up they would soon run out of tape. They began to use the tape sparingly, tying it around trees and bushes to mark the perimeter and around bushes near personal effects—or PE, as they are often called.

As Warner took "before" shots for his photo documentary, he kept losing his balance on the slope, and the going got rougher as the men proceeded from the area below the campsite to the area below the helipad. They were glad they were wearing stout leather gloves. There are porcupinelike bushes in these mountains, and those who have touched them with bare hands are unlikely to forget the burning pain of the quills piercing the skin. In a ravine below the helipad, the two men saw a chunk of fuselage. As they continued to walk east across the ravine, they saw fragments of the cockpit and many PE—shoes and boots, helmets, a mess kit, some B-4 bags. They also found rudder pedals, instrument panels, and a number of bones lying on the floor of the rain forest. These, they decided, marked the center of impact. The men from Manumu hadn't been to the center of the crash, either on their original bird-hunting expedition or on their second trip, for Kelly, but they had told Charlie Obi that they had seen bones during the time they were on the mountain building the helipad. They had probably looked around a bit to see what the Americans were so interested in, and had also traversed part of the crash site on their way to get water from a stream at the bottom of the ravine.

While Huston and Warner were still scouting the crash-site perimeter—from north to south the site covered between 30 and 50 yards, from east to west about 150—Colonel Rosenberg and Sergeant Kelly went to have a look at the wreckage near the campsite. Kelly wanted to verify the plane's tail number. One of the men from Manumu pointed out the general direction of the tail. They came upon the right tail fin lying flat on the ground. Kelly tried to lift it, and couldn't; it was stuck in the ground. He dug around it and saw that there was a hole underneath it. He could see some numbers through the hole but couldn't see them well. With Rosenberg's help, he dislodged the tail fin and set it upright. The top two-thirds was in good shape; the bottom third was completely crumpled. At the top of the tail, Kelly and Rosenberg saw the tail number, 2-41081, painted in yellow. Painted below the number, in white, was a large skull.

"Found a skull! Found a skull!" Kelly shouted, at the top of his voice, in the hope that Hennessy would think he had found a human skull, come running, and take a tumble down the hill.

"Quit that, or Sergeant Hennessy will come running," Rosenberg told Kelly, not realizing that was Kelly's wish precisely.

Lieutenant Colonel David Rosenberg, a soft-spoken, pleasant-looking gray-haired man, was born in 1930. He had been a high-school teacher, with a master's degree in guidance and counseling, and had held an administrative position in logistics at the Pentagon for four years before his assignment to the CIL. The commanding officer of the CIL is always a field-grade officer in the Quartermaster Corps, with a primary specialty of 92—matériel/services management. Fewer than half a dozen field-grade officers in the United States Army are further specialized as 92-Es, or Ninety-two Echoes—memorial-affairs officers. Colonel Rosenberg was not a 92-E. He has described the CIL's young sergeants as "a bunch of kids" and preferred to delegate responsibility for keeping the kids in line to his first sergeant, John Hennessy.

John Hennessy was born in Glen Burnie, Maryland, in 1939. He is a quirky, uncommunicative man who pronounces his *v*'s as *b*'s (he speaks of *b*illages like Manumu, and about *B*ietnam). A licensed mortician, Hennessy has spent more time in the mortuaries of Vietnam and at CIL-HI than any other Fifty-seven Foxtrot. He is held in esteem for his Graves Registration knowledge, but the younger sergeants agree that he is neither a leader of noncommissioned officers nor a follower of orders from commissioned officers who lack his experience in his field.

Hennessy disappointed Kelly by not hurrying over to see the skull. Unbeknownst to Kelly and Rosenberg and the rest of the team, the skull, with crossed bombs below the skull (the crossed bombs could not be seen on 41081's tail because of its crumpled condition), was the symbol of the 90th Bomb Group of the Fifth Air Force. The symbol had been devised by a publicity-minded second lieutenant after Colonel Arthur H. Rogers became the group's commanding officer, in July 1943. To the young lieutenant, an outfit that was led by a flamboyant man named Rogers and flew the high seas seeking Japanese ships to burn and sink should be called the Jolly Rogers and flaunt on the spacious vertical tail surfaces of its B-24s a skull and crossed bombs.

After Huston and Warner had done what they could for the day, they walked most of their teammates through a good section of the crash site, pointing out one of the plane's wings, one of its engines, and certain areas marked off with tape where bones had been found that should not be disturbed by stomping around. Kelly went through the crash site on his own; he was particularly interested in a portion of the plane's nose section and a parachute below the two propellers near the campsite. The team returned to camp shortly after four o'clock. The sun plummets below the horizon around five-thirty in equatorial countries like Papua New Guinea, a land of limited twilight. The men hadn't stopped for lunch—they had munched on crackers and papayas and bananas that they had brought with them—and they wanted to eat dinner before dark. The day had been hot, but by late afternoon clouds had set in and it was chilly.

As the men from Manumu went to their plastic quarters to cook their dinner, the CIL team and Charlie Obi gathered around their campfire. They put a pot of water on to boil, ate C rations and cucumbers, and drank instant coffee or cocoa while carrying on a lively conversation in the early-evening darkness. Suddenly there was a great flapping of wings and a loud shriek. The first shriek was answered by another and another. "The shrieks were like high-pitched screams, like something out of an Alfred Hitchcock movie," Dave Kelly later recalled. Charlie Obi couldn't account for the shrieks, and was dispatched to ask the men from Manumu if they could. He returned with the information that the shriekers were bats, and that they made an excellent meal. The shrieks grew louder as the bats flew closer, and then became faint as they flew off. After an hour, the bats departed. The men read or played cards or listened to the radio or to cassettes. By eight o'clock, Warner was in his hammock and the others were in their tents. Rick Huston smoked a cigarette and thought, We're onto something big. To Dave Kelly, the site looked promising, but he was disturbed by the expended rounds of ammunition: What if some of the men had survived the crash, had shot at some Japanese, and had wandered away? Jay Warner was enthusiastic about being on the mountainside (he had begun to suffer from "hotel fever" in Port Moresby) but apprehensive. This thing is scattered all over God's green earth, he thought. We could be here a month.

A light rain fell on Mt. Thumb during Friday night, but Saturday, April 24, dawned clear and cool. The men from Manumu had finished all the food they were given to eat the previous day. Colonel Rosenberg saw Warner giving the men another day's worth of food and told him to give them the rest of the provisions Warner had brought for them. Warner said that the Colonel was making a mistake—that an Australian had told him that the natives took a feast-or-famine approach to food—but Rosenberg didn't agree. "This is the twentieth century," he reminded Warner, "and doling out food to the men as if they were slaves isn't right." Warner obeyed the colonel's order.

At 6:30 A.M., while the members of the team were still sitting around the fire eating C rations and drinking coffee, they heard a helicopter. It was bringing Bruce Hoy. He had brought with him Peap (Pappy) Tomon, the laborer the National Museum had assigned to him in 1979; Hoy thought it would be a rare chance for Pappy to work on a crash site. The CIL offered its visitors a cup of coffee. Hoy, a single-minded man, didn't want any coffee. All he wanted was to see the plane. He curbed his impatience for a few minutes and was then taken through the crash site, starting in the area below the campsite. Hoy is familiar with the nicknames and symbols of all the bomb groups that served in New Guinea, and was thrilled to see the Jolly Rogers tail (which he pronounced "tile"—fifteen years away from home had not cost him his Australian accent). He told the CIL team about the Jolly Rogers and made it absolutely clear that he coveted the tail for the Aviation, Maritime, and War Branch. As the walk resumed, Hoy was asked to identify components of the plane the team members couldn't recognize. He translated what looked to them like "miscellaneous wreckage" into horizontal stabilizers, ailerons, oleo struts, and a bomb-bay door. He showed them a small piece of a Norden bombsight in the nose section.

Dave Kelly and G.W. Gardner are both parachutists. They went to the parachute that had been found near the nose section. When a B-24 was on a combat mission, its nose gunner and bombardier would sit in the nose. Although 41081 was being used as a transport when it crashed, Kelly and Gardner thought that perhaps one passenger had been sitting in the nose to get a view, had seen the crash coming, and tried to parachute to safety. The parachute was out of its pack and looked more or less as if it had been deployed. Small trees had grown up through it in the thirty-eight years since the crash, and roots were entwined in its shroud lines. Kelly was sure he would find bones at the end of the shroud lines; he guessed that the plane had been at too low an altitude when the presumed man in the nose jumped, and that the parachute hadn't fully deployed. The team made a preliminary search near the parachute but did not find anything. Warner and Huston had kept searching on the east side of the crash site until they could find nothing more and had then marked off the perimeter there, finishing by 8:00 A.M. Colonel Rosenberg and Sergeant Hennessy had opened a couple of B-4 bags to see if the bags contained anything with identification—a watch engraved with a name, clothing with a laundry mark—but had found nothing.

Shortly after eight o'clock, the team started digging on a hill in the area believed to be crash-site center. Rosenberg, Huston, Hennessy, and Kelly worked 5 or 6 feet away from each other. (Gardner worked alongside Kelly, because he lacked Graves Registration training and digging experience.) Kelly happened to wind up in front of a bone that Huston and Warner had marked with engineers' tape. "Rick, I need an X number," he said to Huston at 8:34. "Jay, come take some pictures," he called to Warner. Huston gave Kelly a tag on which he had written "X-1." Part of Huston's job on the crash site was to distribute X numbers. An X number designates the location where unknown remains have been found. Huston gave out the numbers in chronological order whenever a member of the team found a group of bones in a specific area. He recorded the time he gave out each X number and the name of the man to whom he gave it. Kelly didn't find many bones at X-1, but those he did find seemed to belong to one individual. When Kelly thought he had all the bones that were to be found at that spot (Warner had taken photographs at various stages of the digging), he put them in a large clear Ziploc bag into which he had dropped the tag. At five minutes after nine, Hennessy found some bones and asked Huston for an X number; he was given X-2. Warner was summoned to snap photographs. At nine-fifteen, Rosenberg found some bones and was given X-3. Colonel Rosenberg found even fewer bones at X-3 and had no reason to think the bones didn't belong to one person. At X-2, a large number of bones, which Hennessy dug up, seemed to belong to at least three people; he had noticed an inordinate number of vertebrae and duplicates and triplicates of a number of bones, including three left-thigh bones.

When a number of people are killed in a plane crash, their bones are usually commingled as a result of the impact. If an inexperienced group of people had come to the B-24 site, had started digging, and had put all the bones and teeth they found into one bag, it would have been difficult, if not impossible, for Tadao Furue, the CIL's physical anthropologist in Honolulu, to identify all the plane's passengers individually. Although Furue is able to segregate commingled remains to a remarkable extent, it makes his job much easier if the men in the field put each set of bones they find—together with any teeth or personal effects, such as rings or ID bracelets—into a separate bag, with an X number, so that he will have less segregating to do. The CIL team knows how much families value individual identifications and therefore tries to dig carefully. (The family of First Lieutenant Charles W. Springer, a passenger on a P-38 fighter plane whose wreckage the CIL visited on an earlier expedition to Papua New Guinea, had expressed disappointment that Furue had been unable to separate his remains from those of the captain who was flying the plane. Springer's mother and brother hadn't wanted him to be buried with the pilot in a national cemetery— an Army regulation for inseparable remains; they had wanted him buried next to his father.)

By 10:30 A.M., Huston had given out seven X numbers. The digging was tedious; the men were always standing on an incline, so that one leg bore all the weight, and by midday the air was muggy. Around eleven o'clock, they clambered up the steep hill to the campsite and took an hour-and-a-half break for lunch. Shinnying back down to the center of the crash was equally treacherous. Kelly tied a rope to a tree above the parachute and let it run all the way down the hill. He subsequently tied a second rope to a tree below the landing zone; it went down to a propeller near crash-site center. After lunch, the team resumed digging. By late afternoon, Huston had given out eleven X numbers. The men couldn't believe their progress. The remains were surprisingly close together and close to the surface. They didn't have to dig more than 3 to 5 inches to find them. The calls for Huston to give out X numbers and for Warner to take photographs came so quickly that the men recalled Saturday as having a "Eureka!" quality to it. Around 3:45, as Colonel Rosenberg was starting to dig at a new spot, Sergeant Hennessy said he thought he was going to call it a day. He hesitated, did a little more digging, and mumbled that the natives were tired. Colonel Rosenberg, an even-tempered man who almost never swears, was frustrated by Hennessy's indecisiveness.

"God damn it, First Sergeant, are we calling it a day or are we not?" he asked.

"Yeah, we are," Hennessy answered.

The team returned to camp around four-fifteen. By then, the

men from Manumu, who had been kept busy clearing brush and cutting small trees away from the area where the team was digging, were shivering with cold. The team members' backs hurt, and so did their eyes. Bones that have weathered over a period of many years tend to blend in with the metal parts of the plane or with the brown earth; they become difficult to see as the sun dips in a gray sky. As darkness fell, the bats started to shriek again; they played their Hitchcock scene for an hour, as they did every night the men stayed on the mountain. The members of the team sat around the campfire, sharing their C rations with Bruce Hoy and Peap Tomon. Bruce Hoy called his laborer Pappy because his first name sounded like Pappy and also because he was so willing and able that Hoy compared him with a famous Fifth Air Force officer of the Second World War, Colonel Paul I. (Pappy) Gunn, who, among other accomplishments, was renowned for ingeniously converting ineffective medium bombers into effective strafers. Pappy Tomon, a short, wiry man from the southern highlands of Papua New Guinea, has no idea when he was born; Hoy believes he is in his late forties. The only two words Pappy could write were his name. Making change for the soda he sold in the office flustered him, but in a few hours on Mt. Thumb he had revealed such an aptitude for spotting bones ("He has eyes on him like a hawk," Warner said) that the team asked Hoy to let Pappy stay with them after his departure, and Hoy consented.

The CIL is interested solely in recovering and identifying remains, but Hoy's main interest was in gathering souvenirs for his museum. While the team and Pappy Tomon dug for bones, Hoy bustled about the crash site as if on a treasure hunt. He found a silver dollar, a pair of bombardier's wings, and many other artifacts. The team didn't want him to remove too many objects before the crash site had been properly photographed and searched, so Hoy, who would return to Port Moresby by helicopter the next morning, gave Charlie Obi and Pappy a long list of the things he wanted them to set aside for him. Hoy had decided to come back to the mountain with the helicopter on Tuesday.

The team was cheerful, because the first day of digging had gone so well. This is easy, Jay Warner thought. We're really going to get off this mountain in a week. Hoy was overjoyed to be on a spot where no living white man had ever been before. It was also the first time he had been to a plane that had been undisturbed since the day it crashed. "Most of the planes I'd been to had been visited by everyone and his dog, and the wreckage had been moved around countless times and much of it removed," he later recalled. He was happy about the chain of events that had led to his putting the team on such a promising site: the discovery that the RAAF had listed Cox's aircraft as missing in the wrong place; his intuition that there was a plane where Cox's aircraft was supposed to have been, which had prompted him to send Charlie Obi to Manumu in mid-March to learn about the missing plane; his reversing the numbers that the bird hunters had brought back.

The team's luck held on the twenty-fifth. Huston handed out six X numbers between 9:24 A.M. and 1:38 P.M.—X-12 through X-17. Numbers X-15 and X-16 were given to Sergeant Hennessy, who found what he thought were the remains of two individuals in the same spot. One was close to the surface, the other a few inches below the surface. Hennessy put the bones into one bag. Huston gave himself X-17 when he discovered a considerable number of bones and teeth near the spot where he had found another cluster of bones and teeth at X-4 the previous day. He believed the remains he had found at X-4 and those he now found at X-17 belonged to two men. (Tadao Furue later determined that Hennessy had not found two men at X-15 and X-16, and that Huston had guessed wrong about X-4 and X-17.)

Another of Huston's tasks was to record where each cluster of bones had been found. He used a compass to shoot azimuths from crash-site center to each X number to get the bearing in degrees. He also paced off the distance. At Graves Registration School, he had learned that a hundred and twenty of his paces equaled a hundred meters, just as Kelly (who is 2½ inches shorter than Huston) had learned that a hundred and thirty-one of his paces equaled a hundred meters. Huston went back to Honolulu with a list that read, "X-1, 276°, 21 meters; X-2, 330°, 10 meters; X-3, 65°, 18 meters," and so on. This information was put to good use by Tadao Furue for eight months after the team's return.

As the men dug, they often chatted. They observed that they were finding relatively few of the two hundred and six bones in the human body at each X number; they figured that many small bones—toe and finger bones, for instance—had disintegrated in almost four decades, but they wondered why they weren't finding more arm and leg bones. They also worried about the scant number of teeth they were digging up, because they understood the particular significance of teeth in identification; whenever they found a jawbone, they sifted slowly through the soil for loose teeth. They noticed that they weren't finding many dog tags or personal effects. The men passed around the few dog tags they did recover, and speculated on why they weren't finding more. Had most of the plane's passengers not been wearing dog tags? The men put whatever PE they found at an X number in small olive-drab patient-effects bags of the kind used in Army hospitals. (In all his years in the Army, Kelly had seen only one bag that was originally designated a personal-effects bag.) They put whatever teeth they found at an X number in a small Ziploc bag. The patient-effects bags and small Ziploc bags (each with the appropriate X number marked with a felt pen or a grease pencil) went into the larger plastic Ziploc bags that held the bones. At the end of each afternoon's work, the men carried these bags to an empty crate at the helipad.

Sunday had been another productive day of digging; seventeen X numbers in two days was more than anyone on the team had anticipated. The men were grateful that the work was going so well and that the working conditions were so favorable. The weather was benign. At 8400 feet, they were somewhat less energetic and less hungry than they were at sea level, but they felt all right and were bothered by nothing more serious than insect bites around their ankles or their boot tops or belt lines. They treated the bites with a mixture of alcohol, iodine, and scratching. There were no mosquitoes, and the men had convinced themselves that they were "above the snake line," which they had arbitrarily proclaimed to be 6000 feet; they were all leery of snakes.

Charlie Obi was a disappointment. He complained of feeling

sick, and spent most of the day hanging around the campsite.
The team sensed that his education and linguistic ability made
him feel superior to the other Papua New Guineans on the
mountain, and that, as a city boy employed as a clerk, he was
averse to doing manual labor. Pappy, with his sharp eyes and
ready smile, more than made up for Charlie Obi. Three of the
four men from Manumu were hard workers; the fourth seemed
to be genuinely ill. He pointed to his head, and Warner often
gave him Tylenol. (The team later learned that he had malaria.)
All four men were pleasant, and were interested in the CIL's
excavation project. Kelly tried to give them lessons in anatomy,
using sign language, but never was able to teach them the difference between a right-arm bone and a left one. At first, the
men kept to themselves. "They're so quiet and we're such a
bunch of loudmouths, always hollering and yelling and swear-
ing," Kelly acknowledged. By the end of the third day on Mt.
Thumb, two of them joined the members of the team as they sat
around the campfire. They had finished eating almost everything they had been given the previous day and were invited to
share the C rations and listened to the team laughing and remi-
niscing about planes they had visited on previous trips to Papua
New Guinea. After the men from Manumu had listened to the
sergeants talk in a language they scarcely understood, they returned to their plastic haven. They kept a small fire going there
all night, and it was always warm. With each passing day, the
once-clear plastic became a deeper shade of reddish-brown.

At 8:00 A.M. on Monday, shortly after the men had slid down
the rope to the center of the crash site, Hennessy called to Huston for an X number and got X-18. Hennessy found only a
handful of bones, two teeth, two rusty keys, and an old ring
missing a stone at X-18, which was close to X-1, X-5, and X-8,
dug up two days before by Huston and Kelly. The other men
kept digging and found nothing. The villagers were no longer
just clearing brush and trees. They were moving logs and pieces
of wreckage the team had separated with bolt cutters. At this
stage, the team wanted the plane parts out of the way so that
they could search under them. Dave Kelly also took pleasure in
disposing of unwanted objects—some of the many aluminum

oxygen bottles the B-24 had carried. He liked to see how far he could throw them, and he liked to hear the tinny sound they made when they rolled down the ravine and the *boing* they made when they landed.

X-1 through X-18 had been found in different directions from crash-site center, but none farther away than 21 meters. Around noon, a decision was made to expand the site's northern perimeter. At 1:43, Hennessy found X-19, 45 meters from crash-site center down the ravine. He found only a small number of bones, including a fragment of a mandible, and a pair of aviator's goggle frames, a silver watchband, an officer's cap insignia, a cigarette lighter, and three coins. All of a sudden the relative quiet of the mountainside was broken by a gunshot. The loud *bam* startled the team. One of the men from Manumu had killed another parrot. He would sell the parrots' red, yellow, and green feathers in Port Moresby.

By two o'clock, Hennessy had finished digging at X-19; the other members of the team had found no bones farther down the ravine. The sergeants did find a tall tree that attracted them, because it had a sturdy vine hanging from it. Huston cut the vine off at the base, tested it, and then sailed 150 feet into the air. As Kelly was taking his turn, the colonel came along and told him to get off the vine. Kelly thought he was kidding. "God damn it, Sergeant Kelly, I told you to get off that vine!" Rosenberg said, in an exasperated, boys-will-be-boys tone. While Hennessy and some of the others were down around X-19, Kelly, Huston, and Pappy walked west and found the plane's fourth engine and some watches. Kelly and Huston felt grubby after four days of sponge baths, and thought they would venture still farther down the ravine to the stream they could hear, from which the villagers fetched water every day. The terrain was so steep and rough that they gave up. They were to leave the mountain without ever seeing the bats and without seeing the stream the villagers got down to and back from in twenty minutes.

After the main area of the crash was declared cleared, the team climbed the hill, using the rope hand over hand, and went a hundred yards to the tail section and started to dig. A B-24 has very few windows, and the men thought that perhaps one passenger might have been sitting in the tail gunner's position to look out at the scenery. They found no trace of bones or PE. Each evening, the men reviewed the day's discoveries. Hennessy often went to his cluttered tent to consult 41081's Missing Air Crew Report. When some sets of dog tags, an identification disk, and a photograph of an Army Air Corps officer with the officer's name still legible on the photograph were dug up, Hennessy was content, because the names on the dog tags, the disk, and the photograph matched the names of the men on the manifest. "Yup, he's on the plane," Hennessy commented on quite a few occasions. Two items disturbed Hennessy. At X-3, Colonel Rosenberg had dug up a set of dog tags with the name and serial number of James A. Miller. There was no person on the manifest by that name. Hennessy and the other team members wondered if Miller might have been killed a short time before the crash and one of his friends on the plane might have been carrying his dog tags, planning to mail them to Miller's family. Hennessy was also troubled by a silver identification bracelet he had dug up at X-10. The bracelet was inscribed on one side with the name Robert A. Ambrose and a serial number. On the other side was the inscription "ED-RA, 12-25-43." There was no one named Ambrose on the manifest. "Shoot, he's not supposed to be on the plane, either," Hennessy said. It also occurred to the team that Miller or Ambrose or both might have boarded the plane at the last minute—too late for their names to appear on the manifest.

Every member of the team except Jay Warner had served in Vietnam. The sergeants had learned that hitching rides on planes in a war zone was common and that military manifests in Vietnam were not as reliable as passenger lists of commercial airliners in the United States. (In May, 1972, Rick Huston had been on an S-and-R team that recovered the remains of thirty-four men from a CH-47 Chinook helicopter that had crashed on its way to Vung Tau, a Rest-and-Recreation resort on the South China Sea 40 miles southeast of Saigon. There were only thirty-two men on the helicopter's manifest. The S-and-R team learned from the commander of the men's battalion that two soldiers had gone on R and R at the last minute.) On an earlier trip to Papua New Guinea, the team had discovered that Second World War manifests were also incomplete. The original Missing Air Crew Report of a C-47 in the Saruwaged Range which the team had visited in 1979 and 1980 had the names of only four crew members when it went missing, on December 10, 1944. An investigation a year later determined that a fifth man, a captain in the Medical Corps, was a passenger on the plane. The team knew that the original Missing Air Crew Report for 41081 listed a crew of three and eighteen passengers; a nineteenth passenger was subsequently added.

The helicopter brought Bruce Hoy back to Mt. Thumb at 7:00 A.M. on Tuesday, the twenty-seventh, with more food for the men from Manumu (Warner now doled it out a day at a time), a case of South Pacific beer, and a carton of Kools. Kelly had reserved the helicopter for Thursday morning; he figured the team's work at 41081 would be done by then. The helicopter was supposed to come back to collect Bruce Hoy between ten and ten-thirty. It didn't return until one o'clock, and then it was too late to land. Half an hour earlier, clouds had billowed in and covered the site. (It is almost always too cloudy to fly in and out of the Owen Stanleys in the afternoon.) The team had shot off flares, but the helicopter hadn't even come close to finding the helipad. Bruce Hoy was stranded and would be spending the night with the CIL team. The crash site had changed so much in the past two days of digging that Hoy scarcely recognized it. "It looked as if some villagers had dug up a big garden," Hoy said later. "I couldn't find the spot where I had found the silver dollar on Saturday."

At 8:00 A.M. the team had resumed its search for remains around the tail section. The men found nothing. They then formed a skirmish line and searched the rest of the area within the crash-site perimeters. Still nothing. The north side of the perimeter was extended 40 or 50 yards farther; no more bones were found. After several hours, Kelly decided that further digging in the ravine was pointless. He and Huston were drawn to the parachute—they had dug there during a couple of lunch breaks—and they went back to it now. Kelly followed the shroud lines down the hillside. They didn't end in a harness, as he had hoped; they just trailed off.

Hoy and Pappy had dug with the team on the skirmish line. After the search ended, Hoy had a fine day fossicking. Among the relics he carried back to the Aviation, Maritime, and War Branch were a bottle of Atabrine antimalaria tablets (they had retained their bright-yellow color), a pair of binoculars, a metal bandage tin, part of a razor, a bottle of Sheaffer ink (it had not dried up and was still deep blue), part of the parachute, a black comb, a set of navigator's instruments, an electric percolator, a bottle of Listerine mouthwash, two bottles of hair oil, a jar of hand cream that still smelled of lanolin, a bottle of nail varnish, and a fire extinguisher.

Hoy sat happily around the fire with the team. The colonel, the only man present who was old enough to remember the Second World War, asked him a great many questions about the war in the Pacific. The others asked him what it was like to live in Papua New Guinea.

The morning of Wednesday, the twenty-eighth, was a breezy one. At about seven o'clock, the men saw a helicopter right over the landing zone. It hovered. They could see passengers on board. The pilot blinked the helicopter's lights three or four times and flew off. The men were puzzled. Didn't the helicopter have space for Bruce Hoy? Did the blinking lights mean the pilot would return for him on another run?

The CIL team and the villagers spent Wednesday preparing to leave Mt. Thumb. They took up the ropes and the engineers' tape. They carried the digging equipment from the crash site to the LZ to be packed. They took down the tents and stuffed them into a crate. The CIL men repacked the remains: they wrapped cotton around the teeth and skulls they had found, and put the eighteen plastic bags in seven olive-drab waterproof bags. Huston was busy with paperwork: he redrew the crash-site sketch and shot some additional azimuths—this time to get grid coordinates, so that he could show where the crash had occurred on a 1:250,000 scale map of New Guinea he had brought with him from Hawaii. Kelly paid the men from Manumu, again doubling their salary. They wanted their money then, because they seemed to believe they were leaving the mountain that day. Kelly had learned that they preferred to be paid where the other villagers couldn't see how much money they had earned. The helicopter didn't return.

Kelly, Gardner, and one man from Manumu cleared a path

from the tail section to the LZ and carried the right vertical fin to the helipad. Pappy carried up the nose section and a .50-caliber machine gun Hoy wanted. The team also had the villagers cut down all the trees around the plane's right wing, which was intact. Like the rest of the plane's exterior, it was painted olive drab. There was about 2 inches of moss and dirt on it, which Kelly and Warner cleaned off down to the wing's smooth surface. Kelly then went to the LZ and fetched a can of orange fluorescent paint from one of the crates, and Warner got up on the wing. With Kelly and Gardner watching, he sprayed:

U S A CIL-HI
APRIL 82
D.R. J.H. R.H. D.K. J.W. G.W.G.

Warner sprayed the initials of the team members because there was ample space on the wing and because it had been a successful mission. The team had had the villagers cut down the trees so that the painted wing would be visible from the air. After Warner was finished, Gardner said he thought he would add "USMC"—for United States Marine Corps—to the wing. Colonel Rosenberg was at the nearby helipad at the time (as Warner knew) and overheard Gardner. "Go ahead, I don't care," Warner said, for Rosenberg's benefit, handing Gardner the can of paint before he went back to the helipad. "Sergeant Warner, you go back down and make sure that marine does nothing of the kind," Rosenberg instructed Warner.

Bruce Hoy had kept busy fossicking during the day. That evening he was melancholy. The camp struck him as less jolly. With the tents packed (the men would sleep out under plastic that night), it seemed to him to have lost its personality.

The team could get a radio station in Port Moresby on Huston's battery-operated radio, but the station broadcast a lot of music, a little local news, and very little world news. The war in the Falklands had begun in early April. On the mountain, it seemed much less interesting to the men than it might have had they been in Hawaii. Some nights, Kelly, Huston, and Warner had walked from the camp up to the helipad. They could see the lights of Port Moresby from there. (The city was not visible from the helipad by day or from the camp or the crash site at any time.) To Kelly, the city lights far away through the darkness were just "a beautiful view." To Warner, there was something "surrealistic" about them. In six days, the mountain had become his world. Although he missed his wife, being on Mt. Thumb with some natives who had been precipitated from a tribal way of life into the twentieth century in a matter of fifty years beguiled him. He liked Papua New Guinea's "laid-back" quality, and could imagine living there.

The men were up at first light on Thursday for a last meal of C rations around the fire. The villagers covered the trash pit and the latrine. The CIL men finished packing; sleeping bags, blankets, Warner's hammock, and their sheets of plastic went into footlockers or rucksacks. What the men from Manumu wanted almost as much as Bruce Hoy wanted the Jolly Rogers tail fin, was plastic. The team agreed to give them the now cloudy-brown plastic they had slept under. At eight-thirty, the helicopter landed and started to lift the men off the mountain. The pilot explained the puzzle of the previous morning's blinking lights: he couldn't pick up Hoy, although he had space for him, because he had several other people aboard; the combination of their weight and a strong wind had made landing impossible; the lights were a signal that he would return whenever he could get in.

On the helicopter's first three trips, between Mt. Thumb and Manumu, it carried all the men down except Bruce Hoy and Jay Warner, taking a slingload of equipment with each group of three or four passengers. The remains from 41081 traveled inside the helicopter; slingloads have been known to drop. In Manumu, the four villagers were greeted like heroes: a helicopter ride appeared to be a status symbol. Hoy and Warner were the last two men on the mountain. They had kept rucksacks with them and sufficient food for several days, in case they got socked in by weather. The weather stayed good, and in a while the pilot returned for them. Hoy got into the helicopter with the C rations. Warner hooked up the last cargo net—it held the tail fin, the .50-caliber machine gun, and the rucksacks to give it additional stability—and jumped aboard.

The CIL team left Port Moresby for Sydney on an Air Niugini flight on the afternoon of Tuesday, May 11. Bruce Hoy was at the airport to see the men off. On the afternoon of the twelfth, they boarded a nonstop flight for Honolulu. Colonel Rosenberg sat in the no-smoking section. The rest of the team sat in the smoking section, at a calculated distance from the colonel. They drank many small bottles of complimentary wine and got rather loud. The flight attendants had to ask them several times to quiet down. After dinner, a movie was shown. It was *On Golden Pond,* starring Henry Fonda, Katharine Hepburn, and Jane Fonda. In Kelly's judgment, it had been morally wrong for Jane Fonda to go to Hanoi while Americans were being held prisoner there. He refused to see any of her movies, and after her workout book and cassette became popular he wouldn't let his wife buy them. As he flew east across the Pacific, ignoring the screen, Kelly began wondering how many of the men on 41081 Tadao Furue would be able to identify. If he couldn't identify all twenty-two, Dave Kelly was determined to go back to Mt. Thumb and continue digging in the vicinity of the parachute.

PART II

IDENTIFICATION

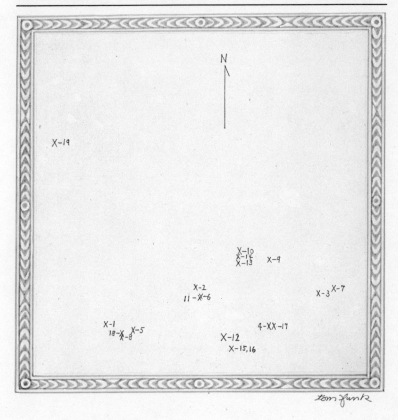

I T IS A TEN-MINUTE DRIVE from the airport to the Central Identification Laboratory, which in 1982 occupied half of a two-story cream-colored cinder-block building (No. 1027) and all of a one-story cream-colored cinder-block building (No. 1028) next door. The buildings are on a down-at-the-heels pier in the international section of the Honolulu port, in the midst of an expanse of blacktop used for unloading and storing cargo. The CIL's windows look out on containers filled with heavy machinery and pallets stacked with lumber—some of the least scenic vistas in the city. Most of the CIL's offices and its conference room are on the ground floor of No. 1027 (Army auditors are known to work overhead but are never heard and scarcely ever seen), and most visitors to the CIL are received in No. 1027. Building No. 1028, which was a United States Customs building in a previous incarnation, is surrounded by a barbed-wire cyclone fence. Affixed to one of its doors—the door that faces No. 1027 and is used most often—is a sign that reads:

NO SMOKING
IN RESPECT FOR THE DECEASED PLEASE REMOVE HEADGEAR
RESTRICTED AREA
AUTHORIZED PERSONNEL ONLY

In No. 1028 are the office of Tadao Furue; an identification-specialist's cubicle; a clerk-typist's cubicle; a small photography lab; and a good-sized records room. The walls of the records room are papered with maps of the world, of Vietnam, Laos, Cambodia, Korea, and Papua New Guinea. Fifty-two locked file cabinets, more than three-quarters of them containing records pertaining to the Vietnam dead, cover most of a linoleum-tile floor. The majority of the building's floor space, however, is taken up by one high-ceilinged room. The room, known as "the lab floor," is almost 60 feet long and 50 feet wide, and Building No. 1028 is often referred to as "the lab." It was on the lab floor that the remains brought back from Papua New Guinea would be identified.

Just before the team's return, Leslie Stewart, an identification specialist, and a sergeant had taken eighteen collapsible stretchers from a storage shed behind Building No. 1028, had set each olive-drab stretcher on the lab floor on waist-high stretcher stands, and had covered each stretcher with a white sheet. Now they and several members of the team opened the olive-drab bags and put one large plastic bag on each stretcher. At the back end of the lab floor were a number of storage racks; on them were stretchers holding remains that could not be identified or were awaiting processing. The remains from the Mt. Thumb B-24 were to spend a few weeks on the storage racks, but for most of the next eight months they were to be on the lab floor.

On May 13, Leslie Stewart and two other men started to wash the remains from the B-24 in two sinks in a corner of the lab floor. Screens were placed over the drains to prevent any possible loss of valuable material. Each large plastic bag was opened separately and its contents washed in cold water. The men used their fingers and soft brushes to remove the soil in which the bones had lain for thirty-eight years. The bones were fragile. If there were any teeth in a plastic bag, they were cleansed with toothbrushes. When the men were finished with the remains from X-1, they placed them to dry on the stretcher that had been tagged X-1, and went on to unpack and wash the bones from X-2. The washing and drying took about two weeks. Stewart then laid out the remains on each of the eighteen stretchers so that the bones occupied their normal positions relative to the other bones of a human skeleton.

The CIL owns two complete skeletons—perfect specimens, of the sort bought from medical-supply firms to teach aspiring doctors and physical anthropologists anatomy. On a lab skeleton, all two hundred and six bones of the human body, which are originally ivory in color, have been bleached white, and the bones have been wired together. All twenty-six vertebrae and twelve pairs of ribs, all fifty-four wrist, hand, and finger bones, and all fifty-two ankle, foot, and toe bones are present and accounted for: the specimens had died of natural causes. Two facial bones (the maxillae) form the upper jaw and serve as the foundation for the sixteen upper teeth. A large horseshoe-shaped facial bone (the mandible) forms the lower jaw and supports the sixteen lower teeth. If any teeth are missing, the chances are they have fallen out. Most medical-supply firms in the United States acquire specimens in India, from poor communities whose residents cannot afford dentists.

The difference in appearance between the lab-specimen skeletons and the bones that Stewart had laid out on the eighteen stretchers was quite comparable to the difference between the B-24 when it took off from Port Moresby on March 22, 1944, for Nadzab, and the B-24 less than half an hour later, after it had crashed into the side of Mt. Thumb. When the CIL team saw the B-24 in April 1982 a few of its large parts were fairly intact and recognizable, but some parts had been damaged almost beyond recognition and others, most of the left wing, for example, were never found; they had probably been consumed in a fire that started after the crash.

The B-24 had flown into the mountainside at a speed of approximately 150 miles per hour. As a result of the impact, a large number of the bones had broken. In addition to the trauma originally suffered by the bones on March 22, 1944, even those that were intact after the crash had deteriorated during the thirty-eight years they spent in the wet soil of the tropical rain forest. (The intervening years had been kinder to the metal parts of the plane.) The small bones, such as the phalanges, metatarsals, and cuneiforms of the feet, are always among the first to disappear in such circumstances. Few were found. The hipbones, which consist of the ilium, the ischium, and the pubis—three separate bones that unite during adolescence—are usually called the innominates, because they bear no resemblance to any other object. The innominates are heavy and tend to endure. The twelve long bones of the upper and lower limbs—the right and left upper-arm bone (the humerus), the right and left bone on the thumb side of the forearm (the radius), the right and left bone on the little-finger side of the forearm (the ulna), the right and left thighbone (the femur), the right and left shinbone (the tibia), and the right and left calf bone (the fibula)—are also quite durable. Long bones consist of a shaft and two ends; the ends are less dense and disintegrate before the more compact shafts. Many long bones were missing from these remains. Some had perhaps been washed away after the crash: the plane had come to rest on a steep hillside, and there was a stream below the hillside.

In the first half of June, when Tadao Furue looked at the remains on the eighteen stretchers, his immediate reaction was that there were indeed remarkably few bones, and that those present were in remarkably poor condition. With twenty-two individuals on the plane, there could have been 4532 bones if they had all been recovered. There were fewer than a thousand. Four of the stretchers—X-2; X-4; X-15, 16; and X-17—appeared quite crowded. Many were rather bare. There were fewer than twenty-five bones each on X-5 and on X-9. Leslie Stewart had put any jawbones and teeth that had been in the plastic bags at the tops of the stretchers. Teeth are by far the longest-lasting parts of the human body (dental enamel is one of the hardest substances found in the natural world) and are the most valuable in the identification of skeletal remains. If each of the twenty-two passengers had had thirty-two teeth and if all these had been recovered, there would have been seven hundred and four teeth on the stretchers; there were a hundred and eighty-one. Furue wished he had more bones to work with: it is much easier to identify an individual if you have two hundred and six bones or a hundred bones than if you have twenty. He also wished there were more teeth. He could see that the team had recovered no teeth for a number of the men who had been on the plane.

The remains on the stretchers had been found by the team in a small area of the crash site and were commingled—a frequent occurrence in plane crashes. The purpose of laying out the bones on each stretcher in proper anatomical order is to provide an early visual awareness of commingling. It was easy for Furue to see that there were the remains of at least three men on X-2, because there were duplicates and triplicates of bones that an individual has only one of—for example, two right femora and three left femora. There wasn't just copious commingling on crowded stretchers, like X-2 and X-17; there was obvious commingling on fully half the stretchers, including some that were almost as sparsely populated as X-5 and X-9. There were only sixteen bone fragments (besides some skull portions) on X-19, yet these included portions of three right humeri and two right femora.

The first step taken by a physical anthropologist in identifying commingled remains is called segregation—the uncommingling of the remains. In remains from a crash like this, with such extensive commingling of bones in very poor condition, segregation is by far the most difficult and time-consuming part of the identification process. An adept student of physical anthropology may learn in a few days or weeks the difference between an intact right tibia and an intact left tibia and the difference between the sixth and the seventh thoracic vertebra on a specimen skeleton. It might have taken such a student years to ascertain whether some of the pale-brown weathered bone segments on the eighteen stretchers were part of thoracic or lumbar vertebrae—an ability that Furue had acquired during three decades spent identifying the victims of plane crashes and other disasters.

Tadao Furue (pronounced Fur-ROO-eh), a Japanese citizen who was fifty-seven years old in May 1982, had studied anthropology at the University of Tokyo, had received his Bachelor of Science degree in 1950, and had become an assistant in the Department of Anatomy of the Nara Medical College. In 1951, General Douglas MacArthur's headquarters had needed a physical anthropologist for five months to identify some Korean War casualties. Furue had asked for a leave of absence and had accepted the temporary job. It evolved into something more permanent: he has now been working for the United States Army for thirty-five years. From 1951 until 1977, he was a "contract" employee and lived in Japan. In the 1960s, difficult cases from Indo-China were sent to him. He was also assigned to Vietnam and to Thailand on a number of occasions, for periods of up to three months, to identify remains from the Vietnam War. In 1977 he moved to Hawaii, with his wife and daughter, and went to work for the CIL as a Department of the Army civilian employee. Furue, who has had more experience in identifying military remains than any other physical anthropologist in the world, says that his work, and particularly segregation, has several requirements to which he lays claim: "nerves of steel," "great tenacity," and "a strong personality."

"If some of the other physical anthropologists I've worked with had seen the eighteen stretchers, they might have written a report to the effect that 'Due to the nature of the crash, individual identification is not possible, therefore it is recommended that the commingled remains receive a group burial,'" he says. "You can't look at shattered bones and either panic or mentally give up. You have to tell yourself that it may take weeks or months to piece fragments together and fit loose teeth into the proper sockets. It takes time to put a puzzle together. I think of my work as solving a high-dimensional jigsaw puzzle."

You also have to like hard cases, Furue adds. He thrives on them, which is just as well, because the CIL receives hard-to-identify remains not only from all branches of the military but also from civilian disasters. Two hundred and forty-one servicemen, most of them marines, were killed when a building that the marines were using as a barracks at Beirut International Airport was blown up by Middle Eastern terrorists on October 23, 1983. The remains of two of the men who couldn't be identified by identification specialists at the United States Army Mortuary in Frankfurt, Germany, the largest military mortuary in Europe, were hand-carried to the CIL in a small card-file box. Furue was able to identify them as two young lance corporals who had been assigned to the arms room at the time of the incident.

Tadao Furue is a perfectionist. He first reviewed Stewart's preliminary work, correcting some errors that had been made in laying out the remains. Right and left humeri and right and left femora had been reversed, and partial femora had been mistaken for partial tibiae and other bones. Stewart had put together with surgical tape only a few long bones that were broken into two pieces. Furue started piecing together many other long bones, as well as vertebrae and the cranial and facial bones of the skull. It was indeed slow, tedious work. He began to commit to memory the bones on each stretcher and to decide which bones on each had once belonged to one individual. Furue is familiar with the procedures followed by the CIL's search-and-recovery teams in the field. He respects the fact that the bags containing bones (and often teeth and personal effects) represent an initial form of sorting. For this reason, the contents of each bag are kept separate while they are washed and laid out on the stretchers.

The greatest single aid in the preliminary stage of segregation, so readily visible on Stretcher X-2, is duplication—and, in this instance, triplication—of bones. After Furue had inspected the remains on X-2, he asked for two additional stretchers, which were tagged X-2A and X-2B. What made it unusually easy for him to see that most of the bones on X-2 belonged to three individuals was the disparity in the length of the limb bones: variation in bone length is a second significant factor in segregation. In Furue's informed opinion, one man had been of medium height. The bones that Furue believed to be his were pieced together and laid out on Stretcher X-2. A second man had been extremely tall. The bones that Furue believed to be his were laid out on X-2A. The third had been extremely short; his bones were put on X-2B. Age is a third critical element in segregation. Furue could tell that the man on X-2 had been in his late twenties and the men on X-2A and X-2B in their early twenties. If segregation consisted of merely examining the pieced-together bones on one stretcher and dividing them up on three stretchers, it would be only a moderately difficult, time-consuming, nerve-racking enterprise. Some of the bones found at the X-2 site didn't belong on either X-2 or X-2A or X-2B, however, and some of the bones that were originally on other stretchers (it eventually turned out) did.

The work of sorting out the femora that Furue found on X-2 gives an indication of what was involved in this one aspect of segregation. There were two right femora. He allocated one to the medium-tall man on X-2, the other to the very tall man on X-2A. There were three left femora. A very long one was put on Stretcher X-2A; it matched X-2A's right femur. Bilateral symmetry is another principle used in segregation. People's left and right arms and legs generally look alike because the bones in their left and right arms and legs do. (Exceptions to the rule include baseball players, and especially pitchers—something that Furue had learned when he was a university student and had the opportunity to examine and measure the arms of the members of a well-known Japanese baseball team.) Furue put a very short left femur on Stretcher X-2B, which at this stage had no right femur. Usually, an individual with short arm bones has short thighbones. The scale of the left humerus, radius, and ulna on X-2B accorded with the very short left femur, as did the scale of such other bones as the left and right clavicles (the collarbones) and the right scapula (the shoulder blade).

Furue realized that the third left femur originally on X-2 didn't belong to the medium-tall individual whose bones were now on X-2. It didn't resemble X-2's right femur, and it differed in appearance from the other bones. It seemed to belong to a man who had been shorter than the man on X-2, though not quite as short as the man on X-2B, and one whose build had been heavier than that of either of those two men, whose bones indicated that they had been of medium build. While Furue is segregating commingled remains, he evaluates each individual's build. Even the spongy inner-bone texture of this third left femur was different from the texture of the other bones on X-2. Bone texture is another aid in segregation. "Bones and teeth will surrender many facts about a person's physical attributes and his cultural patterns, so a good bone detective must make multi-dimensional observations," Furue says.

When Tadao Furue turned his attention to Stretcher X-10, he concluded that most of the bones on it belonged to two people. The one whose bones he left on X-10 had been a man who was quite short and of medium build; the one whose bones he shifted to Stretcher X-10A had been about the same height, but his bones showed he had been far heavier. There was a partial right femur and almost a whole right femur on Stretcher X-10. Furue left the partial femur there, because it corresponded to the other bones on X-10. He saw that the almost intact right femur was too short and too slender for either the individual on X-10 or the one on X-10A. After examining the remains on every stretcher on the lab floor, he found its place: it matched the very short left femur on X-2B perfectly. That left the individual on X-10A without a right femur, but only temporarily: X-10A got a right femur from X-6.

Meanwhile, Furue had been segregating the bones on X-4 and X-17, which had been dug up by a CIL sergeant on separate days but at spots that were not much more than a yard apart. Furue determined that most of these bones belonged to three individuals—to two rather tall men of medium build (they were designated X-4 and X-4-17) and to one who had been quite short and of medium build, X-4-17A. There had been four left femora on X-4 and X-17. One went to X-4, one to X-4-17, one to X-4-17A, and one to X-6. There had been three right femora at X-4 and X-17. One went to X-4 and one to X-4-17. The third right femur didn't match the other bones on X-4-17A. It was the bone of a thinner man and went to X-6.

Thus far, X-4-17A lacked a right femur. It acquired one shortly. Furue had made up his mind that most of the bones on Stretcher X-14 belonged to two individuals—a thin man of medium height, who was designated X-14, and a very tall, thin man, designated X-14A. There were two left femora on X-14—one for X-14, the second for X-14A—and three right femora. One of these was for X-14, another for X-14A; the third wound up on Stretcher X-4-17A: it matched the left femur already there.

When Furue got to Stretcher X-19, he determined that most of the bones were those of two individuals, X-19 and X-19A. There was a partial femur and an almost complete femur on that stretcher. The partial femur, which he pieced together with a fragment of femur from Stretcher X-13, went to X-19A, a slight man of medium height. The almost complete right femur went to X-19, a rather short, heavily built man. The third left femur that had been on X-2 finally found its place—on X-19, where it matched the right femur in size and symmetry. Movement between Stretchers X-2 and X-19 proved to be a two-way proposition: both X-2 and X-2B got partial right humeri from X-19. There was some additional transferring of femora, but one bone that X-2 never did get from any other stretcher was a left femur.

Furue's identifications have so rarely been challenged by the families of those whom he has identified, and so rarely submitted to other physical anthropologists for verification, that he feels he must be extremely severe with himself. "I have only one sister, who lives in Japan, but I imagine that in the lab with me I have a vicious twin brother, another Tadao, who questions everything I do," he says. "When I am segregating remains and I switch a bone from X-6 to X-10A, I can almost hear my twin brother asking, 'Are you sure that's reasonable?' I look at the rough crash-site sketch made by one of the sergeants in the field and redraw it to scale and verify where each X number was recovered. X-6 and X-10 were 14 feet apart. Perfectly reasonable. I also study the photographs taken by another sergeant in the field. I may ask him whether a certain bone was found above or below the surface, or in exactly which position. Before I move a bone from one stretcher to another, I mark it with the number of the stretcher on which it started out, so I won't lose track of it, and if I move, say, a left femur, I make sure that it doesn't fit on any of the other stretchers—even those that already have left femora that seem to belong where they are. I try to create my own system of checks and balances."

Had Furue decided only that there were three individuals on X-2, three on X-4 and X-17, two on X-10, two on X-14, and two on X-19, thereby adding six stretchers to the original eighteen on the lab floor, he might have had twenty-four stretchers, but as he was adding six X numbers he subtracted two. There were about twenty bones or partial bones (plus some partial jawbones and a few teeth) on Stretcher X-5. These bones included a right humerus, a right radius, a right ulna, and a left humerus. There was approximately the same number of bones (and some additional jawbone fragments and teeth) on Stretcher X-8, including a left ulna and a left radius. There were some tiny bone pieces on Stretcher X-18—the largest was a portion of an innominate measuring approximately 2 inches by 4—and still more jawbone fragments and two teeth. To Furue, the remains on the three stretchers appeared startlingly alike; he was convinced that they all belonged to one man, whom he designated X-5.

The skeleton is the body's internal framework. Its primary function is that of support. Just as beams hold up buildings, the skeleton holds the human body erect. Unlike buildings, however, the body doesn't stay still. Where bones meet bones, joints—"articulations," in the language of physical anthropology—make the skeleton flexible and give it movement. Most bones articulate with other bones in one or more places. At its proximal (or upper) end, the humerus articulates with the scapula. At its distal (or lower) end, it articulates with the radius and the ulna; this articulation is the elbow joint. The radius and the ulna articulate with each other at both their ends. X-5's right humerus and right ulna articulated: they fitted together perfectly. When bones do not articulate, it is obvious; trying to force them to do so is as futile as trying to open a door with a key that doesn't fit the lock. Articulation is a cardinal principle of segregation—one that Furue used as often as possible while he was uncommingling the bones on all the stretchers on the lab floor. Furue would have been able to articulate more bones if so many of those that were present had not lacked ends. In the case of X-5, he couldn't articulate the three long bones of the leg—these meet up in much the same fashion as the arm bones—because X-5 had only a fraction of a left femur and a partial right fibula.

Tadao Furue spent a week piecing together X-5's left and right innominates, major portions of X-5's skull, and its axis—as the second cervical vertebra is known. In 1982, Furue was the only full-time physical anthropologist employed by the United States Army to do identification. The Army didn't have an odontologist, a specialist in the science of teeth, assigned to work full time on identification. Furue had made himself proficient in odontology and took pride in his ability to segregate commingled teeth and to fit into their proper sockets teeth that have been found loose. By the time he finished with X-5, he had not only pieced together portions of the maxillae and a number of upper teeth from X-5 and X-8, and portions of the mandible and lower teeth from X-8 and X-18, but had also taken loose teeth from Stretcher X-1 (the remains numbered X-1, X-5, X-8, and X-18 had been recovered by different sergeants on different days in close proximity) and put them in their proper places—one in X-5's right maxilla, the other in X-5's left maxilla. Furue spent more time on X-5 than on any other remains, and recalls this work with special satisfaction. As a high-school student, Furue had planned to be an engineer, but after seeing

Modern Times, Charlie Chaplin's satirical movie about the dehumanizing effects of technology, he decided he wanted to work in a profession that was less mechanical. A remains like X-5 always makes him glad he chose to become a physical anthropologist. "I'm bewitched by the beauty of bones," he often says. "They're not mass-produced cast material. Each set of bones has its own individuality, and so does each set of teeth. Even after a man has lost his life and has lain on a far-off island with others for thirty-eight years, his bones and teeth are often unique, so I may be able to make a human contribution. I may be able to keep him from being forever unknown."

In June, when Furue first saw the remains from the B-24 laid out on the eighteen stretchers at the CIL, he had believed that it would take him three months to identify the remains, if there were no interruptions. There were interruptions, and segregation proved even more difficult than he had originally assumed. When he finished segregating the remains, not a single stretcher on the lab floor had the same bones it had started out with. Originally, Furue had believed that Stretcher X-1 held the remains of only one individual, and had believed the same of Stretcher X-7, but even these stretchers had eventually had skeletal fragments removed: X-1 had provided X-5 with part of the right innominate and with two teeth, and X-3 had supplied X-7 with a right ulna and X-9 with a piece of the left scapula. Even some of the smallest bones had been moved—X-14 contributed a fragment of the right innominate and of the first lumbar vertebra to X-13.

After segregation, there were twenty-two stretchers on the lab floor. Furue had known since the team's return that there were twenty-two men on the manifest of the B-24: the CIL is a small organization and such news travels fast. About forty years earlier, he had read Arthur Conan Doyle and had been impressed by his fictional detective Sherlock Holmes, because Holmes was properly wary of easy assumptions. Twenty years earlier, he had learned that manifests were fallible. While he was working in Japan, he had identified the remains from a Second World War plane crash that was recovered during the mid-1960s. There had been twenty-three men on the plane's manifest. When Furue segregated the remains, he discovered that there had been twenty-four men aboard. The twenty-fourth man had been a hitchhiker and was subsequently identified. Furue hadn't found a single bone on any of the original eighteen stretchers from the B-24 which suggested the presence of an unmanifested passenger.

The twenty-two stretchers were numbered X-1, X-2, X-2A, X-2B, X-3, X-4, X-4-17, X-4-17A, X-5, X-6, X-7, X-9, X-10, X-10A, X-11, X-12, X-13, X-14, X-14A, X-15, 16 (Furue had found some commingling on that stretcher, but most of the bones belonged to one individual, not two, and three bones that didn't were now on X-12), X-19, and X-19A. Many stretchers held fewer bones than they had in June. The stretcher that was the most strikingly bare was X-19A. There were six bones on X-19A—a partial left tibia, a partial left ulna, a small section of the left femur, a portion of the right femur, a major portion of the right innominate, and a modest section of the left innominate. There wasn't a tooth on X-19A.

The CIL's hours are from 7:00 A.M. to 3:30 P.M. Monday through Friday. Furue often stays on alone until the late afternoon, goes home for dinner, and returns to the lab to work into the night. He often works weekends. "X-19A was the hardest case to sell to my evil twin brother," he recalled afterward. "My first impression of the remains, in June, was that there were at least twenty individuals on the stretchers. After several months, I gradually became sure that there were twenty-one. If there had been, I would have finished much sooner. I spent three days in late November checking to see if the six bones on X-19A could possibly belong on one or more of the other stretchers. They couldn't. X-19A's partial right femur and right innominate were morphologically inseparable. No other femur could conceivably match that innominate. Nor could the combination of that femur and innominate fit into the remains on any of the twenty-one other stretchers. The right partial innominates on seventeen stretchers duplicated the sizable part of the right innominate on X-19A. Four other stretchers completely lacked right innominates, but all four had right femora that duplicated X-19A's partial right femur. On the evening of the third day, as I paced the deserted floor of the lab, I said to myself, 'If I've segregated the remains brought back from Mt. Thumb perfectly, if I've reduced the commingling to zero, each stretcher should now have on it all that the team recovered of what were once twenty-two human beings.'"

Furue's next concern was to determine from the remains on the twenty-two stretchers precisely what those human beings' physical characteristics had been on March 22, 1944, just before the B-24 crashed into Mt. Thumb.

There are five primary characteristics that an experienced physical anthropologist can read from unknown skeletal remains. Some bones (particularly those that form the pelvis) disclose sex. The skull and teeth reveal whether an individual is a Caucasoid, a Negroid, or a Mongoloid (the three major races). In March 1977 the Vietnamese had turned over what they said were the remains of twelve American pilots to a special commission of prominent American citizens. According to the Vietnamese, these pilots had been shot down over the North between 1965 and 1968, had died in captivity, and had been buried in several cemeteries around Hanoi, one of which was named Van Diem. Furue determined that one of the twelve was a Southeast Asian Mongoloid man who had been at least fifty years old. The special commission had been told that among the people buried in Van Diem were two hundred and fifty civilians killed in American bombing raids on Hanoi. The Mongoloid remains were presumably those of a Vietnamese civilian.

In early June, Furue had checked to make sure that the remains on the twenty-two stretchers at the CIL were all those of white males; they were. The three other primary characteristics that Furue could ascertain from the bones, which he had used to a significant extent in segregating the remains, would be essential in differentiating them. One was age. The bones of the human body are not fully formed in childhood. In children, most bones—including the long bones—consist of a diaphysis (or shaft) and two epiphyses (end portions), which are separated by a thin layer of cartilage known as the epiphyseal plate. It is this arrangement that enables bones to increase in length. As growth occurs, the cartilage disappears and the diaphysis and the epiphyses unite into one bone; eventually, all that is left of the epiphyseal plate is a vestigial line. Studies have shown that "epiphyseal union" takes place in the long bones of young men in an orderly sequence between the ages of about seventeen and twenty-five. Even when individual rates of growth are taken into account, a physical anthropologist can determine the age of young men with a high degree of precision. Furue can recognize the stages of epiphyseal union—from none, through one-quarter, one-half, or three-quarters united or fused, to completely united or fused—and he is often able to judge how long before death unions occurred by assessing the vestigial lines.

Furue is relieved when an unknown remains has a clavicle, because clavicular epiphyses fuse later than those of the long bones and are useful in determining the age of remains up to the age of thirty. Like all physical anthropologists, he is especially relieved when he sees an innominate, the bone that has been found to be the most accurate indicator of estimated age—one that may be useful up to the age of fifty. The left and right innominates meet in front to form the pubic symphysis, which undergoes a regular metamorphosis and is one of the most useful areas for determining the age of an adult even past the age of fifty.

In life, the younger a person is, the easier it is to assess his age correctly. One may misjudge a baby's age, but not by more than a couple of months. One may overestimate or underestimate the age of a sixteen-year-old, but usually not by more than a couple of years. A person who is forty-five may look fifty or fifty-five, whereas another forty-five-year-old may appear to be thirty-five or forty. In death, too, as a general rule, the younger an individual is, the more accurately Furue can assess his age from his skeletal remains. After Furue studied the bones on Stretchers X-2A and X-4, he estimated the ages of both individuals as between twenty and twenty-two, which is to say that he believed they were at least twenty years old but had not yet reached their twenty-third birthdays. After studying the bones on X-2 and X-3, Furue estimated the ages of both those individuals as between twenty-five and thirty. He could occasionally be fairly precise in estimating the ages of older individuals, especially if a large number of bones was present. "The more bones the better," Furue says. "I need quantity as well as quality. If I have a lot of bones, I can see whether the aging criteria are consistent."

Furue was able to estimate X-12's age as between thirty and thirty-five, because there were many bones on Stretcher X-12, including both clavicles, and it was one of just three remains on the twenty-two stretchers that had well-preserved pubic symphyses. Furue could estimate X-10A's age only as between twenty-five and thirty-five. There were just ten partial bones on X-10A, no pubic symphysis, and no scapula (another bone that Furue finds useful for assessing age in the mid- and late twenties), and the partial right clavicle on X-10A, in Furue's words, "lacked usable areas for estimating age." He recorded the age of each of the twenty-two remains on a "working form"—a copy of Department of Defense Form 892 (a "Record of Identification Processing").

The second characteristic Tadao Furue recorded on a working form 892 was the height of each remains. Anatomists have been measuring bones for centuries—in 1755, an anatomy professor at the Louvre published some measurements he had made for the purpose of providing artists with a means of rendering the human body in correct proportions—and generations of artists and anatomists have known that there is a correlation between an individual's stature and the length of his long bones. It wasn't until the late nineteenth century that physical anthropologists in Europe attempted to estimate stature from the long bones, and it wasn't until the middle of the twentieth century that an American physical anthropologist—Dr. Mildred Trotter—was presented with a sufficient number of subjects to enable her to devise reliable algebraic formulas that could be used to estimate the living height of an unknown from his bones.

In 1948 Dr. Trotter, a professor of anatomy at Washington University in St. Louis, was assigned to Honolulu, where Second World War remains from the Pacific theater which had been temporarily buried overseas were being brought back by the Army Graves Registration Service for preparation for final burial. Dr. Trotter measured the bones of hundreds of these servicemen, who had been measured upon their .nduction into military service, and whose identities had never been in question. The vast majority of the men were white; the rest were black. From her research, Dr. Trotter concluded that the relationship of stature to long-limb bones differs sufficiently among men of different races to require different formulas, and also that the lengths of the lower-limb bones are more highly correlated with stature than are the lengths of the upper-limb bones; therefore arm bones should not be used in the estimation of stature unless no leg bones are available.

The formulas derived from the measurements that Dr. Trotter made in 1948 and 1949 were published in 1952. The table below, for white males, is given in centimeters and is arranged in order of increasing standard error of estimate.

$$1.30 \text{ (Femur + Tibia) + } 63.29 \quad \pm 2.99$$
$$2.38 \text{ Femur + } 61.41 \quad \pm 3.27$$
$$2.68 \text{ Fibula + } 71.78 \quad \pm 3.29$$
$$2.52 \text{ Tibia + } 78.62 \quad \pm 3.37$$
$$3.08 \text{ Humerus + } 70.45 \quad \pm 4.05$$
$$3.70 \text{ Ulna + } 74.05 \quad \pm 4.32$$
$$3.78 \text{ Radius + } 79.01 \quad \pm 4.32$$

X-1 had a femur that measured 46 centimeters and a tibia that measured 36.5 centimeters. Using the Trotter formula, Furue added these two numbers (which came to 82.5 cm), multiplied 82.5 cm by 1.30 (which came to 107.25 cm), added 63.29 cm, and got X-1's height: 170.54 cm. According to the Trotter formula, X-1's height should have been no more than 2.99 cm greater or less than 170.54 cm. There are 2.54 centimeters per inch, so Furue divided 170.54 by 2.54 and got X-1's height in inches: 67.1. The margin for error was 2.99 cm, or 1.17 inches. Because X-5 had only fragments of the lower limbs, Furue had to use a humerus. It measured 35 cm. He multiplied 35 cm by 3.08 and added 70.45 cm, divided by 2.54, and got X-5's height in inches—70.2. The margin for error was 4.05 cm—1.59 inches. He was able to use a femur plus tibia to estimate the height of six sets of remains and a femur to estimate the height of eleven others. He had to make do with a fibula once, a tibia once, and a humerus twice. In only one instance did he have to resort to a radius, where the margin for error is 4.32 cm, or 1.70 inches.

Before Furue was able to employ any of the Trotter formulas, he had to measure the available long bones. Measuring a bone is somewhat trickier than measuring a desk. Bones cannot be measured with rulers. On the other hand, once one has mastered the art of positioning and rotating bones on a device called an osteometric board to obtain their maximum lengths, measuring bones is a great deal easier than estimating the lengths of complete bones from partial bones. During segregation, Furue had been able to measure only four long bones—X-2A's right femur and X-4-17's left femur, tibia, and radius. (He obtained X-4-17's height by using his left femur and tibia; he also measured X-4-17's radius and figured out his height from the radius, but only as one of his numerous self-imposed checks and balances.) He had to estimate the lengths of fifty-six bones before he could estimate the heights of the twenty other remains. There are formulas for calculating the length of long bones from partial bones, but Furue doesn't use them, because he has found them unreliable. Instead, he studies the surface contour of each partial bone. He is familiar with the precise location of all its "landmarks"—its projections and ridges and the openings through which it receives nutrients—and with the distinctive way in which each long bone tapers. He then compares a partial bone with a similar complete specimen bone in the CIL's collection. He says he is usually able to estimate the length of a bone if he has at least one-third of it.

There are no formulas to help Furue assess muscularity, the third, and last major characteristic to be recorded on the working forms, from the remains on the stretchers. He simply holds a bone in one hand, looks at the ridges (to which the individual's muscles were once attached), does the same with many of the other bones on that stretcher, and decides whether they belonged to a man who was of slight muscularity/slender build; of average muscularity/medium build; or of well-developed muscularity/heavy build. He sometimes subdivides builds; for example, a set of bones may strike him as being of subaverage muscularity/medium build. He has been asked if dieting changes the appearance of bones, and has answered that it doesn't. "Prolonged starvation in a prison camp might change the bony substrata, but in estimating muscularity I've never been fooled by weight changes in my years of handling military remains," he says.

All methods of identification use the basic process of comparison. The identification of human skeletal remains requires the matching of physical characteristics derived from the remains with physical characteristics that are a matter of record. Before the search-and-recovery team left for Papua New Guinea in April, the CIL had obtained the Missing Air Crew Report for 42-41081 and also the missing-in-action files of its crew of three and its nineteen passengers. The files held a fair amount of information about each serviceman. Every file had the man's rank, serial number, date of birth, height, and weight, and the name and address of at least one of his next of kin. While Furue was recording the estimated age, height, and muscularity for the twenty-two remains, Leslie Stewart was examining the men's antemortem records. It was much simpler to put the physical characteristics from the records on paper in such a way as to enable Furue to compare the records of the twenty-two men easily with the readings from the remains than it had been to elicit the information from the remains. Stewart looked up each man's date of birth and figured out the man's age on March 22, 1944. He wrote down each man's height and weight. Furue verified Stewart's figures. Three of the men had been measured and weighed more than once. Furue used the greater height and the highest weight when he calculated each man's body-build index, because they were the most recent and, with a few exceptions, he had learned that the latest figures on a record were the most accurate. These numbers would be compared to Furue's readings of muscularity from the remains. To obtain each man's body-build index, he employed a mathematical formula that had been devised by a German physical anthropologist named Fritz Rohrer in 1921. The formula—weight in grams divided by height in centimeters cubed, and the quotient multiplied by a hundred ($g/cm^3 \times 100$)—yielded twenty-two body-build indices, which ranged from 1.00 to 1.67: the lower the number, the more slightly built the man. Figures between 1.00 and 1.15 indicated slender men, figures from 1.15 up to about 1.40 men of medium build, and figures over 1.40 those of heavy build.

The most recent record of one of the three tallest men on the plane showed that his height was 72 inches; his last recorded weight was 180 pounds.

180 lbs. = 81.6 kg, or 81,600 g

100 × 81,600 = 8,160,000

72 in. = 182.88 cm

182.88^3 = 6,116,438.863

8,160,000 divided by 6,116,438.863 = 1.33

So 1.33 was the man's Rohrer body-build index. Furue and his calculator are seldom parted.

Furue filled out a few pages of legal-size paper with a combination of information from the records and body-build indices. (He had used two other indices besides Rohrer's, as a check and balance.) He arranged the information from the records in order of the men's heights, because he regarded height as the most significant single physical characteristic in these identifications. There were three men in the very tall group, ten in the medium-tall group, eight in the medium-short group, and one very short man. The table opposite is an abridged version of the relevant data that Furue wrote down.

Furue arranged the working forms in the numerical order of the twenty-two stretchers, from X-1 to X-19A. Then he compared the physical characteristics of the remains to the data from the records, starting with X-1.

According to Furue's reading of the remains, the man on X-1 had been 67.1 inches tall, he had been of medium build, and he had been between twenty-three and twenty-six years old on the day of the crash. In a crowded room, a person might not notice the difference in height between a man who is 5 feet 7 inches and one who is 5 feet 9 inches. A 2-inch difference in height appears much greater on the bones, and therefore a less conscientious physical anthropologist might not have bothered to compare the man on X-1 with the three men in the very tall category, or even with the ten men in the medium-tall category. Furue, however, compared the man on X-1 with the record of each of the twenty-two men whose names had been on the man-

NAME	HEIGHT IN INCHES	WEIGHT IN POUNDS	ROHRER BODY-BUILD INDEX	AGE (years, months, days)
Allred, Robert E.	72	180	1.33	28-4-25
Holm, Keith T.	72	142	1.05	23-6-28
Shrake, William M.	72	135	1.00	20-7-29
Frazier, Weldon W.	71	156	1.21	25-2-27
Kachorek, Joseph E., Jr.	70½	212	1.67	32-8-16
Young, Emory C.	70½	159	1.26	21-0-28
Atkins, Harold	70	170	1.37	23-0-27
Carpenter, Thomas J., Jr.	70	152	1.23	22-8-5
Samples, Charles, Jr.	70	141	1.14	24-5-28
Loop, Carlin E.	69½	161	1.33	26-3-5
Landrum, Harvey E.	69½	140	1.15	24-8-23
Thompson, Robert C.	69½	130	1.07	22-7-16
Walker, Melvin F.	69	145	1.22	28-0-25
Steiner, Charles R.	68	162	1.43	26-5-18
Ginter, Frank	67½	155	1.40	27-3-2
Staseowski, John J.	67	173	1.59	29-7-11
Barnard, Charles R.	67	148	1.36	23-10-0
Butler, Clint P.	67	120	1.10	20-8-22
Gross, Stanley G.	66½	141	1.33	26-1-18
Lawrence, Stanley C.	66¼	139	1.32	25-1-12
Mettam, Joseph B.	66	168	1.62	24-3-24
Geis, Raymond J., Jr.	64	139	1.47	21-0-0

ifest of 41081, starting with Allred. "The more I do, the less chance there is of error creeping in," he says. "Who knows when an extra look at remains will help me to detect a mistake I may have made in segregation?" Robert E. Allred was not only much too tall to be X-1 but also too old. Keith T. Holm was too tall and too slight of build. William M. Shrake was too tall and too slight (Furue had never seen a lower Rohrer index than Shrake's) and too young.

In the medium-tall category, Weldon W. Frazier was too tall and Joseph E. Kachorek, Jr., was too tall, too heavy, and much too old to be the man on X-1. When Furue compared the readings of the remains on twenty-one of the stretchers on the lab floor with Kachorek's record, Kachorek was easy to rule out. At 212 pounds and thirty-two years eight months and sixteen days, he was more heavily built than anyone else on the plane and more than three years older than the next-oldest man. Kachorek's Rohrer index was the highest that Furue had ever come across. Emory C. Young was too tall and too young to be the man on X-1; Harold Atkins was too tall; Thomas J. Carpenter, Jr., was too tall and a little on the young side; Charles Samples, Jr., was too tall and too slightly built; Carlin E. Loop was too tall and a little on the old side. Harvey E. Landrum was too tall and too slender, and so was Robert C. Thompson (who was also a bit young). Melvin F. Walker was too tall and too old.

When Furue turned to the medium-short group, he had to consider body-build index and age more closely. X-1 was about halfway between the tallest man in the group (who was 68 inches) and the shortest (who was 66 inches), so none of the eight could be ruled out on the basis of height. Charles R. Steiner was a little too heavily built and too old, Frank Ginter was too old, and John J. Staseowski was far too heavily built and too old. Charles R. Barnard was of medium build, as was the man on X-1, and at twenty-three years and ten months he fell within X-1's age bracket. Furue thought that the man on X-1 might be Barnard, but he went on to compare the man on X-1 with the records of the four other men in the medium-short group. Clint P. Butler was too slight and too thin. Furue considered Stanley G. Gross a bit too slender to be the man on X-1, but still a candidate. Stanley C. Lawrence's build was also a bit slighter than medium, but his age was within X-1's age bracket; he, too, might be the man on X-1. Joseph B. Mettam was far too heavily built to be the man on X-1.

Raymond J. Geis, Jr., was about 2 inches shorter than anyone else on the plane. It was easy to rule him out against X-1—and against twenty of the twenty-one other unidentified remains. He was also one of the three youngest men on the plane. Furue sometimes describes himself as "a cold-blooded scientist." It is an inaccurate description. When he wrote down Geis's age, he had thought how sad it was for a man to die on his twenty-first birthday. Although twenty is the age when one officially becomes an adult in Japan, Furue remembered how happy he had been when he celebrated not only his twentieth birthday but also his twenty-first.

While Tadao Furue was still recording the estimated ages, heights, and builds of the twenty-two remains, Leslie Stewart was charting the teeth on the stretchers. Going over Stewart's work, Furue noticed that four stretchers had at least sixteen teeth on them and that nine had between one and fifteen. Nine stretchers had no teeth, although two had small jaw fragments. Stewart also charted the dental records of the men on 41081. When Furue reviewed them, he saw that the files of two passengers contained no dental records. Forms in the files of eleven other men showed only what teeth they had had extracted. When Furue had previously compared the dental remains of Second World War soldiers with their dental records, he had learned that men with extraction-only records did not have otherwise perfect teeth. He had learned that two of the forms put in missing-in-action files in the 1940s did not lend themselves to thorough dental charting: the people who filled out these forms could easily record extractions, but there was little room on either form for them to record other dental work that might have been done. The records of only nine of the men on the plane contained dental charts from their years in the armed services which showed fillings, crowns, or other forms of dental restoration or treatment as well as extractions.

Despite the abundance of information visible on bones which enables a Tadao Furue to make reliable determinations of sex, race, age, height, and muscularity, the information is often not specific enough to lead to a precise identification. According to the bones, the man on X-1 could be Charles Barnard, Stanley Gross, or Stanley Lawrence. Personal identification from skeletal remains is more likely to be accomplished by a study of dentition. The effectiveness of dental identification is naturally related to the recovery of dental remains, which had been limited on Mt. Thumb, and to the caliber of the dental records, which had been dismal for the men on 41081.

Furue does not permit himself to be discouraged easily by things in life he cannot change. He goes on with his work. His next task was to compare the dental charts from the remains with the dental charts from the records. In dentistry, each tooth is assigned a number to simplify its designation. Under the current system used by the armed services, the upper teeth are, from right to left, No. 1 to No. 16. No. 1 is the right third molar (or wisdom tooth), No. 2 is the right second molar, No. 3 is the right first molar, No. 4 and No. 5 are the second and first right bicuspids, No. 6 is the right bicuspid, No. 7 is the right lateral incisor, No. 8 and No. 9 are the central incisors (the upper "two front teeth"), and so on over to No. 16, the left third molar (or wisdom tooth). The lower teeth are No. 17 to No. 32, this time going from left to right. No. 17 is the left third molar (another wisdom tooth), No. 18 is the left second molar, No. 24 and No. 25 are the bottom "two front teeth," and No. 32 is the right third molar (the fourth wisdom tooth). The most commonly extracted teeth are the four wisdom teeth—No. 1, No. 16, No. 17, and No. 32. Furue has learned that they were the most unreliably charted during the Second World War. Wisdom teeth usually erupt between the ages of seventeen and twenty-one, but may erupt as late as the age of twenty-five—or, if they are impacted, not at all. Military dentists often marked a young man's wisdom teeth extracted when in fact they had not yet erupted. The teeth of servicemen were rarely X-rayed in the early forties, so the mistake was an easy one to make.

The teeth from the records and those from the remains had been charted on a Department of Defense Form 897—a "Physical and Dental Comparison Chart." The greater part of the form is taken up with thirty-two lines for charting the teeth. Its left half is for the dental information elicited from the remains, its right half for the dental information from the records. When Furue began his attempt to systematically associate the twenty-two names of the men on 41081's manifest with the remains on the twenty-two stretchers, he had established a "command post"—a table covered by a white sheet, at one side of the lab floor. From his chair at the command post he could see the rows of stretchers. He had filled out a Form 897 for each of the twenty-two men with the man's name on it and only the right side of the form filled in. He now laid the forms out on the table in two rows of eleven. The forms were arranged in order of the men's height. To hold the forms down and let him read them at a glance, he covered each row with a piece of Plexiglas. Furue had made up another set of 897s in the numerical order of the stretchers, from X-1 to X-19A. Only the left side of these forms was filled in. He proceeded to compare the 897s from the remains with the 897s from the men's records, starting with X-1. (See page 68.)

If Furue writes nothing next to a tooth, that signifies that no dental work has been performed on it; such teeth are known as "virgins." Of the teeth on Stretcher X-1, Teeth No. 6, No. 7, No. 8, No. 9, No. 10, No. 12, No. 15, and No. 16 were virgins; six of them had been found in the maxillae, two had been found loose. The symbol PX next to a tooth indicates that the tooth is "posthumously missing"; the tooth had been in place up to the time of the crash, but had come loose upon or after impact and had not been recovered by the search-and-recovery team. Anatomically, a tooth consists of two main parts—the root or roots, which are mostly embedded in the bony structure of the jaw, and the crown, which is mostly above the surface. It was easy for Furue to tell that Teeth No. 11 and No. 17 on X-1 were posthumously missing, because there were large empty sockets where they had been. If X-1's maxillae had shown that a tooth or teeth had been extracted, Furue would have written an X over the relevant number or numbers. Not only is it easy for him to distinguish between a tooth that is posthumously missing and one that has been extracted but he can judge whether the extraction is recent or old. If the extraction is recent, the bone has begun to repair itself and to fill in the socket; if the extraction is old, the bone has finished its job, and the spot on the maxilla or the mandible

This was X-1's form 897:

1	
2	
3	Section of maxilla
4	not recovered
5	
6	
7	
8	
9	
10	
11	PX
12	
13	O-AM
14	OL-AM, O-AM
15 / 16	} found loose
17	PX
18	
19	
20	
21	
22	
23	
24	Major portion of mandible
25	and teeth Nos. 18-32 missing
26	
27	
28	
29	
30	
31	
32	

where the tooth had once been is smooth. He can also see whether teeth have been extracted or have decayed and fallen out; dentists leave telltale signs when they pull teeth. Sometimes, when only a mandible and the lower teeth are recovered they may give Furue information about the upper teeth. If he sees that No. 19 is at a higher elevation than No. 18 and No. 20 and shows less wear than its neighbors, he will suspect that No. 14, the tooth that No. 19 should touch on the left maxilla, has been missing for some time before death, because teeth tend to rise when their opposite numbers are not there for them to meet up with.

Furue, in his role as odontologist, charts the type of substance used to fill teeth and the surface or surfaces of the teeth which have been filled. The substances used to fill teeth in the 1940s included "AM" (dental shorthand for "amalgam," an alloy composed primarily of silver and tin mixed with mercury, used predominantly on posterior teeth) and "SIL" (for silicate, a cement used on anterior teeth because it is similar in shade to the teeth). A tooth has five surfaces, which have been named to indicate the direction each surface faces. The mesial surface (M) is the surface of a tooth nearest the midline of the dental arch. The distal surface (D) is the surface farthest away from the middle of the arch. The lingual surface (L) faces toward the tongue. The facial surface (F) of a posterior tooth faces toward the cheek, of an anterior tooth toward the lips. The occlusal surface (O), the chewing surface of posterior teeth, meets and touches teeth of the opposite jaw. Occlusal amalgam fillings are the most common. The man on X-1 had one such filling on tooth No. 13 and another on No. 14. On No. 14, X-1 also had an amalgam filling that went into two surfaces, the lingual and the occlusal. Furue has worked on numerous dental remains with fillings on all five surfaces of a single tooth and has on rare occasions seen a tooth with eight fillings. He is able to determine whether a filling is recent or old by the amount of grinding, or attrition, it shows.

Although Furue had ruled out the probability that the man on X-1 was any of the members of the very tall group or of the medium-tall group, any of five of the men in the medium-short group, or the very short Geis, because of either one, two, or three physical discrepancies, he didn't compare X-1's dental remains only with the dental records under the Plexiglas on his command post for Charles Barnard, Stanley Gross, and Stanley Lawrence, the three likely candidates to be the man on X-1. The bones of the skull are morphologically related to the other bones of the body, and an individual's teeth age consistently with his bones—facts that Furue had taken into account during segregation. Only four stretchers had an atlas, as the first cervical vertebra is known, and only one of these four also had an occipital bone, the bone that forms the back and base of the skull and articulates with the atlas. Furue acknowledged the possibility that he might have mistakenly put the wrong jawbones and teeth on a stretcher. He compared X-1's Form 897 with all the 897s on the command post; this was yet another check and balance.

Once again, he began with Robert Allred, whose dental record was complete and contradicted X-1's in many ways. Allred had one filling on No. 6, No. 8, and No. 9, and two fillings on No. 10, No. 12, and No. 15; these six teeth were virgins in the man on X-1. Allred had one filling, an O-AM, in No. 14, whereas the man on X-1 had two, an OL-AM and an O-AM. Allred's record also showed that he had had six teeth extracted—all four wisdom teeth and No. 7 and No. 13. Furue did not place much value on the discrepancy between Allred's No. 14 and X-1's No. 14: it was conceivable that the man on X-1 had had an OL-AM filling after Allred's last dental examination. Allred's teeth No. 6, No. 7, No. 8, No. 9, No. 10, No. 12, No. 13, and No. 15 could not, however, have been X-1's. Teeth that have been filled can never again be virgins, and teeth that have been extracted do not reappear. Furue's experience had taught him that except in the case of wisdom teeth dentists were quite accurate in recording extractions unless a tooth—say, No. 19—had decayed and been pulled, No. 18 had drifted into the position of the lost tooth, and a dentist had subsequently marked No. 18 as having been extracted instead of No. 19.

Keith Holm's dental record showed only one thing—that he was missing No. 16; X-1 had this tooth, but it was an unreliable wisdom tooth. Holm, who had been ruled out physically, couldn't be ruled out dentally. William Shrake's dental record, another of the complete ones, was not X-1's. The major discrepancy was that Shrake had a filling on No. 15 and the man on X-1 did not. According to Weldon Frazier's dental record, he was missing all four wisdom teeth. Because the dentist had recorded the dates on which he pulled Frazier's No. 17 (June 8, 1943) and No. 32 (June 16, 1943), Furue regarded these extractions as reliable. Frazier, therefore, was not the man on X-1, whose No. 17 was posthumously missing. Joseph Kachorek's dental record was distinguished by ten extractions, including No. 8, No. 13, and No. 14, teeth that were present in X-1. (Kachorek, it occurred to Furue, was unique dentally as well as physically.) Emory Young's dental record showed him not to be X-1; the principal discrepancy was that Young had a virgin on No. 14 and the man on X-1 didn't. Harold Atkins and Thomas Carpenter were the two passengers on the plane who lacked dental records. Charles Samples had a DO-AM filling on No. 13. The distal surface hadn't been filled on X-1's No. 13, and signs of fillings on tooth surfaces cannot disappear. In addition, Samples' record showed the date that his No. 16 was pulled (January 4, 1944) and the date his No. 17 was pulled (November 24, 1942). The dental records of Carlin Loop and Harvey Landrum revealed only that each of these men had had two wisdom teeth extracted, and didn't lend themselves to comparison with X-1. Robert Thompson's record also showed only two teeth extracted: No. 18, which couldn't be compared with X-1's unrecovered No. 18; and No. 16, a wisdom tooth, on which Furue placed little value. (There were no dates on the extraction-only records of Holm, Loop, Landrum, and Thompson.) Melvin Walker had two fillings on No. 15, the man on X-1 had none; Walker was not the man on X-1. Charles Steiner's record showed only two extractions, but one was No. 14, present in the man on X-1. Like Kachorek, Frank Ginter had had ten teeth extracted, including No. 14, so he could not be X-1. (The first molars—No. 3, No. 14, No. 19, and No. 30—come in when one is six, and get six more years of wear, and, often, of childish neglect, than the second molars, which come in when one is twelve; after the wisdom teeth, the first molars are the teeth most frequently extracted.) John Staseowski's record was another of the undated-extraction-only variety; his Tooth No. 16 (an unreliable wisdom tooth) had been pulled. There were six other extractions, and they were of teeth that hadn't been recovered for X-1, but Staseowski was approaching thirty when he was killed, and the teeth on X-1 were those of a younger man. The next dental chart on Furue's table was Charles Barnard's.

This is what Furue saw when he placed the first seventeen lines of X-1's 897 next to the first seventeen lines of Charles Barnard's record.

X-1's FORM 897 FOR 1-17		CHARLES BARNARD'S FORM 897 FOR 1-17	
1		1	O-AM
2		2	O-AM
3	not recovered	3	O-AM, L-AM
4		4	
5		5	
6		6	
7		7	
8		8	
9		9	
10		10	
11	PX	11	
12		12	
13	O-AM	13	O-AM
14	OL-AM, O-AM	14	OL-AM, O-AM
15	found loose	15	
16		16	
17	PX	17	O-AM

Of the twelve teeth on X-1 that could be compared with Barnard's record, nine agreed perfectly. No. 6, No. 7, No. 8, No. 9, No. 10, No. 12, and No. 15 were virgins on X-1 and on Barnard's record. No. 11 and No. 17 were posthumously missing on X-1 and therefore could not be compared precisely with Barnard's record (on which No. 11 was a virgin and No. 17 had an O-AM filling), but there was agreement in that the man on X-1 had had those teeth at the time of the crash. No. 13 and No. 14 were identical. The one tooth on which there was a discrepancy was No. 16. According to Barnard's record, No. 16 had been extracted. No. 16 was present on X-1. Tadao Furue was inclined to believe that this was an instance of a dentist's marking a wisdom tooth extracted when it had not yet erupted. It is an important feature of dental identification that there be no inconsistencies that cannot be adequately explained between an antemortem record and recovered dental remains. Furue thought it likely that the man on X-1 was Barnard, and kept on going. Clint Butler's limited record showed only that Tooth No. 30 had been extracted; his record couldn't be compared with X-1's. Stanley Gross's record showed only four extractions—of No. 1, No. 16, No. 19, and No. 30—and the notation that No. 32 had been treated on January 23, 1944, for pericoronitis, a painful inflammation that often occurs when a tooth is breaking through the gum. Gross couldn't be ruled out dentally, because X-1 was missing his No. 1, his No. 16 was unreliable, and his No. 19, No. 30, and No. 32 had not been recovered. Stanley Lawrence's record showed that he was missing eight teeth, including No. 12 and No. 13, which X-1 had; Lawrence was not X-1. Joseph Mettam's dental record consisted of three extractions—two wisdom teeth and No. 9, which was present on X-1. Raymond Geis's record showed only that he had four teeth extracted—three wisdom teeth and No. 19, which X-1 did not have. Geis could not be ruled out dentally.

Furue had eliminated nineteen men physically against X-1; eleven of them had also been ruled out dentally. The twentieth man, Lawrence, could have been the man on X-1 physically but had been ruled out dentally. Furue now put a red index card with Charles Barnard's name on Stretcher X-1, even though his vicious twin reminded him that there was still a slim possibility that Stanley Gross was the man on X-1. If Furue had been less certain of X-1's identity, he would have put a blue card on it. No matter what the color of the card on the stretcher, as he turned to X-2 he would treat X-1 as if there were no card on it, and would compare Barnard's physical and dental record with the records of the dental remains on all the other stretchers.

After comparing his reading of X-2's remains with the physical records of all twenty-two men, just as he had done with X-1, Furue decided that the man on X-2 was probably Melvin

Walker. X-2 was one of six stretchers on which there wasn't a single tooth or jawbone fragment. Furue couldn't compare the man's dental record (and Walker had a good one) with the remains, so he put a blue card on X-2. He is far more cautious when he cannot make any dental comparison. X-2A got a red card with the name William Shrake. No one else on the plane was as tall, as thin, or quite as young as Shrake. Furue has devised a system for calculating the percentage of bones recovered for each remains. X-2A had a higher percentage than anyone else on the plane—66 percent. (X-19A had the lowest—8.6 percent.) Furue was positive that the man on X-2A was between twenty and twenty-two, because there were many stages of epiphyseal union for him to observe on the long bones; bones that usually grow together before the age of twenty were completely fused, those whose union usually takes place after the age of twenty-three were not. X-2A also had both clavicles and many vertebrae; most vertebrae have five epiphyses apiece, and these epiphyses, which unite after the age of twenty-three, had not begun to do so. Consequently, the man on X-2A couldn't be Keith Holm, although the two men were the same height and almost equally thin and Holm was only twenty-three and a half when he died. Shrake was twenty and seven months, and was also one of the few men on the plane with the combination of a good dental record and good dental recovery. There were twenty-six teeth on Stretcher X-2A, and the dental record was an extraordinary match, although Shrake's four wisdom teeth had been marked extracted and three that were recovered for X-2A were unerupted—Furue could see them in the jawbones. Furue had found that mistake even more prevalent with men of Shrake's age than with men of twenty-three, like Barnard.

The man on X-2B was between twenty and twenty-three, 64½ inches tall, and of medium build. That could be only Raymond Geis. Just one tooth was recovered for X-2B, but Furue considered it compatible with Geis's record; X-2B got a red card. Methodically, Furue identified X-3 (Charles Steiner), X-4 (Emory Young), X-4-17 (Weldon Frazier), X-4-17A (Stanley Lawrence), and X-5 (Robert Allred). Like Shrake, Allred was a man with a good dental record, and there were fifteen teeth on Stretcher X-5. Eight of the recorded fillings matched those on the remains, and so did four extractions, including two unusual ones—No. 7 and No. 13. Allred was the only one on the plane whose record showed he was missing Tooth No. 7. (Even Kachorek, who had had ten extractions, had Tooth No. 7, although a notation on his record next to that tooth—"periapical abscess"—suggested that it might have been the next one to go.) "I've identified men with no bones and far fewer teeth that matched, just on the teeth," Furue said, putting a red card on X-5, as he had on X-3, X-4, X-4-17, and X-4-17A. Furue also put a red card on X-6, identifying the remains as those of Clint Butler. Despite the fact that Butler's dental record was limited to one extraction (X-6 had had a fair amount of other dental work done), it matched the extraction on X-6, and the remains were unique among the twenty-two men: no one else in the short group was as young and as thin as Butler. Stretcher X-7 (Charles Samples) got a red card. Not only did Samples' dental record and the dental remains match well but Furue noticed that Samples had had his teeth cleaned by a dentist on January 4, 1944. In 1982, with 400-watt mercury-vapor lights shining down from the lab's ceiling on X-7's teeth, Furue was able to see that they had been professionally cleaned not long before the crash of the plane. X-9 got a blue card, X-10 a blue one, and X-10A a blue one. Furue felt quite sure that the man on X-10A was Staseowski on the physical comparison: no one else in the short group was as heavy or as old as Staseowski. Still, there wasn't a fragment of a jawbone or a tooth on X-10A with which Furue could have compared Staseowski's dental record of seven extractions, and at this stage in the identification process Furue never put a red card on a stretcher with no dentition, no matter how distinctive the remains seemed when they were compared with the records of the twenty-one other men aboard the plane. Staseowski was the only passenger on 41081 whose dental record showed that he was missing No. 1, No. 2, No. 3, and No. 4, four teeth that Furue, who has had nine extractions, also happened to be missing.

Tadao Furue, a lean but muscular man of 5 feet 6 inches, often compared himself physically with the men on 41081 who were in the short group. He is extremely conscious of his health. His daily lunch always consists of four or five pieces of fruit and a cup of coffee, usually with a small piece of cake or a couple of cookies his wife has baked. He weighs himself twice a day; he believes that weight is one indicator of physical fitness. In the morning he weighs 145 pounds, in the late afternoon 143. "There's no need for me to go jogging at dawn, because I get plenty of exercise at work—especially when I'm walking from stretcher to stretcher segregating bones," he says. "My wife is an excellent cook. Sometimes she prepares Japanese food, other times Chinese food, American food, Italian food. Her spaghetti is delicious. I'm sure that after one of her dinners my weight goes right back up to a hundred and forty-five."

From Monday to Friday, Furue wears slacks, a short-sleeved shirt, and comfortable shoes with ridged soles to work. On Saturday and Sunday, he comes to the lab in a T-shirt, bluejeans, and sandals. Upon his arrival at the CIL, he puts on a short white coat. He says that the custom of wearing a white coat is a carryover from his student years ("It makes me feel like working"), and that the poor condition of his teeth is, too. "I had bad cavities in 1940, when I was a fifteen-year-old student, but I was too busy preparing for an important high-school examination to have them filled," he recalls in an older-but-wiser tone. "After Pearl Harbor, you couldn't get an appointment with a dentist. You were taken on a first-come, first-served basis, and usually had to wait three or four hours. I didn't want to wait, so I just took aspirin when I had a toothache. When I started at the university in 1945, I went to see a dentist, but by then it was too late. He pulled two of my teeth. Over the years, other dentists pulled five, and I pulled two myself. In addition to No. 1, No. 2, No. 3, and No. 4, I've lost No. 13, No. 17, No. 18, No. 19, and No. 31. I also have three gold inlays, on No. 5, No. 14, No. 30." The gold in No. 5 can be seen when Furue is talking. When he smiles, the empty space where No. 4 used to be is exposed to view; he has had two sets of removable partial dentures made, but both gave him so much trouble that he stopped wearing them. Furue's teeth could not have been X-1's, but he has calculated his Rohrer index, and when he weighs 143 it is 1.38, just .02 higher than Charles Barnard's—and .05 higher than Stanley Gross's.

*   *   *

According to Tadao Furue's reading of the remains, the man on Stretcher X-11 had been between twenty-four and twenty-eight years old, 66³⁄₁₀ inches tall, and of medium build. When Furue compared X-11 to the records of all the other men on the plane, starting with Allred, he was able to rule them out until he came to Barnard. When he compared the man on X-11 with Charles Barnard's record, there was a possibility that X-11 was Barnard, just as when he had compared the man on X-1 with Stanley Gross, the man on X-1 could have been Gross. At twenty-three years and ten months, Barnard was only two months under the bracket for X-11. Furue had deemed Gross a little too slight to be the man on X-1, and now deemed Barnard's build more on the medium side than that of the man on X-11. Gross, at 66½ inches, was closer in height to X-11's 66³⁄₁₀ inches, just as Barnard, at 67 inches, was closer to X-1's 67¹⁄₁₀ inches. Furue thought that the man on X-11 was apt to be Gross, just as he had thought, after comparing X-1 physically with the other men on the plane, that the man on X-1 might well be Barnard. Only one of X-11's upper teeth had been recovered, but the entire mandible had been found. Furue now went through the dental records, ruling out many men dentally, as he had when he compared X-1's 897 with the 897s of the men on the plane. When he got to Charles Barnard's dental record, he spotted two major discrepancies: the man on X-11 had had No. 19 and No. 30 extracted, whereas Charles Barnard's record showed that he had both these teeth and that each had three fillings. Moreover, Barnard's record showed that he had two fillings on tooth No. 18; the man on X-11 had one. When the dental remains on Stretcher X-1 had been compared with Stanley Gross's dental record, Gross could not be ruled out, because only the teeth from No. 6 to No. 17 had been recovered among the remains on X-1, and Gross's dental record for these teeth was too limited. Because X-11's mandible and lower teeth had been recovered, Barnard could convincingly be ruled out dentally against X-11. There was also favorable agreement between X-11's mandible and Stanley Gross's record. Both the man on X-11 and Stanley Gross were missing No. 19 and No. 30. Something that particularly impressed Furue was their agreement on No. 32. Gross's record showed that he had been treated for pericoronitis for that tooth on January 23, 1944. Next to X-11's No. 32 Furue had written "recent eruption." Wisdom teeth often break through the gums painfully and require treatment to relieve the pain. After Furue had finished comparing X-11's dental chart with the records of Stanley Lawrence, Joseph Mettam, and Raymond Geis, he put a red card on X-11 for Stanley Gross.

Fingerprints are the most widely used scientific method of identification in the United States. The Federal Bureau of Investigation has over 167 million sets of fingerprints in its current collection, which is believed to be the world's largest. No two fingerprints that the FBI has examined since it went into the business of collecting prints, in 1924, have ever been found to be alike. The prints of identical twins bear no more resemblance to each other than to the prints of strangers. In the case of skeletal remains, dentition is the most effective method of identification. A basic premise of dental identification is that no two mouths are alike. There are a hundred and sixty dental surfaces (thirty-two teeth times five surfaces) that may have decayed and been filled with various substances; there are a vast number of possible combinations of one or more missing teeth at various spots; there is the possibility of an almost infinite variety of porcelain crowns, bridges, and dentures, all of which make dental identification the second most specific method of comparison after fingerprints. Computers have been used to demonstrate that there are more than 2.5 billion possibilities in charting the human mouth.

In the population at large, it is likely that millions of people will have an O-AM filling on No. 13 and OL-AM, O-AM fillings on No. 14, in combination with eight virgin teeth—No. 6, No. 7, No. 8, No. 9, No. 10, No. 12, No. 15, and No. 16—as X-1 did. If just six more teeth had been recovered for X-1 and if No. 1 and No. 2 had the same fillings, No. 3 and No.18 the same two fillings, and No. 19 and No. 30 the same three fillings as those on Charles Barnard's dental record, there might only be tens of thousands of people in the population at large whose dental records would match X-1's dental remains.

Odontologists and physical anthropologists never have to concern themselves with the population at large. Circumstances narrow the probable population involved. In this instance,

Furue had to consider only the twenty-two men on 41081's manifest. While he was processing the twenty-two sets of remains simultaneously, he had to keep repeating the two-step pattern: he had to prove that the man on X-1 was Barnard, and he had to prove that the man on X-1 was not any of the other men on the plane, which he had now done when X-11 became Stanley Gross.

Before very much more time had elapsed, there were red cards for the man on X-12 (whom Furue was sure was Kachorek), X-14A (Holm), and X-19 (Mettam), and blue cards for those on X-13, X-14, X-15, 16, and X-19A. Stretchers X-12 and X-19 were the ones that included jaw fragments but no teeth. The information provided by these jaw fragments was compatible with Kachorek and Mettam's records. On X-12, for instance, a fragment of the right side of the mandible showed that No. 30 had been extracted and No. 31 and No. 32 were posthumously missing. Kachorek's record showed that No. 30 was one of his ten extractions and that he had had No. 31 and No. 32 at the time of his death. Thus, there was no dental contradiction between Kachorek's record and the jaw fragment on X-12. The information from X-12's jaw fragment did contradict the dental records of sixteen of the twenty passengers who had dental records. The jaw fragment also matched Kachorek's unique physical remains morphologically and was incompatible with the remains of the three other men whose dental records could not be ruled out when they were compared with X-12's No. 30, No. 31, and No. 32. It was also morphologically incompatible with the remains of X-13 and X-15, 16, who lacked dental records.

"Comparison equals identification" is a physical-anthropological/odontological axiom, but there is no generalization governing the number of points of comparison that must exist before a positive identification can be made. It is up to the individual physical anthropologist or odontologist to make this decision. When, in late 1982, Furue put a red card with the name Robert Allred on X-5 and commented that he had identified men with no bones and far fewer teeth that matched, he was thinking of Stanley Campbell. In 1979 a CIL team had visited a C-47 that had crashed into a high peak in Papua New Guinea's Saruwaged Range with five men aboard. Only a partial maxilla and three teeth had been recovered at the site. When Furue compared the maxilla and teeth with the dental records of all five men, they matched the record of Second Lieutenant Stanley D. Campbell, the plane's pilot, and failed to match the records of the four other men—who were thus, in Furue's words, "excluded from association by negative comparison." He recommended that "this maxillary bone and teeth be identified as the only recoverable remains of Stanley Campbell." His recommendation was accepted. "Identification by exclusion" is also in the lexicon of physical anthropology and odontology.

After Furue finished comparing the physical and dental remains on the twenty-two stretchers with the twenty-two physical records and the twenty dental records (a formidable number of comparisons), there were red cards on fourteen stretchers and blue cards on eight. Six of the stretchers with blue cards were those that had no dental remains: in addition to the remains of X-2 (whom Furue believed to be Melvin Walker) and X-10A (whom Furue believed to be John Staseowski), there were those of X-9 (believed to be Carlin Loop), X-10 (believed to be Frank Ginter), X-14 (believed to be Robert Thompson), and X-19A (believed to be Harvey Landrum). The two other blue-carded stretchers were X-13 (Furue thought the man on X-13 was Thomas Carpenter, who lacked a dental record) and X-15, 16 (Furue thought this man was Harold Atkins, who also lacked a dental record).

Furue next attempted to "validate the last eight identifications," as he put it. In the absence of dentition, he had to resort to the use of personal effects or military equipment as a secondary means of identification, to corroborate his comparisons of the remains and the records.

The CIL team had dug up a small number of personal effects, or PE, on the crash site. Australian coins from the early forties had been recovered at eight X numbers. This wasn't surprising—in March 1944 American servicemen stationed in New Guinea were paid in Australian currency—but the coins could not help identify a particular individual. The same was true of a Honolulu Rapid Transit token stamped "Good for One Full Fare" found at the X-15, 16 site: during the Second World War, most servicemen traveled to the Southwest Pacific by way of Honolulu, and many had ridden buses during their layovers. A camera had been found at the X-13 site. There was a roll of film inside, but when one of the sergeants attempted to develop it at the CIL he discovered that it had been ruined by the climate. The team had brought back a number of items that were referred to as PE but were actually "military equipment," because they had been issued by the government. Five GI Elgin watches had been recovered at five X numbers; there were serial numbers on the watches but no Elgin serial numbers on the men's records. The team had also returned with fifteen dog tags. Two dog tags stamped with the name Melvin F. Walker had been recovered at the X-2 site; they were the first pair that caused a blue card on a stretcher to be replaced with a red one. At the X-10 site, a set of dog tags and a silver disk with the name and serial number of Frank A. Ginter and a pair of dog tags on a long silver chain with John J. Staseowski's name and serial number enabled Furue to replace two more blue cards with red ones. At the X-14 site, a single, chainless dog tag with Robert C. Thompson's name eliminated a fourth blue card. Additional dog tags and personal effects, with the names of men on the plane's manifest whose stretchers already had red cards, persuaded Furue that these objects hadn't scattered when the plane crashed but had stayed with the remains. (On other crash sites excavated by CIL teams, both the remains and the personal effects had been recovered over much wider areas, and not always together.) At the X-4 site, the team had found Emory C. Young's dog tags, a silver bracelet engraved with his name, and a tattered leather wallet containing a faded picture, on which his name could still be read. At the X-4-17 site, the team had found Weldon W. Frazier's dog tags, at the X-6 site Clint P. Butler's, and at the X-11 site Stanley G. Gross's.

Furue is aware of such soldierly practices as swapping dog tags, and wasn't troubled that the team had also recovered a set belonging to a James A. Miller (upon the team's return to Hawaii, the CIL ascertained that Miller had survived the war) and a bracelet with the name and serial number of Robert A. Ambrose. The serial number on Ambrose's bracelet, found at the X-10 site, was 20283081. Frank Ginter's serial number was

20283103. In a Special Anthropological Narrative that Furue later wrote about 41081, he pointed out the closeness of the two service numbers and suggested that they might help clear up the mystery of the presence of Ambrose's bracelet at the crash site. Eventually, they did. It was subsequently learned that Staff Sergeant Ambrose was a buddy of Frank Ginter's. They had enlisted at practically the same time. Ginter, as a favor, took the bracelet to Sydney to have Ambrose's serial number inscribed on it. (In 1983 Ambrose, who now lives near Buffalo, was astonished when the bracelet was returned to him.) Furue was convinced, as he stated in his Anthropological Narrative, that on the basis of "exclusive physical matching . . . supported by the recovery of identification tag(s)/disc or bracelet" he had independently identified Walker, Ginter, Staseowski, and Thompson.

Blue cards were still left on four stretchers—those for X-9 (believed to be Carlin Loop), X-13 (believed to be Thomas Carpenter), X-15, 16, and X-19A (believed to be Harvey Landrum). Both good and bad statistical luck had come into play in the partial recovery of the twenty-two thirty-eight-year-old, weathered remains. It was bad luck that Atkins and Carpenter lacked dental records: there was a fine recovery of teeth at the X-13 site and an excellent recovery of teeth at the X-15, 16 site. Furue's comparisons of the dental remains of X-13 and X-15, 16 with the dental records of the other men on 41081 had shown that both were compatible with these remains. As good statistical luck would have it, the four men who lacked either dental records, dental remains, or personal effects were sufficiently different in age and muscularity to enable Furue to satisfy himself and the other Tadao that he could tell them apart. He could differentiate between X-9 and X-19A because his readings of the remains indicated that the man on X-9 was older than the man on X-19A and more heavily built, and this was confirmed by Loop's and Landrum's records. Furue had estimated X-9's and X-19A's ages as older than Carpenter's, and here, too, Loop's and Landrum's records proved him correct. Furue had judged the man on X-15, 16 to be more muscular than either Carpenter or Landrum and younger than

Loop: he had accurately estimated X-15, 16's age as between twenty and twenty-five (Atkins was twenty-three) and X-9's as between twenty-five and thirty (Loop was twenty-six).

It could have worked out otherwise. If, for example, the last four men for whom the team had recovered only bones had been Young, Carpenter, Samples, and Landrum, Furue would not have been able to tell them apart. Furue had estimated the man on X-4 as 70½ inches in height, from twenty to twenty-two years old, and of average muscularity/medium build, and X-13 as also 70½ inches in height, from twenty to twenty-five years old, and of average muscularity/medium build. According to their records, Young (X-4) was 70½ inches tall, weighed 159 pounds, had a Rohrer body-build index of 1.26, and was twenty-eight days past his twenty-first birthday, and Carpenter (X-13) was 70 inches tall, weighed 152 pounds, had a Rohrer index of 1.23, and was twenty-two years and eight months old. Furue had estimated the man on X-7 as 69⁴⁄₁₀ inches tall, from twenty-three to twenty-six years old, and of slight muscularity/medium build, and the man on X-19A as 69⁶⁄₁₀ inches tall, from twenty-three to twenty-seven years old, and of slight muscularity/medium build. Samples (X-7) was 70 inches tall, weighed 141 pounds, had a Rohrer index of 1.14, and was almost twenty-four and a half years old. Landrum (X-19A) was 69½ inches tall, weighed 140 pounds, had a Rohrer index of 1.15, and was twenty-four years and eight months old.

If the men with the last four X numbers had been Young, Carpenter, Samples, and Landrum, Furue would have asked a CIL team to return to Mt. Thumb to try to recover additional remains. In 1978, a CIL team had recovered remains from a B-24 in Papua New Guinea. The reluctance of native helpers had forced the team to leave the crash site before it had completed the recovery, but Furue had been able to identify eight of the eleven men on the plane's manifest. Two tarsal bones had been kept at the CIL after Furue made these identifications. He was certain that they didn't belong to any of the eight men. Another CIL team went to the crash site in 1980 and recovered more bones and teeth. Furue was then able to identify two more passengers; the tarsal bones belonged to one of them. An elderly native who had seen the B-24 go down in 1945 had told the team that one man aboard had survived the crash. He was badly injured but had walked away. His remains were never found.

The CIL had been prepared to return to Mt. Thumb if Furue had been unable to identify as many as twenty-two remains. When the team left the mountainside in April of 1982, one member, Sergeant David Kelly, was convinced that he would find bones in the vicinity of the partly deployed parachute if the team had to return. Kelly would not have minded going back to Mt. Thumb: unlike some other crash sites, this one had not required long uphill-downhill walks to get in to and out of; he thought the helipad the men from Manumu had built would still be usable in the summer of 1983. The CIL did not have to return to 41081, because, as Furue wrote in his Special Anthropological Report on January 14, 1983, "upon anthropological and odontological evaluation 22 mutually exclusive identities were simultaneously established; all other hypotheses were scrutinized and nullified."

Sergeant Kelly came to believe that the parachute had been aboard the plane and had deployed itself upon impact.

In October 1982 Tadao Furue went to Japan on a long-planned and often postponed trip to visit his sister. He was back at the lab in early November. Furue, who has no Ph.D. or M.D., has been called Doc by almost all the Americans he has ever worked with. During the summer and fall of 1982, while he was segregating the remains from 41081, his colleagues at the CIL often asked, "How many, Doc, how many?" There was great rejoicing at the CIL when, in late November, Furue was able to answer "Twenty-two."

Furue lives, with his wife, Saeko, and their daughter, Yuko (a nurse with a B.S. from the University of Hawaii, whose hobbies include hula dancing), in a three-bedroom condominium on the twenty-first floor of an apartment building in downtown Honolulu. His father was a banker who traveled extensively; Furue was born while his parents were living in Taipei. His father worked in the United States for four years, and to this day Furue wishes he could speak English as fluently as his late father did. Furue's father was of mixed Shinto and Buddhist heritage, and his mother's family were Buddhists. When Tadao was growing up, he accompanied his father on visits to Shinto and Buddhist shrines. During the Second World War, when turkeys were in short supply, he and his sister also accompanied their parents each Christmas Day to a restaurant on the Ginza, downtown Tokyo's main thoroughfare, where they ate a turkey dinner. Tadao and Saeko Furue (who is of Buddhist origin) are as cosmopolitan as his parents were. They sent Yuko to a Protestant high school in Japan, they maintain a Buddhist shrine in their bedroom, they go to the Japanese Consulate General in Honolulu on Japanese national holidays, and they celebrate Thanksgiving. "I check the epiphyses of the turkey to determine its age when I carve it," Furue says. "It's a professional reflex."

The Furues also send Christmas cards and decorate a plastic tree. Their apartment is elegant, and ample in size (Furue uses the third bedroom as a study), but its storage space is limited. He keeps the Christmas tree, along with its lights and ornaments, in a storage shed behind the lab. When he came home from work on December 9, 1982, he saw that Saeko had covered one of the living-room coffee tables with a red-and-green cloth. The table had obviously been prepared for the tree. In late fall, Furue had promised himself that he would complete the identifications of the men on 41081 in time for the CIL to send their remains to their families before Christmas. He knew in early December that he wouldn't be able to keep his promise; too much paperwork remained to be done before the remains could leave the CIL. Because he had been unable to keep his promise, he didn't feel that it was appropriate for him to celebrate Christmas that year. He told his wife he wouldn't be bringing the plastic tree home. "Saeko is a traditional Japanese woman," he says. "She keeps house, does most of the grocery shopping, so that I can concentrate on my work, and sews all of her own clothes and most of Yuko's. She understood."

Photographs, sketches, processing charts, forms, and narrative accounts dealing with the recovery and identification of the remains from the Mt. Thumb B-24 would be sent from the CIL to the Directorate of Casualty and Memorial Affairs, in Alexandria, Virginia, and, later, to the relatives of the twenty-two men. Some of the paperwork—a crash-site sketch by Sergeant Richard Huston, for example—had been completed in the first half of 1982.

In June 1982 Sergeant Jay Warner had taken a photograph of the eighteen stretchers covered with remains from the crash-site prior to segregation. For some months, each of the segregated remains had lain on a white sheet on one of the twenty-two stretchers. The sheets were wider than the stretchers and were always folded over the remains at the end of Furue's working day and unfolded in the morning. In January 1983 each remains that Furue had identified was transferred to a stretcher with a sheet folded double. Warner would take a photograph of each remains: the doubled sheet provided a background with more contrast. Every family was to receive a June photograph of all the stretchers and a January photograph of one of them.

Among the last forms to be completed for each man was a Department of Defense Form 892. During segregation, Furue had just written numbers on the left half of the copy of this form with one of the many pens that filled many pockets in his white lab coat—an estimated age, an estimated height, bone measurements—along with a few words describing the estimated muscularity. The right half of an 892 consists of a diagram of a human skeleton. While Furue was segregating the remains, he had only jotted down on the skeletal diagram the X numbers of bones that had been transferred from one stretcher to another. In January everything from the copies had to be typed up on the 892 and other information added to it, and every bone or partial bone that was missing from a stretcher had to be filled in with black ink on the skeletal diagram. It was slow, painstaking work. In a box on the lower-left side of the 892 for "Remarks or Statement of Anthropologist," Furue commented on each man's "dexterity," or right- or left-handedness. He had concluded that nine of the men on 41081 were right-handed and two left-handed. To assess right- or left-handedness he generally required both humeri and/or radii, ulnae, and scapulae. He lacked sufficient bones to assess the handedness of eleven men. "Dexterity: UTD" (i.e., undetermined) was typed on their 892s. Comparisons of the handedness of a remains with recorded handedness have been of use to Furue on some occasions, but handedness was not included in the records of any of the men on 41081.

In early January, twenty-two 897s also had to be typed up, so that anyone reading one of the forms could easily compare the dental chart of the remains with the dental chart from the man's record. There was a line on the lower-left side of the 897 for the estimated height of the remains and another for the estimated age, and corresponding lines on the 897's lower-right side for the man's height and age of record.

In 1958, Dr. Mildred Trotter wrote that 68 percent of all white men whose heights were derived from measuring their femurs and applying her formula would fall within the formula's plus-or-minus-3.27-centimeter standard error of estimate and 95 percent would fall within the range of two standard errors. The other 5 percent would deviate even more. Textbooks on physical anthropology recommend that, when using Trotter's formulas, "to be on the safe side, double the margin for error." It was striking to see, on the line for height on the 897s, how accurate Furue's estimates had been, no matter which bone or bones he had used to determine them. In two cases, his estimated heights and the men's recorded heights were identical; in twelve the deviation was between ¹⁄₁₀ and ³⁄₁₀ of an inch; and in six it was between ½ and ⁷⁄₁₀ of an inch—all well within the standard error of estimate. In one case, in which he had used a femur, he was off by 1½ inches—¹⁄₇ of an inch outside the standard margin of error. And in a case in which he had used a humerus he was off by 1⁸⁄₁₀ inches—¹⁄₅ of an inch outside the standard margin. (It was later discovered that Bob Allred had added an inch when reporting his height for the records when he was commissioned, which accounted for a large part of the discrepancy.) "People who have no experience measuring bones or people who are measuring the bones of a heterogeneous population may have to double the margin of error," Furue says. "I've measured the bones of thousands of individuals, and I'm fortunate that the military population I usually work with is homogeneous. If I doubled the standard margin of error, someone whose height I estimated from his femur as being 69 inches could be anywhere from 66½ inches to 71½ inches. That would cover sixteen of the men on 41081." Furue's age estimates all proved to be accurate when they were compared with the ages on the records. They were still accurate (he learned in 1983) when it turned out that two men were a year younger and another man two years younger than they had claimed to be when they entered the armed forces.

There were boxes for "Remarks" at the bottom of both the left and the right sides of Form 897. Furue is able to read many things from remains in addition to race, age, sex, height, muscularity, and dexterity. He had observed that William Shrake's left ulna was deformed, had taken a photograph of the bone, and had commented in the box on the lower-left side of Shrake's 897 that there was an indication of an old elbow injury on the left ulna. (Shrake's record made no mention of any such injury.) On most forms, in fact, nothing had been typed in the right-hand box, for remarks from the record, except the man's race and the last military unit with which he was known to have served. Emory Young's record showed that he had fractured his right great toe in 1931, but none of his toe bones had been recovered. According to Joseph Mettam's record, he had once suffered a skull fracture and had a "skull indentation over the right orbit." To see this, Furue would have had to study the frontal bone of Mettam's cranium; it had not been recovered. Robert Allred's record showed that he had a deviated septum and flat feet. Allred was missing the bones that Furue would have needed to see either condition. Flat feet had figured in a number of identifications that Furue had made in the past. A case that stood out in his mind was that of Captain Robert J. Thomas, one of eleven men whose remains the Vietnamese had turned over in 1978. The Vietnamese had given the names of seven of the eleven men but had given only the dates of death of the four others. Thomas, a B-52 copilot, had been turned over as Walter Ferguson, another member of the crew of the B-52, which was hit by a surface-to-air missile on December 18, 1972, during a bombing raid over Hanoi. Furue had found that the remains turned over as Ferguson's matched Thomas's physical and dental record. The remains had flat feet. Ferguson didn't. Thomas did. (Furue identified Ferguson as one of the four men the Vietnamese hadn't named on that turnover.) Furue rarely hears how the families of the men he has identified regard his work, but in Thomas's case someone sent him a copy of a 1979 newspaper story in which Thomas's widow, Earlyne, was quoted. "They showed me pictures of the remains, and went over the information they had, but I guess it was the flat feet that convinced me," Mrs. Thomas told the newspaper reporter who spoke to her about her husband. "He had very flat feet."

Another form that would be sent to Casualty and Memorial Affairs, a Department of the Army Form 2773-R, gave a brief account of the crash and of the recovery of the remains by the CIL team; a paragraph describing the condition of the remains; a short account of the segregation and identification process that had taken place at the lab; and a list of all the passengers and crew members on 41081. Form 2773-R and Furue's Special Anthropological Narrative, a six-page account of the identification of each of the twenty-two men, were among the last documents typed. When Furue signed the Special Anthropological Narrative, he told Major Johnie E. Webb, Jr., the commanding officer of the CIL, that the twenty-two remains from 41081 were "the hardest I've ever worked on."

On Tuesday, January 11, 1983, Major Webb telephoned Lieutenant Colonel William R. Flick, an officer with Casualty and Memorial Affairs in Alexandria, to say that the CIL would be making positive recommendations on all twenty-two men aboard 41081. The CIL can only recommend identifications. A Board of Officers must approve the recommendations. In January 1983 the Board of Officers for Second World War cases was composed of three officers in the Directorate of Casualty and Memorial Affairs—Flick, Lieutenant Colonel James W. Gleisner, and Colonel J. E. Gleason—and two civilians, both of them identification specialists who worked for Casualty and Memorial Affairs. Webb told Flick that the CIL would be sending all the 41081 paperwork off to Alexandria on the fourteenth.

The paperwork reached Casualty and Memorial Affairs on January 17. At 4:00 P.M. on January 20, the Board of Officers "convened" and approved the identifications of all twenty-two men on 41081. Actually, the board members merely scanned the documents submitted by the CIL and then "duly" approved the identifications without formally convening. No board had ever rejected a recommendation made by Furue. It is doubtful whether the colonels and civilians who sat on the board, none of whom were physical anthropologists, were capable of judging what might have taken Furue days, weeks, or months to do. They could not have identified the remains in the first place. No relative of a Second World War casualty had ever questioned a Furue recommendation, and although the families of a number of Vietnam servicemen had asked to have his work reviewed by dentists or physical anthropologists, no dentist or physical anthropologist had ever overruled Furue.

One example of a family's requesting verification of a board-approved Furue recommendation had occurred less than a year before. Early in 1982, the CIL had received two paperboard boxes that were believed to contain the remains of a United States serviceman missing in Laos. These skeletal remains had reportedly been recovered by Laotians from a crash site, and the Laotians had given the location of the crash site. After segregating the remains, Furue said they were the remains of one individual. On February 26, after he had compared the remains, which were reasonably complete and included a mandible and Teeth No. 17 through No. 32, with the records of all the men missing within 200 miles of the crash site, he recommended that the remains be identified as those of Nicholas G. Brooks. Lieutenant Commander Brooks, a bombardier-navigator, had been shot down while his A-6A was making a strike over the Ho Chi Minh Trail on January 2, 1970. Gladys and George Brooks, two of the most active members of the National League of Families of American Prisoners and Missing in Southeast Asia, had reason to believe that their son not only had survived the crash but had been captured and had escaped from captivity at least once. In March they had their son's remains flown to their home in New York state, and had their family dentist, who had taken care of Nicholas Brooks' teeth until he entered the United States Naval Academy in 1962, examine the dental remains. He recognized some of the work he had done on his former patient's teeth.

"Are you as sure as if it were your own son?" the Brookses asked.

"Positively," the dentist replied.

George and Gladys Brooks wanted any additional information they could obtain about the cause of their son's death, the date of his death, and the spot where the remains—described by

Furue as weathered—had lain between the time of his death and their exhumation. The military sent the remains from New York to Washington, D.C., and there they were examined by Dr. J. Lawrence Angel, a curator of physical anthropology at the Smithsonian Institution's National Museum of Natural History. Dr. Angel answered the Brookses' questions to the best of his ability. Neither the date nor the cause of death could be definitely determined, he stated. In an opinion he wrote on March 22, 1982, he said that the remains had lain in reddish, very acid soil for ten or more years, and that he would not have been surprised if the time were longer than the twelve years that elapsed between the date Nicholas Brooks' plane was shot down and the time his remains were turned over. He also said that his observations of the remains "fit the life data of Lt. Cmdr. Nicholas G. Brooks." Dr. Angel had estimated Brooks' height as between 68½ inches and 71½ inches and his age as between twenty-two and twenty-nine. Furue had estimated his height as 70²⁄10 inches and his age as between twenty-five and thirty. Nicholas George Brooks was 70 inches tall, and on January 2, 1970, his age was twenty-six years seven months and fourteen days. In another case of Furue's that was reviewed by a distinguished physical anthropologist, not only were the anthropologist's age brackets wider than Furue's but the actual age of the individual involved was not within the brackets. The anthropologist had to be asked to rewrite his opinion. One physical anthropologist who has worked with Furue says that many other members of their profession have far greater experience in other realms of knowledge—such as assessing the antiquity of remains dug up on archeological sites—but that no one can hold a candle to Furue in identifying remains from the country's last three wars. Some go as far as to say that reviewing Furue in his special area of expertise amounts to an academic exercise, because no other physical anthropologist has his experience in dealing with thousands of skeletal remains not only from the military but also from civilian plane crashes and, occasionally, coroners' offices.

Recently, some of Furue's Vietnam-era identifications have been the subject of controversy. Last year, the CIL received remains from a site in Pakse, Laos, where an American airplane had crashed in 1972 with thirteen men aboard. After working with the remains for four months, Furue recommended that positive identifications be made of all thirteen. The Armed Services Graves Registration board accepted Furue's recommendations. Family members of some of the men who had been identified refused to accept the identifications, pointing out, in several cases, that Furue had claimed a positive identification on the basis of only a handful of bones. In response, the Army commissioned an independent review of the CIL's overall work by two physical anthropologists and an odontologist. The review panel spent three days at the CIL studying Furue's recommendations on thirty sets of remains, including those of the Pakse victims. "We did not find that any of the bodies in question had been misidentified," one physical anthropologist wrote, but he added, "We were not able to make many of the identifications in these cases." Regarding the thirteen Pakse cases, the panel concluded, in part, "Two of the bodies were acceptably identified, and there is no real reason to doubt any of the others. However, we did not feel that there was sufficient evidence to establish the other identities either." Furue stands by the identifications.

The panel made a number of recommendations that it felt might improve the "credibility" of the identification process, including the hiring of a dentist with training in forensic odontology and the hiring of a nationally or internationally known forensic anthropologist, who would validate the CIL's identifications. "This person should be at the academic level of full professor, full curator, or laboratory director," the panel wrote. "He or she should also be a diplomate of the American Board of Forensic Anthropology or have some similar form of established credentials." The panel recommended that forensic anthropologists and odontologists be added to the review board that approves the CIL's identifications. The panel also recommended that Furue be retained as senior anthropologist. The Army is now putting these recommendations into effect.

The scarcity of the remains from Pakse was unusual. Ordinarily, when Furue identified Vietnam-era remains, such as Nicholas Brooks', he had much more material to work with than he did with Second World War remains. The dental records were always more precise, and almost always included X-rays taken during the time of military service. Nicholas Brooks' teeth had been X-rayed ten times between 1961 and 1969. Ante-mortem X-rays reduce the opportunities for dentists to make errors in charting teeth. X-rays will show whether a wisdom tooth has been extracted or has not yet erupted, and whether a second molar has drifted into the position of a lost first molar. If there had been X-rays in Charles Barnard's missing-in-action file, Furue not only would have known that No. 13 had an O-AM filling and No. 14 an OL-AM, O-AM filling but would have been able to see the shapes of these fillings and could have compared them with postmortem X-rays he would have taken of X-1's teeth. If two people have fillings on the same surfaces of the same teeth, the fillings will usually appear different in X-rays. X-rays also reveal the precise shapes of jawbones and teeth, the spaces between individual teeth, and the angles at which they fit into their sockets.

Over the past dozen years, when Furue has not been working evenings and weekends identifying remains he has spent his free time perfecting "cranio-facial superimposition," a process that makes the identification of skeletal remains still more specific. The setup he uses to do superimpositions consists of lights, mirrors, a fine-mesh screen, and a 35-mm camera, and enables him to place a photograph of a known individual (often his high-school-yearbook or his wedding photograph) over a photograph of an unknown individual's skull taken from the same distance and the same angle as the photograph to see if they match. Those who have observed Furue's demonstrations of photographs that do match—and photographs that don't—are almost always impressed. Tadao Furue used cranio-facial superimposition as a supplementary method of identifying Nicholas Brooks. He has since carried superimposition a step further: in recent years, he has been superimposing antemortem and postmortem X-rays to make even these comparisons more specific. In late 1983, when Furue was given the scant remains of the two young men killed in the Marine barracks in Beirut whose remains could not be identified at the Frankfurt mortuary, he successfully superimposed an X-ray of a partial mandible of one of the two unknown remains on a dental X-ray of Lance Corporal David M. Randolph, and he successfully superimposed a postmortem mandibular X-ray on an antemortem dental X-

ray and also on X-rays of a skull suture and a sinus of Lance
Corporal Curtis J. Cooper. "Without superimposition, I couldn't
have identified either young marine, because of the scarcity and
condition of the remains," Furue says. By December 1983, after
identifying Randolph and Cooper, Furue had seen newspaper
photographs of some of the men on 41081. He wished he had
had the photographs a year earlier, so that he could have tried
superimposing them.

The colonels and civilians assigned to Armed Services Graves
Registration boards respect Tadao Furue's integrity as well as his
expertise. Most of them have worked with him in Japan, Vietnam, Thailand, or Hawaii, and they know that if he lacks sufficient remains to identify an unknown individual he will always
say so. They also know that he will not identify a remains, no
matter how complete it is, if he isn't convinced that it matches a
record. By January 20, 1983, the day the Board approved
Furue's recommendations of all twenty-two men on 41081, an
extraordinary amount of pressure had been put on the CIL to
identify a young American whose remains were recovered in
1972 on the perimeter of a military camp near An Khe, in South
Vietnam. The remains had traveled from An Khe to the mortuary at Tan Son Nhut, then to Thailand, and finally, in 1976, to
Honolulu. By 1981, the unknown remains, tagged X-15, had
been unsuccessfully compared with the relevant records of all
the nearly 2500 unaccounted-for Americans. In 1982, X-15 was
compared with the records of the known Vietnam deserters; it
did not match the deserters' records, either. Casualty and Memorial Affairs attempted to persuade Furue to say that the remains were those of a young man who had perished in the same
general area as X-15; they weren't, and he refused. On January
2, 1983, a record that had been misfiled at Fort Benjamin Har-
rison under "Discharged in absentia" surfaced and was sent to
Alexandria, where an identification specialist thought he recognized it as X-15's. (X-15 was missing Tooth No. 8, a front upper
tooth, which was an even rarer tooth for a soldier to be missing
in the 1970s than in the 1940s.) The record was sent to the CIL.
It took Furue only a few minutes to say that the long-found
remains matched the long-lost record.

* * *

In 1973 Congress directed the Secretary of Defense to select an unknown Vietnam serviceman to represent all the dead of the war that had divided the country more than any other since the Civil War. In 1975 a crypt was built at Arlington's Tomb of the Unknowns to contain these remains, but for years it stayed empty. In 1921 when the first unknown soldier—a casualty from the First World War—was buried at Arlington, there were more than 1600 unidentified remains to choose from. On May 30, 1958, when an unknown soldier from the Second World War was honored, there were over 8500 to choose from. The same day, an unknown soldier from Korea was also interred, and there were over 800 to choose from. Because of the prompt evacuation of the dead and wounded by helicopter, improved military record-keeping, and scientific advances in identification techniques, there had never been more than four Vietnam un-knowns at the CIL at any one time. Groups like the National League of Families had successfully fought the selection of a Vietnam unknown, because they feared that it would lead to a slackening of government efforts to search for the individuals still unaccounted for. In the spring of 1984, however, the pres-sure from groups like the Veterans of Foreign Wars and the American Legion combined with the Administration's eagerness to make a controversial war more respectable by honoring those who had fought in it resulted in a Defense Department decision to choose a Vietnam unknown from the four remains then at the CIL.

In choosing an unknown from earlier wars, an administrative procedure of forgotten origin was followed: only remains that were as much as 80 percent complete were selected. These so-called "best" remains of the 1920s and 1950s were the worst choices in the 1980s, because of the progress in identification techniques, so the criterion of 80 percent was waived for the Vietnam unknown soldier. X-15 was 26 percent complete but had been identified once the right record was found.

One of the four remains at the CIL in early 1984 was ruled out because it was 95 percent complete. A second remains, which had been turned over by the Vietnamese in 1983, was not a candidate, because Furue had successfully superimposed a scapula from the remains over a chest X-ray from the record of one of the unaccounted-for, and in the CIL's opinion there was an excellent likelihood of identifying him if the Vietnamese turned over additional remains. The third remains at the CIL had been part of a 1978 turnover of four from Laos. One of the four had been identified as an American Air Force pilot, but two others had proved to be Southeast Asian Mongoloids. The bones of the fourth were those of a Caucasoid, but there was no evidence that he had been a soldier.

The fourth remains at the CIL at the beginning of 1984 had been found by a South Vietnamese Army reconnaissance team in late 1972 near a town about 60 miles north of Saigon. The remains were eventually given the number X-26. They consisted of six bones. Along with the remains, which were only 3 percent complete, the reconnaissance team had brought in a few objects such as remnants of a flight suit, of a pistol holster, and of a parachute, and a one-man inflatable raft. Furue determined that X-26 was a Caucasoid man of average muscularity, whose height had been approximately 68.4 inches and who had been between twenty-six and thirty-three years old. The only men in the killed-in-action/body-not-returned category within a 2500-square-mile area of where X-26 had been found were two men in a helicopter and the pilot of a fighter plane; both aircraft had crashed, as it happened, on May 11, 1972. Several sergeants at the CIL were convinced that X-26 was one of the two men from the helicopter, but Furue was not certain. The Vietnamese reconnaissance team's report had been disturbingly vague, and the condition of the six bones—they showed no evidence of trauma—was at variance with accounts of both crashes. Furue was asked to go to Washington and recommend to the National League of Families that X-26 be chosen as the Unknown Soldier of the Vietnam War. He declined to go. He believed that if additional remains of X-26 were ever found he could identify him. On April 13, 1984, Caspar Weinberger designated X-26 as the remains that would be buried at Arlington.

Johnie Webb and Tadao Furue refuse to discuss the Vietnam Unknown. "Putting X-26 in the Tomb of the Unknowns was politically expedient," a former CIL sergeant says. "At best, it was premature. I'll bet Doc considered him unidentified but not unidentifiable. Perhaps it was appropriate to the Vietnam War. So much else about it was political. Everything connected with X-26 has been ordered shredded, but you can't shred what's in men's minds. If we ever get into South Vietnam, the way we got into Laos, and find additional remains that match those in Arlington, there could be a problem."

The CIL is always under pressure to identify remains from Vietnam, but in this case it was under pressure to identify the twenty-two remains found on Mt. Thumb as well. On April 29, 1982, as soon as Bruce Hoy had returned from the crash site to his office, he telephoned the editor of the country's leading English-language newspaper, the *Post-Courier*. Hoy is eager for publicity, because he believes that it will help him promote the Aviation, Maritime, and War Branch and thus stir up interest that will lead to the discovery of more missing planes. A *Post-Courier* photographer took photographs that day of three CIL team members standing in front of 41081's tail, and one of its reporters interviewed Lieutenant Colonel David C. Rosenberg, Major Webb's predecessor as commanding officer of the CIL, and Bruce Hoy. That evening, Hoy was also interviewed by a representative of the Australian Associated Press. By May 1, an AP story about the CIL's recovery had started to run in newspapers all over the United States. The AP story, often accompanied by a *Post-Courier* photograph of 41081's tail, quoted Hoy and Rosenberg and mentioned the date of the crash, the plane's itinerary, the number of men aboard, and the units to which some of them had been assigned.

Among the millions of Americans who read the AP story in their local newspapers were relatives of Robert Allred, Frank Ginter, Keith Holm (the plane's navigator), Melvin Walker, and Emory Young. The relatives had kept the letters they had received from the headquarters of the Army Air Forces and from the Department of the Army in the 1940s. The facts in these letters—the date of the crash, the plane's itinerary, the type of plane, and the plane's use as a transport on March 22, 1944—jibed with the facts in the AP story. Within a few weeks, the relatives got in touch with the CIL. On May 20, Andrew Ginter, of Clarence, New York, a small town on the outskirts of Buffalo, wrote to Honolulu to say that the report he had read in the Buffalo *Evening News* about the B-24 wreckage found on Mt. Thumb sounded as if the plane might be the one his brother Frank had been on; he said he would appreciate any information the CIL might be able to send him. A week later, Andrew Ginter received a letter from Colonel Rosenberg, which read in part:

> A review of the manifest of the aircraft shows that Staff Sergeant Frank Ginter, 20283103, was on the aircraft when it became missing on 22 March 1944. However, we do not know whether or not your brother was among those recovered.
>
> All remains recovered from the aircraft are now in the laboratory, here in Hawaii, undergoing forensic examination. At this time, we are not certain how many remains were actually recovered, and no specific identities have been determined. The laboratory examination will take some time before any positive identification can be established.
>
> This is all the information that is available at present. Should you have additional questions, you should contact Mr. John Rogers, Casualty and Memorial Affairs Directorate, office of the Adjutant General, Headquarters, Department of the Army, Alexandria, Virginia 22331. You may call Mr. Rogers collect at Area Code (202) 325-7960.

The CIL also received letters from people whose brothers, uncles, and cousins had been aboard other planes that disappeared in New Guinea during the Second World War. Until Colonel Rosenberg left the CIL, on June 7, 1982, for a new assignment, he answered a number of these letters. "Records available to this organization show that Staff Sergeant Stoeber was assigned to a B-25, tail number 41-12515, that became missing on August 30, 1944, in the vicinity of the Poi River, western New Guinea, which is called West Irian, and is now part of the country of Indonesia," Rosenberg informed one correspondent. "The aircraft was en route from Nadzab to Owi Island. We have no other specific information on Staff Sergeant Stoeber, but he was definitely not on the aircraft mentioned in the article. Thank you for your interest. It has been a pleasure to have been of service to you."

It did not surprise men like John Rogers, a civilian, who by 1982 had worked at Casualty and Memorial Affairs as an Army identification specialist for thirteen years, that there were so many inquiries. He knew of many mothers who had gone to their graves without giving up hope of hearing something about the fate of their missing sons. In 1970, the year of her death, Carlin Loop's mother read a brief newspaper account of an American Second World War plane that had been found by a Lutheran missionary on a mountain near the north coast of New Guinea. When she wrote to the Army to inquire whether her son had been on the plane, she was informed that the plane the missionary had happened upon was an A-20, which had failed to return from a bombing raid on March 12, 1944, ten days before her son's plane disappeared.

The relatives of Allred, Ginter, Holm, Walker, and Young wrote or called John Rogers during the summer and fall of 1982 to give him the dates they would be away from home on vacation or to ask if the identifications had been completed. Rogers telephoned them once or twice to report that he had no news for them. On November 22, 1982, Colonel Flick wrote to the relatives of the five men to give them "an update on the processing of the remains recovered," which, he explained, had taken much longer than was originally anticipated. "We cannot predict when the identification processing will be completed, but please rest assured that you will be notified immediately of the scientific results," he wrote. He said he regretted the delay and realized the anxiety that it was causing the relatives. He did not, of course, mention the pressure that the AP story was putting on the CIL or the anxiety felt by Furue, whose work could not be expedited by the knowledge that the relatives of five men had been waiting for months for him to complete it. In December, while the paperwork was being completed at the CIL, John Rogers and Douglas L. Howard, a sergeant in Casualty and Memorial Affairs, were given the job of tracing the next of kin of the seventeen men on 41081 whose families had not read the AP story. Rogers wrote down the names, ranks, and serial numbers of the five men with whose relatives he had been in touch, and the relatives' names, addresses, and telephone numbers, on five pieces of legal-size, lined yellow paper. On seventeen similar sheets of paper, Douglas Howard recorded the names, ranks, and serial numbers of the seventeen other men and the name or names and the address or addresses of their next of kin as they had been listed in the men's missing-in-action files. Some men had listed only one next of kin (a mother or a father), some had listed two (a wife and a mother, or two brothers). Rogers did some preliminary work on the next of kin, which consisted primarily of consulting out-of-town telephone directories in the Pentagon library and long-distance-information operators. He checked to see if Joseph Kachorek's mother, Stella Kachorek, of 2477 South Fourth Street, Milwaukee, Wisconsin, was still listed in the Milwaukee telephone book.

On January 11, 1983, the day Webb and Flick spoke on the telephone, Rogers was instructed to call the relatives of Allred, Ginter, Holm, Walker, and Young and tell them that the five men had been identified. On the twelfth, he and Howard started calling the relatives of sixteen of the other men on 41081; Colonel Gleason, of the Board of Officers, had said he would find the family of the seventeenth man.

The most useful tool for tracking down the next of kin was the telephone directory. It took Rogers one call to find the relatives of John Staseowski. His father had died when he was three, and his mother had remarried. She was listed in his missing-in-action file as Mrs. Veronica Rybski, of 166 Homestead Avenue, Holyoke, Massachusetts. A Walter Rybski, of 418 Homestead Avenue, was in the Holyoke phone book. John Staseowski, one of Mrs. Rybski's nine sons and daughters by her two marriages, was her oldest child and the only one who was no longer alive; Walter Rybski was a half brother of John Staseowski. His first reaction to the news that Rogers gave him was astonishment. He had long since given up hope that John would be found, as had the brothers and sisters, if not the mothers, of the other men on 41081. He had no idea that anyone was still looking for Second World War missing planes in New Guinea. Walter Rybski's greatest regret was that his mother hadn't lived to learn of the recovery of her son's remains. "It's an odd thing about the number twenty-two," he said a few months later. "The plane crashed on March 22, 1944, with twenty-two men on board, and my mother died on March 22, 1980."

Clint Butler was from Little Rock, Arkansas; his mother, Grace, who was listed as his next of kin, was dead, but he too was from a large family—he was one of eleven children—and five of his brothers lived in Little Rock and were listed in the telephone directory.

Joseph Mettam's mother had lived in Solana Beach, California, when her son went off to war. She had died years earlier and there were no Mettams in Solana Beach, but an information operator found a listing for a Mettam in nearby Encinitas; he proved to be a cousin of Joseph Mettam's, and furnished Rogers with the telephone numbers of Joseph Mettam's sister and brother, who lived elsewhere in California.

Harvey Landrum's parents had lived in Kilgore, Texas. Some years earlier, his only sister had separated from her husband and had returned to Kilgore to be near her parents. After her mother died, in 1978, she had moved into her parents' house and had cared for her father until he died, in 1979. She had stayed on but had never got around to changing the listing in the telephone directory, so in January 1983, John Rogers had found her by calling the number of her late father, whose name was also Harvey Landrum.

Charles Barnard had grown up in Wadsworth, Ohio. There were three Barnards in the Wadsworth telephone book. Two of them, including the first one Rogers called, A. Gary Barnard, were nephews of Charles Barnard. Gary Barnard telephoned his father, Amos, who had moved to Florida. Amos Barnard called his brother Charles's widow, who had remarried and was living in a small town in Missouri. She in turn telephoned her daughter, Nancy Barnard Linthicum, who was living in another small town in Missouri.

Of the twenty-two men on the plane, nine had been married, and four had children born shortly before or after the crash. Carlin Loop and his wife had been living in Salina, Kansas, when he went off to New Guinea; a nephew who was listed in the Salina telephone directory put Rogers in touch with Loop's son, Larry, who was also living in Missouri.

Weldon Frazier was from a small town in Texas, Thomas Carpenter from a small town in Alabama, and William Shrake from a small town in Indiana. It was easy for Rogers and Howard to get in touch with their brothers, who still lived in or near those small towns.

Where telephone directories failed to turn up relatives, postmasters were sometimes of assistance. Harold Atkins had listed two brothers as his next of kin; one had lived in Rosebud, Montana, the other in Gallatin Gateway, Montana. There were no Atkinses listed in the telephone books of either small town. Rogers called the postmaster of nearby Bozeman, Montana, who gave him the name, address, and telephone number of another brother, who was living in San Francisco. A postmaster in West Virginia helped Rogers trace the family of the late Charles Samples, of Smithers, West Virginia. "Everyone in rural West Virginia seems to know someone living on a hill or in a hollow," Rogers commented several months later.

It took the police to help the Army find the families of three of the men on the plane. Stanley Lawrence's father had lived in Eau Claire, Wisconsin, until his death. The police found one of Stanley's brothers in nearby Chippewa Falls—Myron Lawrence, who had been flying an American flag outside his home ever since Stanley's plane went missing. (Not the same flag; Midwestern winds had shredded about two flags a year.) The police in Robert Thompson's home town, Anniston, Alabama, found a stepbrother of his there; he got in touch with Thompson's sister, who had moved to Georgia. Joseph Kachorek's file listed his mother, Stella Kachorek, of Milwaukee, as his next of kin, but she was not listed in the Milwaukee directory, nor were any other Kachoreks. The police led the Army to one of Joseph Kachorek's three brothers, all of whom still lived in Milwaukee. The three brothers had kept the family's original surname, Kaczorek. Rogers learned that Joseph had changed the spelling of his surname before entering the Army and had also changed the spelling of his mother's name on his Army record.

Colonel Gleason had offered to trace the family of Charles Steiner, of Navarre, Ohio; Gleason had grown up near Navarre and still had a sister living there. Within a few hours, Velma Zimmerman, of Canton, Ohio, one of Steiner's two sisters, was on the telephone with Gleason.

By Monday, January 17, members of all but one of the families of the men on 41081 had been located. Sergeant Howard couldn't find any relatives of Raymond J. Geis, Jr., who had been the plane's copilot. The last address that the Army had for Geis's wife and his mother was in Chicago. There were only fifteen Geises in the Chicago directory. Howard called them all, with no luck. Earlier, Howard had found Stanley Gross's widow, Carmen, whose 1944 address was also Chicago. There were about three hundred Grosses in the Chicago telephone book, but there was just one Carmen Gross. Of the nine widows of the men on 41081, Carmen Gross was the only one who had not remarried. After the crash, the Army Air Forces had encouraged the mothers and widows of the men on the missing plane to keep in touch and had sent them a list of each other's names and addresses. For a year or two, some had exchanged letters. Carmen Gross and the former Mrs. Raymond J. Geis, Jr., had stayed in touch longer than most. Maria Geis had remarried in 1949, and Carmen Gross had been a guest at her wedding. When Sergeant Howard talked to Mrs. Gross, he told her that he couldn't find any of Raymond Geis's relatives. She couldn't remember the surname of Mrs. Geis's second husband or the name of the town in Illinois to which he and Maria had moved in the 1970s.

John Rogers recalled that in 1981 the Army had spent four months trying to find the next of kin of Corporal William Wohlgemuth, whose remains had been recovered in 1980 from another Second World War plane crash in Papua New Guinea. Furue's recommendation on Wohlgemuth had been approved by a Board of Officers on July 31, 1981. Wohlgemuth's address of record was Alhambra, California, a city near Los Angeles, and the record also showed him to have been a member of the Catholic Church. Army officers looked through local records, asked civic and church organizations for assistance, and made a door-to-door search in Wohlgemuth's last-known neighborhood in an effort to trace surviving relatives. In early December, the Army released a dispatch about its fruitless search for Wohlgemuth to the Associated Press and United Press International. A friend of one of Wohlgemuth's brothers read a wire-service account in his local newspaper, and within four days the Army was in touch with the brother, who lived near San Francisco.

On Wednesday, January 19, 1983, the Army again turned to the press. A dispatch was prepared and submitted to the AP and the UPI for distribution to newspapers, radio stations, and television stations. It recounted the story of the crash, gave the names of the twenty-two men who had been identified, said that the families of twenty-one servicemen had been notified, and asked anyone with information that could help locate the family of Second Lieutenant Raymond J. Geis, Jr., "to notify the Adjutant General's Casualty Office with a collect call to (202) 325-7960," the main number for Casualty and Memorial Affairs.

On the evening of Wednesday, January 19, 1983, Maria Ulrich was watching TV in the family room of her home, in Ingleside, Illinois, a small town 50 miles from Chicago, with her husband, her mother, and two neighbors. Shortly after 9:00 P.M., the telephone rang. It was Maria Ulrich's cousin Helen, who lived in Oak Lawn, a Chicago suburb. Cousin Helen, who suffered from arthritis, listened to the radio a great deal. She had been listening to the nine-o'clock news on WBBM, a popular Chicago radio station. After the newscaster read the wire-service story about the plane and the appeal for help in locating Geis's family, she dialed Maria's number. Maria answered the telephone.

"Do you have the radio on?" Helen asked.

"No," Mrs. Ulrich said. "I'm watching the idiot box."

"Are you sitting down?"

"No. I'm in the family room, and the phone down here is on the wall."

"Well, please do sit down," Helen said.

Maria Ulrich followed her advice.

"I don't know whether I should tell you this, but I think I'd better," Helen continued. "I've just heard on the radio that the Army has found the plane Ray was on. They've identified the twenty-two men aboard, and they've notified twenty-one families. They couldn't find you." Helen asked if she might give the newscaster Maria's telephone number. Maria consented, but when he telephoned her, wanting to interview her for the ten-o'clock news, Maria Ulrich had to decline: she was too unnerved to speak to a stranger. The neighbors were tactful and left quickly; like most of the Ulrichs' friends and relatives, they had no idea that Maria had been married to Raymond Geis on November 3, 1943, the day he graduated from Army Air Forces pilot school and received his wings, and that she had become a widow four months later.

After the neighbors' departure, Maria Ulrich made a call—to Carmen Gross.

"Where the hell have you been?" Mrs. Gross inquired.

The two women had a fairly long conversation. Carmen Gross spoke of Sergeant Howard as a very kind man. She passed on the information he had given her about the recovery of the remains and told Maria Ulrich she had learned from Sergeant Howard that the Army would bury the remains of each of the men on the plane in accordance with his family's wishes. Mrs. Gross said she hadn't yet reached a decision about where to bury her husband. Before Maria Ulrich went to bed, still in a state of disbelief, she tried to telephone a cousin of Ray Geis's, a dentist who lived in Joliet, Illinois. There was no answer at his home.

The Ulrichs subscribed to the Chicago *Tribune*. The paper delivered to them on the morning of January 20 carried a story about Emory Young, of Macomb, Illinois. "I'd have had a heart attack if I'd seen the *Tribune* before Helen telephoned," Maria Ulrich said later. She remembered that Emory Young's mother had visited her and Raymond Geis's mother in Chicago not long after the plane's disappearance. That morning, the Ulrichs had to drive to Waukegan, Illinois, for a hearing on the property taxes on their house. The station had called the Adjutant General's Casualty Office the previous evening with Mrs. Ulrich's telephone number. When Sergeant Howard telephoned Maria Ulrich on the morning of the twentieth, her mother answered, and explained that she was out for a few hours. He called back around two o'clock that afternoon, and reached Maria Ulrich. He brought up the matter of who would serve as "primary next of kin," the relative who would assume responsibility for burial arrangements. Mrs. Ulrich told Sergeant Howard that she hadn't corresponded with Raymond Geis's mother for a while; the last she knew, Mrs. Geis was living in a trailer court in a small town in California. She said she believed she could find Mrs. Geis if she was still alive. With the help of the town's Chamber of Commerce, she reached two people at the trailer court, and learned that Mrs. Geis had become quite senile and was living in a nursing home in California. When Maria Ulrich passed this information along to Sergeant Howard, he advised her not to disturb Mrs. Geis by telling her that her son's remains had been found, but Maria Ulrich thought that telling her was the proper thing to do. Raymond Geis had been her only child. She reached her former mother-in-law on a day when she was lucid. Mrs. Geis told Maria Ulrich she felt that Maria was the one best qualified to make any decisions that had to be made. "He belonged to you," Mrs. Geis said. Mrs. Ulrich reported the phone conversation to Sergeant Howard and also mentioned Raymond Geis's cousin in Joliet. Howard said that the cousin was a rather distant relative, and suggested that she might want to honor her former mother-in-law's wish that she serve as primary next of kin; she accepted the responsibility.

On January 21, when Maria Ulrich had just agreed to become primary next of kin and was starting to think about where to bury Raymond Geis, most of the sixteen other families that Howard, Rogers, and Gleason had traced had had between four and nine days to make these decisions; the five families that had read of the plane's recovery in May 1982 had had eight months. In twelve cases, including that of John Staseowski, the primary next of kin would be a brother. In three cases, it would be a sister: Harvey Landrum, Charles Steiner, and Robert Thompson had no brothers. In three cases, including those of Maria Ulrich and Carmen Gross, it would be a widow. And in three cases it would be a child. Nancy Barnard Linthicum, Larry Loop, and Melvin Walker were all devoted to their stepfathers but had always been interested in their real fathers, and they took the opportunity to do something for these men they had never had a chance to know. By January 21, most of the families had decided where to bury the men from 41081; the others would make their decisions soon. Twelve were to be buried in family plots in private cemeteries—often alongside the graves of their parents. Three were to be buried in the military sections of private cemeteries; either their families had no plots in these cemeteries or the plots had been filled. The private cemetery in Massachusetts where John Staseowski's father was buried had lost the location of his grave, and donated a plot; John Staseowski would be buried near the graves of his mother and stepfather. Six other men, among them Raymond Geis, would be buried in military or national cemeteries. Maria Ulrich's husband, Chris, had served in the Army at Fort Sheridan, Illinois. He drove her there on a sunny day to show her the post cemetery. She liked its tranquility and the view of Lake Michigan. She described the cemetery to Carmen Gross, who decided that she would bury Stanley Gross in an adjacent grave. Both women seemed to feel that since the two men had lain together for thirty-eight years on Mt. Thumb it would be fitting for them to lie together for the rest of time.

It was not easy for Nancy Linthicum to decide where to bury her father. One possibility was the Barnard family plot in Wadsworth; she ruled that out, because only her two cousins lived there, and Ohio was a long way from Missouri. Her uncle, Amos Barnard, proposed Arlington National Cemetery, but that was even farther away. Nancy Linthicum had learned from John Rogers and Doug Howard that the Army would pay as much as $1400 if she chose to have her father buried in a private cemetery. If burial was to be in a national cemetery, like Arlington, virtually all costs would be taken care of by the Army and $75 would be allotted for such items as death notices and flowers. Whatever cemetery Nancy Linthicum chose, the Army would not pay for her transportation to or from it, or for the transportation of her two sons. For that reason and for another, more compelling one, she eventually chose to have her father buried in Kansas City, Missouri, in a pretty cemetery near her office and her home. She wanted to be able to visit her father's grave regularly, and that would be possible only if he was buried in Missouri.

While Rogers and Sergeant Howard were calling the relatives of the men on 41081, another branch of Casualty and Memorial Affairs was procuring a Survivor Assistance Officer for each primary next of kin. SAOs must be the same rank as the deceased or higher, and must be active-duty members of the Army. They are chosen from places as near as possible to the homes of the next of kin. A number of the SAOs selected were men who taught military science to ROTC students at universities (Nancy Linthicum's SAO taught at Central Missouri State

108/ SUSAN SHEEHAN

University; Velma Zimmerman's was a professor at the University of Akron) or men assigned to Army Recruiting Commands, although Carmen Gross's, a woman, was a captain assigned to the Alcohol and Drug Control Office at Fort Sheridan. On January 21, 1983, the day after the board met, Colonel Flick sent each SAO a letter with enclosures and instructions. One enclosure was the CIL's paperwork pertaining to the serviceman in question, along with "four disposition options for remains of World War II casualties." Colonel Flick's first instruction to the SAO was "Familiarize yourself with the enclosures," and the second was to please call John Rogers or John F. Manning, another identification specialist with Casualty and Memorial Affairs, before getting in touch with the family. Most of the men and women SAOs had never served in that capacity before. They were given advice by Rogers and Manning on how to telephone the families, and had access to Department of the Army Pamphlet 608-33, a "Casualty Assistance Handbook," which spelled out how "Initial Contact with NOK (Telephonic)" was to be made:

> In your call, identify yourself and the fact that you will be assisting. Do not say that you have been "appointed" or give an impression that assisting is a chore of inconvenience to you. BE SINCERE IN YOUR OFFER TO HELP. Extend your own sympathy and condolence. Tactfully explain there are, or shortly will be, a number of matters which will require the NOK's personal attention and decision. Ask to meet with the NOK as soon as possible, in the home or at a place the NOK designates. The first telephone contact is crucial. Your courtesy, sincerity, honesty, understanding of the situation, and ability to answer questions will help to establish the needed rapport between you and the NOK. If you don't "make the grade" here, you will find it hard to succeed later.

Pam 608-33 (there is little that the Army hesitates to abbreviate) goes on to address "First Visit with NOK" in another paragraph:

> The first visit with the NOK may be difficult for you. However, try to appear poised and self-assured. The NOK will rely on you for strength and expect to find you fully competent. Be sure that

your uniform is proper, clean, and neatly pressed whenever you meet with the NOK. Keep your relationship with the NOK on a professional level at all times. Never become personally involved, seek favors, borrow money, etc. As a representative of the Secretary of the Army, you must be the epitome of a professional soldier in conduct and appearance.

Despite their lack of experience, the sincere, neatly pressed, professional men and women "made the grade" with the relatives. Over the telephone, they had informed them of the CIL documentation they would be bringing on their first visits. When SAOs perceived that relatives were still wrought up over the unanticipated recovery of the remains, they warned them gently that the skeletal diagram and photograph were a bit graphic, and proposed that they put the paperwork aside for a while. Most of the relatives studied the paperwork, including the diagram and photograph, but not all of the children and brothers serving as primary next of kin shared them with the men's mothers. Nancy Linthicum was pleased that her father's remains had been found together in one place. The family of William Shrake was impressed by the quantity of remains found and the excellent dental comparison. When Shrake's mother saw the photograph of the deformed ulna, she remembered exactly when he incurred the injury, playing basketball. A number of relatives didn't understand Form 892 or Form 897. Some had never heard of humeri and tibiae, much less the significance of measuring them. A fair number of relatives accepted the identifications simply because their son, brother, or father was on the manifest of 41081, the plane had been found, his remains had been identified by the Army, as had the remains of all the other men on the plane, and none of the twenty-two had ever turned up elsewhere.

In mid-January, the remains of twenty-one of the twenty-two men on 41081, having been put in aluminum transfer cases, were driven from the CIL to Hickam Air Force Base, flown to Travis Air Force Base, California, and driven to the United States Army Mortuary in Oakland, which is the port of entry for remains from Asia. In Oakland, each remains was wrapped in a blanket, laid out in a metal casket, and covered with a uniform.

Flick's final instruction to every SAO in his letter of January 21 was to send a telegram to the Directorate of Casualty and Memorial Affairs after the family member he or she was assisting had chosen a funeral home or government cemetery and a date for burial. Casualty and Memorial Affairs would transmit this information to Oakland. Each remains would be flown to the airport nearest the cemetery of choice, accompanied by an escort officer from the Oakland area.

The first telegram was dispatched on January 24. By February 12, eighteen funerals had been held. Once most of the relatives had got over their initial shock and had made their decisions, they wanted to give the men the burials they had never received.

In late February, as the remains of two of the men were about to be flown from California to the Midwest for burial—one in Illinois, the other in Kansas—a couple named Juanita and Alvin Beck were setting off in the opposite direction. They flew from their home in Des Moines, Iowa, to Los Angeles, changed planes, and continued to Honolulu. The Becks were going to attend the funeral of the one man whose remains had stayed in Hawaii, because his family had chosen to have him buried there—at Punchbowl, the National Memorial Cemetery of the Pacific. The man was Mrs. Beck's first husband, Lieutenant Robert E. Allred, the pilot of 41081.

PART III

PILOT

R OBERT E. ALLRED'S Army Air Forces record says that he was born on October 27, 1915. The Army chaplain who conducted a brief funeral for Second Lieutenant Allred on March 3, 1983, almost thirty-nine years after his death in a plane crash in New Guinea, mentioned the same date of birth as he spoke in general terms about a man who had been killed when the chaplain was only four years old. By March 3, the date was already on Robert Allred's tombstone, in the National Memorial Cemetery of the Pacific, because the former Mrs. Robert Allred believed that it might cause too much confusion to set the record straight. She was afraid that the process might delay the chiseling of the stone, which she wanted to see in place at the graveside ceremony. Then, too, after so many years, the date didn't really seem to make any difference.

Back in March 1937 it had made a difference to Bob Allred, whose actual date of birth was October 27, 1916. In the spring of 1937, he had just dropped out of the State University of Iowa, in Iowa City, where he had spent two and a half years collecting C's, and had returned to his home in Des Moines, where he had an opportunity to get a job driving a truck for the Railway Express Company. He had to be twenty-one to get the job, so on March 22, 1937, he went with his father, Henry Allred, to the Bureau of Vital Statistics in Des Moines, the state capital and the seat of Polk County. In those years, a new birth certificate could be obtained on the affidavit of a relative. Mr. Allred was willing to fill out a form stating that Bob was born on October 27, 1915, in Corydon, Iowa, a small town in Wayne County: in 1937, a good job was hard to find.

Robert Edward Allred was the youngest of Mary Corbett Jennison Allred's six children. Mary Corbett was born on a farm near Corydon in 1876. When she was twenty, she married Merton Jennison, a farmer. The Jennisons had three daughters: Emily, born in 1899; Hazel, born in 1901; and Margaret, born in August 1903, four months after Merton died of Bright's disease. At the time of Merton's death, the Jennisons were living on a farm in Confidence, Iowa, not far from Corydon. By then, the Corbetts had moved into Corydon, and Mary went to live with her parents for a while. She had fifteen steers in a Confidence feedlot, sold them not long after Margaret's birth, and bought a small house in Corydon with the proceeds. She supported herself and her daughters by housecleaning and washing and ironing for the more affluent Corydonians for 15 cents an hour. In 1904 she met Henry Allred, who lived across the street with his parents.

Henry took a fancy to Mary Jennison. William and Louisa Allred didn't consider a widow with three children a suitable match for their son and let him know it. In 1906 Henry Allred left Corydon—some believed he wanted to escape his father's criticism—and went to Oklahoma. While he was visiting relatives there, he picked up a trade: be became a housepainter. In March 1908 Mary Jennison moved to Des Moines; household jobs there seemed to pay better and to be more plentiful. Henry had gone farther west. He wrote Mary a letter from the state of Washington proposing marriage. Mary and Henry were married in Des Moines in August 1908. Henry worked in Des Moines for a year as a painter before setting off to do some farming. His father had been a farmer until he moved to Corydon, around the turn of the century, and went into Republican politics.

Merton Jennison, who called Mary Marie, had taken her to northern Iowa (where Emily was born) and to Wisconsin (Hazel's birthplace). Henry called Mary Mollie, and took her and the three girls to Kansas and Missouri. Their son Howard was born in 1911, on the second of two Kansas farms they couldn't make a go of (droughts caused crops to fail two years in a row), and their daughter Louise was born, in 1913, in the Ozark Mountains of southern Missouri. Some forty years later, Henry showed Howard the Missouri farm. "I don't know why anyone bothered to call that small, rocky place a farm," Howard Allred said recently. "When I saw it, a guy was harboring goats on it, and the goats weren't faring too well."

Henry and Mollie returned to Corydon in 1914 and rented a hotel. "The water system for the hotel was on the roof," Emily Allred recalls. "The system was fed by a well, so the water had to be pumped to fill the tank each day. If a tramp who could do the pumping didn't come around to the back door for food from the kitchen, Margaret, Hazel, and I had to pump." Howard simply remembers the small-town hotel as being "in the same category as the Ozark farm: no star." In 1932, when Bob Allred was an eleventh grader, he submitted an autobiography to his high-school English teacher. It stated that after a year or two of running the hotel, which Bob described as "strenious" work, his parents moved to a small house. "And it was in a small but pretty home on October 27, 1916 their son Robert Edward came to bless them," he wrote. Mollie, who had only a grade-school education, had won spelling bees and prizes in public speaking. Her youngest blessing inherited her talent as a debater but not her ability to spell: "strenious" is in good misspelled company in Bob Allred's youthful autobiography.

When Bob was a year old, Henry, Mollie, and their six children moved back to Des Moines, and Henry went to work painting Army barracks outside the city. The job didn't last long, and for the next ten years he worked on and off—mostly off—as a painter for a contractor. In 1930 he became a painter at the Equitable Building. Henry was paid a dollar an hour—a fairly lofty sum during the Depression—but painting was seasonal and part time, and he hardly ever worked forty hours a week. The largest sum of money he earned in a year was $1800, and that was after 1945, when he had retired from the Equitable Building and moved to California, and was working as a free-lance painter.

Henry Allred is remembered with affection by his children as a quiet, easygoing man, who asserted himself only when necessary. A few months after his marriage to Mollie, one of the Jennison girls informed Henry that he wasn't her father and so she didn't have to obey him. He gave her a licking, to let her know who was boss. From then on, Henry was her father, too.

He treated all six children equally, and they became a family in which the terms "half sister" and "half brother" were not used. From then on, he was content to let his wife resume her role as family disciplinarian.

Whereas Henry wasn't a hard worker—he rarely sought supplementary employment when painting was slow—Mollie is remembered with respect as a woman who could outwork most men. There was never a year in which she canned fewer than 400 quarts of fruits and vegetables. Whatever she didn't grow in her garden or on a vacant lot she bought from hucksters who drove their wagons around every summer peddling tomatoes, beans, peas, and corn. She was a good haggler, always getting thirteen ears of corn for the price of twelve. At various times, Mollie worked as a cook at a country club and as an unlicensed practical nurse caring for patients in their homes. She took in male boarders and at election time she solicited votes for local Republican politicians, who paid her by the telephone call. Her in-laws came to like her—especially William Allred, who, Howard has said, lived to be ninety-two without learning that "damn Democrats" was two words. She was also paid by Polk County's Juvenile Court to care for babies up for adoption until their adoption papers were complete. She became so attached to the babies that she found it difficult to give them up, and instead gave up that job after a couple of years.

"There was never any extra money in the house," Howard recalls. "I once asked my father for a few dollars to go to a prom. 'Son, I just don't have it,' he said." Louise remembers a year shortly after the end of the First World War when the family couldn't afford a Christmas tree. That December, Mollie made what looked like a pie. The gifts she could afford were put inside the pie. Each gift had a string on it and the recipient's name, so that the recipient could pull out his or her present. Howard didn't know that the pie was an inexpensive substitute for a tree; he just thought that it was a "nifty idea." Until they were grown, the children never realized how poor they had been—partly because so many people were in straitened circumstances in those years, partly because Mollie made a dollar do the work of four or five, and partly because there was always enough food on the table for them, and an extra plate for any friends they invited. Mollie was a strong advocate of Prohibition, belonged to the Woman's Christian Temperance Union, and didn't want any of her children to use alcohol in her house. Henry did make home brew. One evening, he got sick when it was time to bottle the home brew. Mollie's Scots heritage got the better of her hatred of liquor, and she bottled it for him. She then quit the WCTU, but she kept a dry house long after Prohibition was repealed.

Mollie, a stern, domineering woman, had a clear sense of right and wrong, which she was determined to impart to her children. She believed in living by a set of rules. Children who broke those rules got punished—not in the hereafter but swiftly, and often quite forcefully. She kept a supply of yardsticks in the four houses the Allreds occupied in Des Moines while Howard, Louise, and Bob were growing up, and used them on the three younger children as liberally as she had on the three older girls until they were twelve or thirteen. The second of the four houses had no furnace; it was heated by a large coal-burning stove in the living room. One morning, young Bob had done something especially naughty. Mollie looked for a yardstick and couldn't find any. Spring was coming, and the stove wasn't in use every day. A few days later, when she opened the stove door, there lay all the yardsticks, broken into small pieces. Her youngest son was regarded by his sisters and brothers as Mollie's favorite child and also as her most defiant. All the older children addressed their parents as Mother and Dad. In high school, Bob started to call them Mollie and Henry, and got away with it.

In his autobiography, Bob Allred bragged about his youthful pranks. He had launched his business career at the age of three by taking his sisters' love letters out of their dresser drawers and selling them to some high-school boys. When a boy from up the street wouldn't lend him a tricycle, he had knocked him off the tricycle seat and climbed on. ("From then on Jack and I were the best of friends although we had our childish arguements.") He had slid down the poles of a nearby firehouse when the firemen were out on calls. One day when a special-delivery boy left a motorcycle in front of the house, Bob had decided to see what made it go. In the course of his explorations, he wrote, "I pulled the thing over and caught my leg between it and the curbing.

The results were one broken leg. At first I did not mind lying in bed, because all the neighbors brought me little delicasies and my sisters were continually buying toys and story books." Four decades after Bob Allred's death, his contemporaries recall, with a certain awe, that he was the only child they had ever known who was suspended from the first grade—for giving his teacher a bad time.

Once Bob started school, there were yardsticks he couldn't break and conceal, but there were always rules to be broken. "When I was in third grade my teacher Miss McPherin and I were constantly crossing each other and of course I received the punishment consisting of the weekly sessions with the yardstick," he wrote in his autobiography. "I don't believe anyone got more spankings than I did." In fourth grade, he continued, "again my evil spirits got the best of me, and I was deprived of my recesses for fighting."

Bob Allred remembered his graduation from elementary school as "a grand affair: parties, picnics, and all the glory of a sixth grade student about to go to Lincoln." (In 1928 Abraham Lincoln was a new combined junior high and high school on the south side of Des Moines, a working-class section in which, according to Howard, only one man earned enough money to pay income taxes.) An intelligence test given by the school board to all sixth graders gave Bob an "opportunity to shine in studies," he wrote. "I had always been rather low in report card ratings, but in this test, I placed third." In junior high school, Bob Allred participated in sports, held minor class offices, and developed interests in football, oratory, and dramatics, all of which he pursued in high school.

In the 1930s, Lincoln had two graduating classes a year, two plays, and two junior-senior proms. Lincoln's winter production in January 1933 was a play called *The Family Upstairs*. Bob Allred, a junior, was cast in the role of the father; the part of his daughter was played by Juanita St.John, a senior. Juanita took a liking to Bob during rehearsals. One afternoon, she overheard two girls talking in a corridor. "I'm going to get Bob Allred to take me to the prom," one said to the other. "We'll see about that," Juanita remembers saying to herself. She later ran into Bob

Allred and a group of his friends standing near the school's front entrance. "Hi, Daddy," she said, waving as she walked by. She started to date Bob Allred, went to the January prom with him, appeared with him in the spring play, and went to her last prom at Lincoln with him. Juanita was only two days older than Bob—she had skipped a grade. Her mother, Jessie St.John, had allowed her to go out in coed groups when she was fifteen, but she wasn't allowed to go out on single dates until she turned sixteen, during the fall of her senior year. Bob Allred was the first boy she dated seriously.

Juanita's father, Fremont (Monte) St.John, was a contractor who had specialized in custom-built houses until 1930, when the crash brought residential building in Des Moines to a virtual standstill. In 1933 he found work as a deputy county auditor in the Polk County Courthouse, and kept the job until 1948, when the postwar building recovery was under way. The St.Johns struggled during Juanita's high-school years: her mother went back to work; her maternal grandparents and two aunts came to live in their small house; Juanita wore adult hand-me-down black and green satin dresses that were remade for her; and she worked at Woolworth's after school and on Saturdays. She didn't know until she arrived at the store which department she would be assigned to, but she has never forgotten that she was in kitchen utensils and pots and pans the day Bob showed up at Woolworth's to ask her for their first prom date. After graduation, she took a job as a secretary to an attorney. Juanita continued to date Bob Allred steadily during his senior year. Her six-day-a-week job prevented her from seeing him play football on Saturday afternoons, but she went to his two senior proms and watched him star in his two senior-year plays. When he graduated, he received the certificate for drama, which she had won the previous year.

After high school, Emily, Hazel, Margaret, and Louise also had to go to work, and they were expected to pay room and board to Mollie and Henry until they married. Girls of slender means had virtually no opportunity to go to college, and in the twenties and thirties usually only one or two boys went directly to college from Lincoln. Mollie made it clear to Howard from the time he was four that he was going to go to college. Her attitude toward a college education was pragmatic. It was desirable not so that Howard could appreciate Plato and Shakespeare but so that he could earn more money than a house painter.

Howard made up his mind to be a lawyer, and studied hard. When he graduated from Lincoln, in January 1928, he was president of his class and also first in his class; he won the certificate for scholarship. Since the age of twelve, he had sold newspapers, caddied, and worked as an office boy both during the school year and during the summer to pay for his own clothes. In February 1928 he got a job as an office boy and, after asking his mother to waive room-and-board charges, he began to save some money. He went to the State University of Iowa in September 1928, with $110. In the twenties and thirties, it was possible to complete college and law school in six years. After three years as an undergraduate, Howard entered the State University of Iowa law school; he received his B.A. after his first year of law school and his J.D. two years later. Mollie and Henry were unable to assist him; in 1930 the Des Moines bank in which they kept their money went broke, and they lost $200. It was a lot of money for them. All that they had. Howard was able to graduate from law school in 1934 as a result of a combination of hard work, good jobs, and a $750 loan from two insurance men whom Margaret had once worked for—a loan he couldn't pay off until 1940.

Mollie was equally ambitious for Bob. Her ambitions are revealed in the last section of his eleventh-grade autobiography, entitled "Future," which reads, "My plans for the future are not very definite. My Mother wants me to accept an opportunity to enter the United States Naval Academy at Annapolis which she has secured for me through her friend Congressman C. C. Dowell. I would like to do this, but there is no opportunity to take up law, the profession which my brother has chosen and which I would like to take. But at Annapolis all expenses are paid and a salary of $700.00 a year while six years at the State University of Iowa would be quite expensive. However, I have another year or two to think this over and in the meantime I am preparing myself for Annapolis."

Bob Allred's preparations for Annapolis were invisible to others. They did not include studying. His classmates, who remember him as a popular, outgoing cutup, with a sense of humor that made him the center of attention at many a party, also remember that he ranked twenty-third in his graduating class of ninety-three, and attribute this to his high intelligence and low diligence. In September 1934 he enrolled at the State University of Iowa. One contemporary, who says that Bob had never contemplated going to Annapolis, no matter what his mother wished, recently looked back on his friend's choice of colleges and observed, "Bob Allred always followed his own flight plan."

There were a few prosperous students at the State University of Iowa in the 1920s and 1930s—students whose parents paid their school bills, gave them allowances, and provided them with cars—but most were as poor as Howard Allred had been and as his younger brother was about to be. They lacked train and bus fare, and hitchhiked to and from school. They sent their laundry home in cardboard boxes with canvas tops, for twenty-seven cents postage. They paid for their lodgings, tuition, books, and lab fees out of their savings and their earnings from summer jobs. (Like Howard, Bob had worked since he was twelve and had bought most of his clothes.) They paid for their food by taking "board jobs"—jobs for which they were paid one meal for every hour they worked—and they found additional jobs to pay for incidental expenses. Howard had worked at the Hawk's Nest, a restaurant on one of Iowa City's main streets, and Bob's first college job was washing dishes there three hours a day. He eventually improved his lot by getting a three-meal-per-day job loading food carts in the dietary department of the State of Iowa's University Hospitals.

During his freshman year, Bob roomed with Ralph Harper; they had answered the same ROOM FOR RENT sign posted in the window of a house in Iowa City. During his sophomore year, Bob shared a room with Noble Irving, Lincoln High '33, who had appeared with him in school plays. Their room was near campus, in the home of a Mrs. Weber. They paid her $1.50 a week each—less than it cost to live in a regular college dormitory. Bob Allred and Noble Irving, a premed student who went on to become a physician, had one of two small bedrooms

on the second floor of the Weber house; two other boys from
Des Moines had the other bedroom, and the four shared a
bathroom (Mr. and Mrs. Weber and their daughter lived down-
stairs.) Irving remembers that his roommate thought that board
jobs should include fringe benefits, and acted accordingly. One
cold evening, he brought a gallon of Neapolitan ice cream home
from the Hawk's Nest; the boys ate some and set the rest out on
a window ledge. The next day was warm, and when they returned from classes they saw chocolate dribbling down one of
the white walls of Mrs. Weber's frame house, got a bucket, and
washed the wall.

Another evening, Bob, who had a capacious jacket, used it to
conceal two heavy blue wool blankets with UNIVERSITY HOSPI-
TALS woven into them in large white letters. A room at Mrs.
Weber's included linens but only light blankets; Bob gave Irving
a blanket and put one on his own bed. The next day, Mrs. Weber
asked Allred where he had got the blankets. He told her that Mr.
Pangborn, the man in charge of hospital supplies, had lent them
to him for the year. "She believed him," Irving recalls. "He was
lucky she never checked out his story with Mr. Pangborn, who
happened to be one of her close friends. But if she had Bob
would have talked his way out of that, too. He was a great con
artist. If he had survived the war, I think he would have gone
into politics or sold the Brooklyn Bridge. He led me to believe he
was going to return the blankets, but at the end of the school
year he sold both blankets to a young married couple at the
university. We took our belongings home each summer, and he
must have known Mollie wouldn't be as easy to con as Mrs.
Weber."

Bob's sister Louise remembers another of her brother's fresh-
man-year con jobs. In 1934 a man named James Allred was
elected governor of Texas. He was only distantly related to the
Iowa Allreds, but Bob developed a Texas drawl and claimed to
his new acquaintances at college that he was Governor Allred's
son. He boasted of getting away with this to Louise, who held
herself to Mollie's high standards of truth and disapproved of
Bob's lies. When she asked Bob why he told lies—they were
usually lies to make himself seem more important rather than
lies to harm others—he answered, "It keeps me on my toes. I

have to remember what I've told people, so that I won't get caught." Louise prefers to look back on her younger brother's good side. In the summer of 1935, when he was at home working to pay for his sophomore-year tuition, a boy he knew tried to wade across the Skunk River south of Des Moines; the water was too high, the boy was swept downstream, and he drowned. Bob and some of his friends spent most of the night diving for the body. Bob caught typhoid fever, had to stay in bed for several weeks, and temporarily lost some of his hair, but was soon none the worse for wear. Several years later, Louise's infant daughter caught scarlet fever. For five days, she ran a temperature of 105°. It was before penicillin, and the doctors were unable to treat her. Bob came over to Louise's house, sat and held the baby for hours, and cried. Louise and her husband didn't get scarlet fever; Bob did.

There were times during the 1935–1936 academic year when Irving didn't have three cents to mail a letter, but in May 1936, he had about $6 from laboratory-fee refunds, and Bob had somehow saved up $6, too. They decided that as soon as final exams were over they would hitchhike to Indianapolis to watch the 500-mile car race over Memorial Day weekend. Bob's last exam—accounting—was a day or two before Irving's. While Irving was taking his last exam, Allred went to the Commerce Building, where the grades in accounting had been posted. He saw he had flunked the exam and the semester course. He left Irving a note in their room at Mrs. Weber's: "Dear Nobe, I flunked Accounting, I'm no good. I'm going to make it somewhere else. Would you mind calling my mother and Juanita to tell them I'm running away. Bob." When Irving found the note, he called Louise and read it to her. She wasn't upset, nor was Juanita, although she considered it uncharacteristic of Bob to run away from a problem. He hadn't been unduly concerned about flunking French the previous semester, and, like Irving, Louise and Juanita knew that Bob tended to talk his way out of trouble.

That evening, Irving and a friend went to a soda fountain–poolroom near campus. When Irving glanced up from the pool table, there was Bob. "What the hell did you come back for?" Irving asked. "I had it all arranged for you to be away."

Bob sheepishly explained that he had hitched a ride with a truck driver, who had listened to his troubles, helped him put them in perspective, and persuaded him to go back to college. Irving was glad to see him: he had been looking forward to the race. The boys left for Indianapolis the next morning, had a splendid time, returned to the university with 50 cents apiece, and then headed home for the summer.

During the first semester of his junior year, Bob Allred got six C's. He then left the State University of Iowa for good. There was no way he could earn or borrow enough money to pursue a law degree at Iowa for three and a half more years. And there was the prospect of a decent job at home: the opening at Railway Express, where Emily had once worked. She recommended him for the position, Henry helped him acquire the birth certificate that made him twenty-one, and he became an expressman. Bob planned to work for a year and a half and then enter the Des Moines College of Law, a night law school, for four years. It would take longer, but the Des Moines College of Law charged lower tuition than Iowa, it admitted students with only two years of college, granting them an LL.B. after four years, and he could continue to work days while studying law at night. In 1934, he had been keen on going away to college and receiving his J.D. degree from the State University of Iowa (a more distinguished school and degree), but he was more fun-loving and less studious than Howard. After being a big fish in a small high-school pond and getting B's without really trying, he never quite adjusted to being a small fish in a big state-university pond. He also missed home, and Juanita.

Before Bob left for college, Juanita had told him she would no longer go steady with him. She knew he would date girls at the university—he had gone steady with seven girls at one time before she met him, and was reputed to be a ladies' man—and she had no intention of sitting home alone while he was out amusing himself with a blue-eyed blond co-worker in the dietary department. Bob and Juanita saw each other when he came home for weekends and vacations. One weekend early in his sophomore year, Bob returned home unexpectedly. Juanita had a date. Bob asked her to break it, and she refused. They didn't speak for several months, and saw each other infrequently over the next year and a half.

In the spring of 1937, Bob Allred telephoned Juanita at the Atlas Finance Company, where she had been working for a year as a cashier, and invited her out for lunch. She was paying her parents room and board but was able to afford some new clothes on the layaway plan on her $18-dollar-a-week salary. (The black and green satin party dresses she had had to wear during her high-school years were not what a teenager would have chosen.) She was pleased that she was dressed up in a new red coat with a fur collar the day Bob happened to call. They ate sandwiches and drank malts in his parents' car—she had a strict sixty-minute lunch hour—and although they had scarcely seen each other since the fall of 1935 he asked her to marry him.

"Isn't this a little sudden?" she inquired.

"After all these years?" he replied.

She accepted his proposal, he bought her a diamond engagement ring, and they set their wedding date: they would be married in August 1938, a month before he started law school.

During their long engagement, Juanita worked steadily at Atlas and saved for the wedding. Bob, except when he was laid off for brief periods, drove a truck for Railway Express and saved for law school.

The St.Johns had lived in Fort Des Moines, then an unincorporated town outside the city limits, since 1914, and attended the Fort Des Moines Presbyterian Church. Juanita Alice St.John and Robert Edward Allred were married there in a double-ring ceremony on Friday, August 5, 1938, at eight in the evening. At seven-thirty, a thunderstorm had caused a power failure. Candles were lit, but the lights came back on just as Juanita started to walk down the aisle on her father's arm. The wedding photograph shows a pretty, dark-haired, slender bride, who looked younger than her twenty-one years, wearing a white georgette wedding gown with a train, and a tall, dark, and handsome bridegroom in a white summer suit. (At 5 feet 11 inches, Bob was by far the tallest member of the Allred family. Mollie and Henry were plain-looking and of average height.) The church was small and simple, but Monte St.John, who was a carpenter by trade, had decorated it by building a wooden arch, which he painted white and covered with wisteria. The wedding party posed in front of it. Juanita and Bob had eight attendants. Howard, who was on his way to becoming a successful insurance-company lawyer, was his brother's best man. Ralph Harper and Noble Irving were ushers. Juanita's only sister, Marilyn, who was twelve, was the junior bridesmaid. A traditional tiered wedding cake, unspiked punch, coffee, nuts, and mints were served to two hundred guests at a reception in the church basement immediately following the ceremony. Howard drove the bride and groom, still in their wedding finery, from the church, by way of a hospital, to a furnished apartment they had rented. One of Juanita's aunts, who was supposed to have been her matron of honor, had fallen ill at the last minute, and Juanita had promised to visit her before the evening was over.

Juanita and Bob took their annual two-week vacations and spent their honeymoon at home. There were many wedding presents to open, many thank-you notes to write, and no money for a wedding trip. In September, Bob would have to pay $85 for his first semester of law school. Just before her two-week vacation was over, Juanita received a letter from the office manager at Atlas Finance Company informing her that she had been fired and should come in to clean out her desk. Years later, the owner of Atlas asked Juanita why she had quit, and told her she could have become a topnotch loan officer; the office manager's letter seemed even more mysterious then than it had in 1938. Getting fired proved to be a stroke of luck. With Mollie's help, Juanita found a job as a clerk in the Polk County Juvenile Court, under Judge Joseph E. Meyer. The pay was better, and the work more to her liking. "Putting an occasional kid on the right track was more worthwhile than figuring out the interest on someone's loan," she said recently. Judge Meyer was a kind man—after Bob went into the service he gave Juanita a leave of absence whenever she had an opportunity to be with him—and she worked at the Juvenile Court for more than ten years.

Bob put in long hours—behind the wheel of his truck, attending law classes, and studying in the law library or at the dining-room table. He had learned that he couldn't coast through law school, and worked hard to earn B's. Juanita worked at the court and kept busy with household chores. Although she remembers the four law-school years as "a struggle," she also remembers that she and Bob had their share of inexpensive good times. A neighbor might bake a cake and ask them over for coffee, cake, and a game of cards. They went on picnics, and invited friends for Sunday dinner. Sunday evenings, they took their leftovers to Mollie and Henry's, where all the children who still lived in Des Moines were expected to gather for a potluck supper. Bob and Juanita never owned a car, but they went on an occasional long drive with the St.Johns or the Allreds, most often to visit relatives. In 1939 they moved from the furnished apartment to an unfurnished house—they wanted more space—and started to acquire some furniture, borrowing a piece here, buying a piece there. They also bought an English bulldog, which they named Lord Jeeves.

The dog enjoyed a friendly round of wrestling on the floor with Juanita and Bob, chewed up all four legs of their wedding-gift card table, looked ferocious (in appearance, he was a perfect watchdog), but was always gentle with children. When Bob's young nieces came to visit and played too rough, Jeeves, though he weighed 75 pounds, disappeared, and returned after their departure; Juanita never discovered his hiding place. In 1940 the Allreds borrowed money from a savings-and-loan association and started to build a house of their own on Diehl Avenue, in Fort Des Moines, three blocks from the St.Johns' home. Monte St.John and Bob Allred did most of the planning and labor but had considerable help from Bob's four brothers-in-law and from Henry Allred, who painted the house outside and in. Juanita and Bob moved into their new house, which had two bedrooms, in the summer of 1941. That September, the Des Moines College of Law closed; its president was planning to enlist in the military. Drake, the only other law school in Des Moines, agreed to accept its students, to continue night classes for them, and to award them their law degrees.

In March 1942, three months after the Japanese attack on Pearl Harbor, Bob Allred sought recommendations from his boss at Railway Express, from an assistant Polk County attorney who was a family friend, and from Polk County's deputy auditor, Monte St.John. He attached these three recommendations to his application to join the Army Air Forces. The Army

Air Corps had come into existence in 1926 as a result of the effort of Army airmen to establish a separate air service. In June 1941, nine months before Bob Allred sought admission to this elite outfit, the Army Air Corps became the Army Air Forces, acquiring greater autonomy from the rest of the Army, but the term Army Air Corps continued to be used even in some official correspondence until an independent Air Force was established in 1947.

As a student and a married man, Bob Allred could have waited for the draft to catch up with him—if he had been willing to take a chance on his military destiny. He was disinclined to wind up in the infantry. Infantrymen walked. He was an adventurous, socially ambitious, cocky young man. He preferred to fly. To become an aviation cadet, you had to be between the ages of eighteen and twenty-six. According to his revised birth certificate, Bob Allred was twenty-six and a half in the spring of 1942 and had no time to waste. In April, when he first approached an Army Air Forces recruiter, Bob Allred flunked the eye test. He went to an optometrist, did a great many eye exercises, drank gallons of carrot juice, and passed the eye test on his second try. On May 2, 1942, right after finishing his last law-school exam, he walked from his house to the recruiting station at Fort Des Moines. He took a stiff written examination, which tested his vocabulary, his reading comprehension, his math, and his ability to reason. One of his future acquaintances recalled a typical question: If you had to make a 600-mile flight and you flew one-third of it at a 150 miles per hour, one-third at 180 miles per hour, and one-third at 200 miles per hour, how long would the flight take? Bob Allred passed the written exam, was given another physical, and enlisted in the Army Air Forces.

In 1942, the United States had to transform the small Army Air Corps into the mighty Army Air Forces. Hundreds of thousands of young men were as eager as Robert Allred to go off "into the wild blue yonder." Although only a small percentage of the multitude of applicants passed the aviation-cadet exam, the country lacked sufficient schools, instructors, and facilities to accommodate those who did; prospective cadets usually faced a wait of quite a few months. In late May, Private Robert E. Allred,

17067422, was sent to radio school at Scott Field, Illinois. He did his basic training there and began to acquire a Military Occupation Specialty as a radio operator while marking time for his orders to report for cadet training. On August 15, his wait was over. Robert Allred, LL.B. (Drake had granted him his law degree on June 6 in absentia, and he had been admitted to the Iowa bar without taking the bar exam, a courtesy extended to all law-school graduates who entered the service at the time), was sent to the San Antonio Army Air Corps Center, a large base with a newly opened cadet section, and was officially appointed a cadet. He and the thousands of other cadets were at San Antonio for two purposes. The first was Classification. During their first two weeks at San Antonio, they were given physical examinations for flying and a series of tests to determine whether they would be classified and trained as pilots, bombardiers, or navigators—or eliminated from the program.

There were many tests for manual dexterity. One entailed rolling five BBs into five shallow holes within a prescribed period of time. Once the first was in place, the trick was to keep it there while getting the others into holes. There were also tests for depth perception. The cadets had to look at two posts through the narrower end of a long, lighted box. Two strings coming out of the box were attached to the posts. The objective was to manipulate the strings until the two posts were lined up. Pilots naturally required the greatest degree of physical coordination and dexterity; bombardiers also required a considerable amount, and superior depth perception; navigators needed the least. Henry Webster, a future acquaintance of Bob Allred's, hoped to become a pilot when he went to a Classification Center at Santa Ana, California, in December 1942; he couldn't get the posts closer together than 6 or 8 inches and was classified as a navigator. Like Allred, 90 percent of the cadets wanted to become pilots, but there were a few—some former math instructors, for instance—with a definite preference for navigation. Some of these got their first choice; others were classified as pilots. "The bottom line was always what the Army Air Corps needed on any particular day in any particular place," a mathematician who was classified as a pilot recently recalled.

Classification took between two and three weeks. Allred was

classified a pilot and moved from his tent in the Classification
Center to a barracks for five or six weeks of Pre-Flight training,
the second purpose of his presence at San Antonio.

Allred's contemporaries recall Pre-Flight as a mixture of basic
training—there was a daily dose of calisthenics, close-order rifle
drill, marching (to and from the mess hall, among other places),
running, polishing belt buckles, and dusting footlockers—and
an abridged version of plebe year at West Point. Cadets in Pre-
Flight were made to respond instantly to orders and were disciplined for any failure to carry them out. In some Pre-Flight
centers, "upperclassmen" (cadets who had started Pre-Flight a
few weeks earlier) hazed the new cadets. Officers conducted
Saturday-morning inspection, wearing white gloves. Sometimes
an officer ran a clean white glove he was wearing on his right
hand over ledges and footlockers and then, at the end of the
inspection, held up the dirty white glove he had been wearing on
his left hand. "Cadets could be assigned to march up and down
on a tour with or without a parachute strapped to their backs for
any infraction," Robert Dent recalled. Dent and William Bauder
were two cadets who went through Pre-Flight training at San
Antonio at the same time as Allred. Bill Bauder remembers
being scheduled from reveille (6:00 A.M.) to taps (10:00 P.M.)
seven days a week. If he wasn't outdoors, he was in a classroom
being taught subjects like aircraft-and-ship identification. "Cadets could go to church for two hours on Sunday if they wanted
to," Bill Bauder says, "but if they chose not to go they didn't stay
idle. They studied." They didn't get off the base, either. Many
Second World War pilots still look back on their weeks in Pre-
Flight as a period of quarantine. There was a reason for the
testing of nerves and discipline: those who made it through
cadet flight training would be commissioned second lieutenants.

In September of 1942, Juanita asked Judge Meyer for time off
and took a train from Des Moines to San Antonio to be near
Bob. It was her first train ride, and she remembers feeling
frightened as well as naive because she didn't know how to find
the bathroom on a train. In San Antonio, Juanita stayed at the
house of a childhood friend whose father, a career Army officer,
was stationed there. She found work typing tax statements in a
San Antonio courthouse—a boring job—just to make a little

money and have something to do. "I occasionally got on a bus and rode out to the base, but that didn't mean I'd see Bob," Juanita says. "Most of my contact with Bob in San Antonio was by telephone. During the weeks I was in San Antonio, Bob got off the base just once." The wives of other cadets were in a similar predicament. Bill Bauder's wife, Helen, worked for a dentist in San Antonio and saw her husband three times in two months.

Prior to 1941, Primary, Basic, and Advanced Flying Training— the three principal phases in pilot training—had taken a year. Once the country was at war, the tempo of flight training was accelerated. Each phase was cut to nine weeks, with nine weeks added for Classification/Pre-Flight. When Robert Allred's Pre-Flight course at San Antonio ended, on October 10, 1942, he and his fellow cadet-pilots were dispersed to numerous Primary Training Schools. Bob Allred and Bill Bauder were among the cadets transferred to Hicks Field, 15 miles north of Fort Worth. One reason was alphabetical. The great majority of men from various Pre-Flight schools who were sent to Hicks had surnames beginning with the letters *A, B, S, T,* and *W;* there were virtually no men whose last names began with *C, D, P,* or *R* at Hicks that October. (Bob Dent was sent to Primary School at Grider Field, in Pine Bluff, Arkansas.) When Allred, Bauder, and Dent entered Pre-Flight, they had become members of Class 43-D, because if they completed their pilot training on schedule they would receive their wings in April 1943. The alphabet was also imposed on the calendar: *A* designated January, the first month of the year. April, the fourth month, was *D.*

Primary was where most cadets—including Robert Allred, who had never flown before he went into the service—were introduced to an airplane. The plane was most likely to be a Primary Trainer 19, or PT-19, a slow, single-engine two-seater with dual controls, which one of Allred's contemporaries has described as "a nice plane to learn on—it was very forgiving." In Primary, each cadet was usually given a brief ride in a PT-19 (or a similar plane), just to get him used to being off the ground. The instructor told him to tighten his safety belt and pull his goggles down, and to "hold on" as the instructor taxied, took off, climbed to 300 feet, made a left turn, made another left turn, and then made two more left turns (this was called "the pattern"), descended, landed, and taxied back to the edge of the field. The next day, the instructor would take the cadet up for half an hour and let him handle the controls on level flying and making gentle turns; he would show him some stalls, spins, and rolls. If the cadet reacted favorably (some, during the first or second demonstration, got airsick), the instructor would begin to teach him how to do takeoffs and how to "shoot" landings. After eight or ten hours of instruction, the cadet was expected to be ready to solo. Some men who found themselves up in the air alone for the first time lost their nerve. Just before they were to touch down, they would give the plane the throttle, go around again, come in for a landing, "give it the gun," and repeat the pattern several times before they found the courage to land; once they finally got back on the ground, they were through with flying. Many men couldn't get the feel of flying or were slow learners; in 1942, if a cadet wasn't soloing after ten hours of instruction the Air Corps couldn't afford to keep him and washed him out. Allred loved flying from the first day, took to it easily, and soloed after seven hours and forty-six minutes. Once a cadet had soloed, the instructor taught him simple acrobatics and more advanced maneuvers—loop, barrel rolls, Immelman turns, and spin recovery.

During Primary, whenever the cadets weren't airborne they were attending ground school. Again, they were shown silhouettes of Japanese, German, British, and American airplanes and ships. They undertook studies of aircraft engines and airframes, weather, communication in code, and aerial navigation, and they were drilled, inspected, disciplined, and kept occupied for between fourteen and sixteen hours a day, six or seven days a week. Some recall a couple of Sundays when they were free to go off base.

When Bob Allred completed Primary Training School at Hicks Field, on December 10, 1942, he had a total of sixty hours' flying time—about twenty-six and a half hours' dual time, logged with an instructor, and about thirty-three and a half hours' solo time—enough to put him approximately on a par with a civilian pilot able to pass a private-pilot's-license test and a written exam. Two hundred and twenty men started Primary at Hicks in October 1942. A booklet called "The Men of Hicks, Class of 43-D" includes photographs of the cadets who made it through Primary. It has head-and-shoulders shots of only a hundred and thirty-nine young men, wearing leather jackets and helmets, their goggles resting on their foreheads. Between July 1939 and August 1945, 193,444 pilots graduated from flying school and about 124,000 trainees washed out, mostly during Primary, among them the 81 at Hicks Field in the fall of 1942.

Juanita followed Bob from San Antonio to Fort Worth in October. In December she returned to Des Moines. She had been away more than two months and couldn't afford to lose her job. Bob Allred had a shorter journey. On December 16, 1942, he began Basic Flying Training at Perrin Field, in Sherman, Texas, a country town about 80 miles north of Fort Worth.

Basic was essentially a continuation of Primary in a larger, faster, more powerful, and more sophisticated two-seater—generally a Basic Trainer 13, or BT-13. In Primary, the instructors were civilians. From Basic on, they were Army Air Forces officers. In Primary, the cadet-pilots flew visually; in Basic, they started to learn flying with no visual reference to the ground—instrument flying. They spent hours in a Link Trainer, a small, boxlike ground-training device that enclosed a simulated aircraft cockpit, with flight controls, a radio, and full blind-flying instrumentation. The cockpit interior was filled with an eerie purple haze, produced by ultraviolet lighting, which also caused the instrument markings to give off a luminescent, greenish-yellow glow. A Link Trainer was no place for someone with claustrophobia. The cadet-pilot was locked away in a solitary violet-and-yellow world, his only contact with the outside coming through his headset—a gentle intoning of radio signals or, occasionally, the voice of the instructor issuing directions for practice maneuvers. An hour of this was considered a good workout for a beginner. At the close of the session, the cadet would alight from his box to view the results of his efforts: a tiny tracing pen, called "the bug," had recorded his many turnings on a roll of paper. The instructor would point out errors and make suggestions for more precision in instrument flying. For training in the air, a hood installed over the student's portion of the cockpit limited his vision to the aircraft interior. The fledgling pilot could then practice instrument flying while the instructor served as lookout and safety pilot.

During Basic, the cadets were introduced to formation flying and were also allowed to fly short cross-country hops, both day and night, instead of simply flying in the vicinity of the home airfield. They would make up a flight plan to get from Point A to Point B, select an alternative airport, at C, in the event that B was socked in, and figure out how much fuel they would need to get from A to B, on to C, and back to A, with thirty minutes' fuel to spare. Ground school continued, and so did limited time off base, but Allred's contemporaries remember receiving slightly better treatment in Basic, because, as Bob Dent puts it, "the brass figured we'd be around longer."

Shortly before Bob Allred successfully completed Basic Flying School at Perrin, where he had flown a total of eighty hours and forty minutes, he was asked to express a preference for Single-Engine Advanced Flying School (where half the class would be sent) or Multi-Engine Advanced (where the other half would go). Most Second World War fighters had one engine; most transports and fighter-bombers had two engines; and heavy bombers had four. Allred and Bauder wanted to fly bombers, and got their wish: on February 18, 1943, they reported to the Army Air Forces Advanced Flying School at Altus, Oklahoma. A majority of the airbases in the country were in the Southeast or in Texas or California, where the weather permitted year-round flying.

At Altus, Allred and Bauder flew two types of two-engine advanced trainers—the AT-9 (which Bauder considered "a very difficult craft to fly and a real test for student pilots") and the AT-17 ("easy to fly and reliable"). Their cross-country flights were longer; a higher percentage of their flying was done at night; they continued to do their own radio communicating and to perfect their formation flying. The instrument-flight "check rides" they were required to pass grew more difficult. The demand for increasing precision in proper radio procedures and in navigation, and for strict adherence to prescribed altitudes and compass headings, continued to weed out the less competent cadets. By the time Bob Allred passed his last test at Altus, on April 15, he had flown more than a hundred and nineteen hours in Advanced, about sixty-nine of them as pilot, the rest as copilot. During the following week, he was discharged from the Army, commissioned a second lieutenant in the Army Air Forces, assigned an officer's serial number, 0-679012, to replace his enlisted man's serial number, and given a $250 clothing allowance. He gave himself an extra inch when reporting his height on his new records. A week later, his new uniforms gleamed with a second lieutenant's gold-plated bars and a pilot's sterling-silver wings.

Several weeks earlier, Juanita had joined Bob at Altus, a small town with little to offer in the way of housing and less in the way of employment. She lived in an attic bedroom in the house of an elderly couple, wrote letters home, often ate alone at a café in the town square, and did some cooking (the room had kitchen privileges) when Bob was able to get off base. Juanita was there for a dinner dance held in the Armory at Altus on Wednesday evening, April 21, and she and also Mollie and Henry, who had driven out from Des Moines, were in the Post Theater at nine o'clock the following morning to see Bob graduate from the Army Air Forces Advanced Flying School of Altus, Oklahoma, with the Class of 43-D.

The men were prouder of the silver wings than of the gold bars. Bob bought a pair of wings for his wife and a pair for his mother. Mollie wore hers until her death, eleven years later. Some of the men had been lured from the infantry, from field-artillery units, and from low-paying civilian jobs into the Army Air Forces by money as well as glamour: in 1942, privates were paid $50 a month, aviation cadets $75 a month. As the Army Air Forces recruitment posters advertised—posters that featured pretty girls smiling at cadets—second lieutenants were paid $150 a month plus $75 a month in flight pay for every month they flew at least four hours. Bob Allred began to earn $225 a month in May.

On April 22, the graduates were given ten-day leaves. Juanita and Bob drove home to Des Moines, where they were entertained at a round of parties. Before leaving Altus, the second lieutenants had been handed their next assignments. Some would be going to a troop-carrier group in Del Valle, Texas; some were bound for Pyote, Texas, to train in B-17s; Allred and Bauder were two of thirty men from Altus 43-D assigned to Four-Engine-Transition School at Tarrant Field, a new field on the outskirts of Fort Worth, where they would learn to fly B-24s.

In 1969 David Becker, a pilot who had flown a B-24 across the Pacific the same week as Bob Allred, wrote a letter in the form of a memoir to his son. Becker, a jeweler in Terre Haute, was then nearing the age of fifty. "Looking back, I cannot say that to me my life has been dull, but I must admit that it has been quite routine and undistinguished," he wrote. "However, there was one four-year period in my life that was neither routine or un-eventful. Those were the years that I spent in the service in World War II during 1942, 1943, 1944, and 1945."

It was those four years that Becker dwelt on in his letter-memoir. He recalled that he got his first glimpse of a B-24 in the spring of 1943, at an airfield near Houston where he was taking Multi-Engine Advanced Training. He wrote:

> Honest to God, it was the biggest damn plane I had ever seen. The lieutenant who had flown it in said we could enter through the forward bomb bay, walk along the catwalk, go through the hatch, get up into the flight deck, and look around. I had never seen so many instruments, dials, radios, knobs, and buttons in my life. I was sure then that I wanted to fly a B-24, but I remember thinking, How in the devil could a guy learn to fly a monster like that? Don't forget, at that time it was the biggest bomber in the United States. The B-29, our first super-bomber, was only being tested in early '43. The B-24D was 66 feet 4 inches long and had a wingspan of 110 feet. It had four Pratt & Whitney 1,200-horsepower engines. The propaganda put out about it said it would fly easily at 25,000 feet, carry a bomb load of 8,800 pounds, go 2,850 miles without refueling, and travel at a maximum speed of 300 miles per hour. Several months later, when I started flying B-24s, I learned that some of those numbers were misleading. The plane went up to 25,000 feet if its engines were new and it carried a minimum crew and a minimum amount of gas, but in training I was flying ancient clunkers and the highest I ever got in one was 19,000 feet and so help me we couldn't have gone an inch higher if I had thrown out

the crew to lighten the ship. It would carry four tons of bombs if it carried a minimum of gas. It would fly 2,850 miles without refueling if it carried *no* bombs (for long flights extra gas tanks were installed in the forward bomb bay), and it would go 300 miles per hour if you put the nose straight down in a full power dive. But all in all it was one helluva airplane for its time.

On May 1, 1943, Bob Allred reported to Tarrant Field. On May 2, a year to the day after he had enlisted in the Army Air Forces, he went up in a B-24 for the first time. The B-24 was a far different plane from the AT-17, the last plane he had flown at Altus. The cloth-covered AT-17 was made primarily of wood, held five passengers, was powered by a pair of 245-horsepower engines, and cruised at 130 miles per hour. "Some men just couldn't cut it in four engines and were reassigned to troop-carrier squadrons," Bob Dent recalls. (Dent had been assigned to Tarrant after completing Basic and Advanced at bases near Waco, Texas.) Allred, however, took a liking to the B-24 and found it surprisingly easy to fly, and fly it he did—for sixteen days in May and twenty-three days in June. In May an instructor was usually aboard with three students, who took turns in the pilot's left-hand seat, the copilot's right-hand seat, and sitting between them on the flight deck and watching. By June two B-24 pilot trainees with an engineer but no instructor were usually on their own, occasionally taking the plane up at night and flying longer cross-country flights.

At Tarrant, Allred added 114.2 hours of pilot time to the 260 he had when he got his wings. He also put in more hours on instruments and did a good amount of reading. On June 15, he signed a paper certifying that he had read and understood ninety-two subjects newly listed in the table of contents of the "Pilots' Information File," such as "Flying Over Populous Areas and Crowds," "Flying Multi-Engined Airplanes with One or More Engines Inoperative," "Flight Status After Taking Sulfa Drugs," "Psychology and Flying," and "To Bail or Not to Bail." On June 30, he was rated a first pilot. Four days later, he received his next orders. After a fifteen-day leave, he was to report to Clovis, New Mexico, a hot, dusty town that one of his acquaintances later described as "about as close to nothing as I had ever seen in the service." Allred spent his leave partly in Des Moines and partly hitching plane rides there and back, and got to Clovis on July 19, about a week after David Becker did. Becker, a member of the Class of 43-F, had been sent to Clovis to learn to fly B-24s without the benefit of two months of Four-Engine-Transition School. He put in almost twice as many hours in B-24s at Clovis as Allred did, and was checked out as a first pilot in two weeks. "Everyone's career in the Army Air Corps was like everyone else's, only different," Becker explains.

Special Order No. 225 was posted on a bulletin board at Clovis on August 13, 1943. Partial crews for fifty heavy bombers were directed to proceed to El Paso, Texas. Each was composed of a pilot and five enlisted men. Second Lieutenant Robert E. Allred 0-679012, and Second Lieutenants Bauder, Becker, and Dent were among the fifty pilots. After a week's leave (Allred was becoming a commuter to Des Moines), the three hundred men reported to Biggs Field, near El Paso, where, on August 22, a bombardier and a sixth enlisted man were added to each crew. Six days later, the crews were again expanded, each acquiring a copilot and a navigator.

The customary crew of a B-24 in combat was ten men—four officers and six enlisted men. The three officers assigned to Allred's crew were Second Lieutenant Laverne Nusbaum, the copilot; Second Lieutenant Oliver E. Clark, who had received his bombardier's wings and his second lieutenant's commission after completing Bombardiers' School at Albuquerque, New Mexico, on July 31; and Second Lieutenant Keith T. Holm, who had won his navigator's wings and gold bars at Mather Field, in Mills, California, on July 31, 1943, and had been married four days later. The six enlisted men who were to go overseas with Bob Allred were Sergeant James H. Pitts, his engineer; Sergeant Horace D. James, radio operator; Sergeant John R. Campbell, a gunner; and three other gunners, who had come together from gunnery schools around the United States.

Combat-crew training at Biggs consisted of teaching each of the ten men his exact job as it related to a B-24 and then teaching the ten to perform as a crew. Of the ten men in Allred's crew, only Allred himself had ever flown in a B-24 before Clovis, and before Biggs none of Allred's 174.5 B-24 hours had been devoted to mock bombing or gunnery missions. Much of the flying done at Biggs was for the benefit of the bombardiers. The controls that opened the bomb racks and the bomb bays were different on a B-24 from those on the AT-11 that Clark had trained on at Albuquerque. Many days when Allred and Nusbaum took off from Biggs, they headed for New Mexico, where they had to hold the plane steady so that Clark could drop 100-pound sand-filled blue practice bombs on one of the bombing ranges near towns like Alamogordo. Other days were spent on gunnery missions. Sometimes the gunners aimed at targets on the ground—billboards with bull's-eyes painted on them or a heap of cars that had been junked in the desert. Sometimes aerial gunnery was part of the day's agenda, with the gunners firing at cloth targets towed on long cables by small planes. Lengthy day and night missions were flown, so that the navigators could practice keeping the plane on course, while the engineers mastered the art of transferring fuel from one tank to another. Instructor-pilots, instructor-navigators, and instructor-bombardiers sometimes went along to check the performances of individual crew members. Many of Becker's friends had no trouble getting their B-24s up to 25,000 feet, but they seldom pushed them beyond their cruising speed of 200 miles per hour.

On October 16, about midway through his stay at Biggs, Bob Allred sent a letter to his brother Howard. He wrote,

> Things here, as you might expect, are in the continued uproar that seems to go with combat training. The weather is still perfect so flying is going on at a helluva pace, fly 8 hours at a stretch—that means take off at 8 A.M. & land at 4 P.M.—or, take off at 5:30 P.M. & land at 1:30 A.M., which gets rather tiresome. Lots of .45 cal. pistol, .50 cal. machine gun & skeet shooting with 12 gauge pump guns too, along with Ground School, Intelligence lectures, etc. to keep up the pilots interests & not let him sleep.

In his letter, Allred described a recent B-24 crash at Biggs, which he blamed on a fuel-transfer error made by the crew's engineer. He went on to praise his own crew, calling Clark "the best damn bombardier on earth" and Nusbaum and Holm "a perfect copilot and navigator." After stating that the enlisted men were "all swell," he continued, "All in all, I've got a good bunch of boys. All work hard, fight hard, drink hard & are wolves on their nights off. Thank God *I* go to church whenever I'm off duty. I wouldn't want to have people think I've found the cutest little blue-eyed brown haired lovely 5-ft. nurse (Lt.) in the Army. No sir, not me!"

Bob Allred was not a man to let his days on duty keep him from having a good time. One fall day after completing a training mission, he decided to buzz the Rio Grande. Ollie Clark, who was at his position in the nose next to the bombsight, thought Allred was going to fly under a bridge that spanned the Rio Grande, but he pulled up at the last minute and followed the meandering river at an altitude of about 30 feet. Clark could see ducks on the water. The birds would rise a bit and then settle back down. Suddenly, Clark spotted a flock of ducks flying in to land. The ducks became confused and couldn't get out of the plane's way in time. Clark saw that it was too late for Allred to pull up and miss them. Clark had a clipboard with him and held it up to protect his face. One duck hit a Plexiglas nose panel, broke it, and wound up on the floor of the nose. Other ducks hit the steel rim around one of the engines.

Allred knew he was in trouble. The ground crew responsible for maintaining the plane would see the damage and would have to repair it. Work orders had to be issued for all repairs. He told the crew that if they were asked about the incident they should say he was flying at 3500 feet when he hit the ducks. When the colonel in command of his group at Biggs saw the broken panel and the feathery mess around the engine rim and questioned him, Bob Allred failed for once to talk himself out of a predicament. The colonel knew something about Allred's flying habits and something about ducks' flying habits, too. Ducks of that species didn't fly at high altitudes, the colonel informed the pilot. Word of Allred's skirmish with the ducks got around Biggs, and for weeks to come Allred was asked, "Hey, Bob, seen any more ducks with superchargers lately?"

Lee Shelton, another pilot at Biggs, remembers the time Allred struck the ducks while buzzing the Rio Grande. Shelton, who made the Air Force his career, retiring as a colonel in 1969, disapproves of buzzing. "Unless the training or tactical situation demands that airplanes be flown at low altitudes, I do not think the pilot has the right to endanger the lives of the nine other men aboard," he says. "It shows poor judgment." He acknowledges that probably a third of the pilots he flew with in training in the United States and, later, in the Southwest Pacific during the Second World War were called "hot pilots," who indulged in buzz jobs. Shelton remembers one pilot who flew a B-24 so low in New Guinea that he inadvertently bounced it off a beach, returning to base with crumpled rear-bomb-bay doors and sand in the back of the aircraft. Another pilot landed with shreds of palm fronds lodged inside the engine housing from a close encounter with a coconut tree.

It is Bob Dent's recollection that some hot pilots were luckier than Allred, inasmuch as they didn't get caught with the goods, and that even those who did get caught, like Allred, weren't kicked out of combat-crew training, because by then the Air Corps had too much invested in them. "I never flew with Bob Allred, but we flew with many of the same instructors at Biggs," Bill Bauder says. "They all said he could make an airplane do what it was supposed to do. He was a capable pilot."

Crews had been assigned at random at Clovis and Biggs. Hy Webster, a 43-G Mather alumnus, could have been made Allred's navigator instead of his classmate Keith Holm. Crews also kept changing. Bauder's original navigator and radio operator had to be replaced, because they couldn't withstand high-altitude flying. On November 10, 1943, Laverne Nusbaum was transferred to the crew of a pilot named Andrew Sheerin; Paul Harvey, who had been Sheerin's copilot, became Allred's.

Paul Harvey was born in 1921. Five years younger than Allred, he was his physical opposite: short (5 feet 7 inches) and pudgy (159 pounds in 1943), with reddish-brown hair, blue eyes, and a ruddy complexion. He had had a year of junior college and had received a license to fly small single-engine planes before he enlisted in the Army Air Forces, in the spring of 1942. He got his wings and bars in February 1943, and spent the next four months flying B-25s in Kentucky and South Carolina. He expected to be sent to Europe as first pilot on a B-25, a two-engine bomber. Instead, in July he was sent to Ohio and given training in B-17s— four-engine bombers—and then, in August, was ordered from Ohio to Clovis and taught to fly B-24s.

Harvey, Class of 43-B, was more than a little miffed to find himself assigned as a copilot to Allred, Class of 43-D, but he was one of many former B-25, B-17, and A-20 first pilots who ended up at Biggs sitting in the right seat next to men who had been commissioned later than they had. There are countless toggle switches in the cockpit of a B-24. Harvey and other copilots resented being told to toggle the switches that opened and closed the cowl flaps on each engine, and those that synchronized the propellers, while the pilots flew the plane. They formed an organization called the Toggle Joes and wore on their flight jackets a cloth patch designed by one of their members that expressed their resentment: it depicted a six-armed creature wearing a pilot's helmet. "You needed almost as many arms as an octopus to toggle all those switches," Paul Harvey says. There were only two flying weeks left at Biggs after Harvey was put on Allred's crew in November—time enough for Harvey to take a dislike to his new pilot. "Allred ordered me around just because he was boss," Harvey says. "I didn't socialize with him and the rest of the crew at Biggs. I went around with the other Toggle Joes."

Doris Holm had joined her husband a few weeks after their marriage. In mid-November, Juanita took a second long leave of absence from Juvenile Court and went to El Paso, where the Allreds and the Holms shared a two-bedroom apartment. To many of the pilots, El Paso was "just another Texas town," but it did have a redeeming feature: Juárez, right across the Mexican border, where mixed drinks at the bars that lined the main street cost fifteen or twenty cents, there was no shortage of bottled liquor, and many items that were rationed in the United States were readily available. Juanita and Bob went to Juárez to see a bullfight and to do their Christmas shopping. In December the Allreds and the Holms also went on a sixteen-hour (7:00 A.M. to 11:00 P.M.) bus excursion to Carlsbad Caverns, where they met up with Ollie Clark, who had gone there the previous day. In a photograph of Juanita and Bob Allred and Doris and Keith

Holm taken at Carlsbad on December 7, 1943, the two men are in uniform, and the two women are turned out as elegantly as if they were going to church instead of a series of caves. Juanita is wearing pumps, a hat, and the red coat with the fur collar she had worn the day Bob proposed, six and a half years before that day at Carlsbad.

Forty-odd years later, Doris remembers that outing with pleasure—especially the descent into the Big Room, with its majestic formations and its stalactites and stalagmites. She sat with Keith on a bench in silence and darkness while the hymn "Rock of Ages" was played and electric lights slowly illuminated the main chamber. Doris has a few other happy memories of Biggs—it was there that she was introduced to bacon-lettuce-and-tomato sandwiches and iced tea, for which she has retained a lifelong fondness. Her mother-in-law mailed her and Keith chocolate angel-food cakes packed in popcorn to keep them from being crushed, and her mother sent the hometown paper, but it was Doris's first time away from her family; she was lonesome and never felt like a carefree young bride. "We knew the men would soon be going overseas," she says.

In October, when Bob had written to Howard, he believed he would be going to the Southwest Pacific, and had sounded pleased; at Clovis, when he was asked to state an overseas preference it was his first choice. On the evening of December 6, Bob wrote to Emily to thank her for some Christmas presents she had sent. Training at Biggs was over, and he knew he would be on his way to Topeka, Kansas, in ten days. "The general doesn't think it wise to turn us loose for 10 days so close to our sailing date for several reasons, mainly venereal disease and boys going over the hill for extended time—so we have to report every day for a lecture, a movie (sex, Art of War, etc.) and P.T.," he wrote. "It's looking more & more like we will go to either England or the Mediteranean theatre & that will be by boat." He did not look forward to the prospect of going to Europe, of getting there by boat, or of moving to Topeka. He reported that he had seen snow only once since the spring of 1942: 3 atypical inches had fallen on El Paso the previous week and had melted in haste. "The southern climate agrees with my lazy disposition," he wrote.

*   *   *

On December 17, 1943, the Biggs crews went by troop train to Topeka, which Hy Webster was to remember as "the land of ice and snow," saying, "We never saw the ground the whole time we were there." They were given a briefing about their forthcoming voyage to Europe, but when they were issued sheepskin-lined pants, jackets, and boots—standard issue for high-altitude flying in Europe—some of them joked that they were actually bound for Greenland, which the United States had occupied in April 1941, to help protect American and British shipping from German submarines. The wives shivered in their spring and fall coats and wished they had been issued winter clothes to wear in Topeka's cold.

Allred and his crew had their photographs taken in their Arctic gear in front of an early-model B-24 named Lil' De Icer, which had been chosen as an artistic backdrop because of a scantily clad lady painted on its fuselage. Rank had its privileges: the officers' names were capitalized on orders; the four officers stood in front of Lil' De Icer while the six enlisted men crouched in front of them in deep snow. As the year was ending, the men were called out one night and told they wouldn't be going to Europe after all—they would be going to the Pacific. The men didn't fly in Topeka—it was the first month since Allred got his wings that he hadn't collected his $75-a-month flight pay—and they had little to do there except sit around the Officers' Club and play cards. Some took unofficial leaves at New Year's. The Allreds returned to Des Moines, borrowed Mollie and Henry's car, and drove it back to Topeka.

Early in January 1944 the pilots learned they would be getting brand-new B-24s, and on January 7 they were told to report to a specific office to sign the papers for their B-24Js and engines. "There were about 35 or 40 of us in line," David Becker wrote in his letter-memoir to his son. "About the third or fourth man got up to the desk and we heard him say, 'I don't sign unless I see what I sign for.' We all had to wait until they took him over to the flight line so that he could make sure 'his' plane was really there, and so that he could count the engines. The brass was not amused, but the other pilots thought it was funny."

In the eyes of most beholders, the B-17 was a beautiful plane but the B-24, with its boxcar-shaped fuselage, was homely. Officially designated the Liberator, it was more generally known as "the flying boxcar." Allred's boxcar was an olive-drab B-24J, with the serial number 42-100210. The plane had all four engines, but the gas tanks were leaking fuel, and on January 8 it went into the depot for repair. Three days later, the men tested 210. (Planes were commonly referred to by the last three digits of their serial numbers.) Allred flew the plane to Des Moines and took it low over Abraham Lincoln High School and some of the city's other substantial buildings. Forty years later, Jim Pitts remembered hearing him say that from the day he had become a pilot it had been his ambition to buzz his hometown. Pitts also remembered Harvey's displeasure. "Watch those smokestacks, Bob, watch those smokestacks," he had cautioned.

Within a few days of signing for their new planes, the crews got orders to proceed to Fairfield-Suisun Army Air Forces Base, in Fairfield, California. A few planes left Topeka each morning. No. 210 departed on January 13. The men got up at five o'clock. Juanita and Bob said their goodbyes at the rented room in Topeka where they had been staying, but some of the wives went to the airfield to watch the flyaway. Doris recalls that the plane dipped its wings after takeoff, and that it was a pretty sight in the early-morning sun. The planes all stopped in Tucson to have extra gas tanks added in the forward bomb bay. A day or two before they left Topeka, the crews had been issued, and required to wear, side arms—.45 caliber Colt semiautomatics. In Tucson, Pitts removed the protective Cosmoline (a thick grease) that the factory had put on the pistol. He and two other enlisted men stayed at the plane on the thirteenth and fourteenth to keep objects stored on it from being stolen. On the second night, he, James, and Campbell felt bored and amused themselves by riding around the hangar on some three-wheel scooters parked there. Allred often heard about his enlisted men's escapades but rarely chewed them out, perhaps because of his own youthful larking, and they were fond of him.

No. 210 left Tucson for Fairfield-Suisun on the morning of the fifteenth and arrived there that evening in a cold, driving rain. The weather at Fairfield stayed bad, and for the next several days Allred and his crew did little except sleep, play poker, and watch the rain. By the nineteenth, it had cleared, and Allred's crew and five others received orders to proceed to Amberley Field, near Brisbane, Australia. Their orders said they were to report to "Commander, Fifth Air Force Replacement Center, Amberley Field, Brisbane, Australia for assignment to the Fifth Air Force." On the morning of the twentieth, they took the plane up for an hour and fifteen minutes to make sure that the fuel would transfer properly out of the new bomb-bay tanks. At 11:30 P.M., Allred set off for Hawaii. There were dozens of planes leaving Fairfield-Suisun that night, but when Harvey called the tower to say that Boxcar 210 was ready for takeoff the tower responded, "Roger, Boxcar 210—and good luck." Allred flew south over the Golden Gate Bridge and down the coast before turning west to the sea.

The flight to Hawaii—almost 2400 miles southwest of Fairfield—was the longest leg of the transpacific journey. It took Allred's boxcar fifteen hours to reach Hickam Field, on the outskirts of Honolulu; all but three of the hours were flown at night. Although it was the crew's first flight over water, all the enlisted men except James, the radio operator, slept a good deal of the way. The officers could also trade off, and for most of the way the plane was set on autopilot, but Holm stayed up all night. He later wrote to his aunt that he had used quite a bit of celestial navigation between California and Australia but more radio, because it was "a lot easier for position reports." After landing at Hickam, on January 21, the men cleaned up and went sightseeing. The next day, some of them went swimming at Waikiki Beach. The crews had been briefed on the flight to Australia before they left the United States. They were always rebriefed by Air Transport Command personnel, however, before embarking for the next island on their itinerary.

On the twenty-third, Allred took off for Canton Island, 1650 miles southwest of Hawaii. Canton Island is a coral atoll about 4 miles wide and 8 miles long that rises only a few feet above the ocean. In the fall of 1942, it had become a renowned speck in the Pacific, which is a sheet of water of 70 million square miles and covers a third of the globe. In October 1942 Edward Vernon Rickenbacker, America's No. 1 Ace of the First World War, left Hickam for Canton Island on a B-17. He was carrying a secret message from President Franklin D. Roosevelt's Secretary of War, Henry L. Stimson, to General Douglas MacArthur, commander-in-chief of the Southwest Pacific area, who was then in Brisbane. The B-17, with a crew of five and three passengers, missed Canton Island. The pilot ran out of fuel before he could find it by "boxing the compass" (going west for forty-five minutes, then north, east and south). He managed to land the heavy plane safely in the water. The eight men climbed into two life rafts. Seven of the eight, including Rickenbacker, survived a three-week ordeal before they were rescued.

Rickenbacker's experience placed a psychological burden on pilots and navigators headed for Canton Island in 1943 and 1944. Holm had no trouble finding it—210 touched down on Canton Island eleven hours and forty minutes after taking off from Hickam—but Becker's navigator got slightly lost, and the plane had to fly a square search until the men sighted Canton. In the 1980s, with jumbo jets flying from Hawaii to Australia in ten hours, the island that Rickenbacker's plane missed is once again obscure. Canton Island lingers in the memories of Allred's contemporaries as a rim of coral around a lagoon, an island so desolate that the only thing they saw growing there was one palm tree.

Allred and his crew left Canton Island on the morning of the twenty-fourth, crossed the International Date Line, and arrived eight hours later—midafternoon on the twenty-fifth—at their next port of call. This was Nandi, a landing strip on Viti Levu, which is the largest of the Fiji Islands and was a British colony in 1944. On Canton Island, Allred and the other pilots had been warned about the runway at Nandi. The strip was an optical illusion. After you landed, you would be going uphill, and it would appear that the crest of the hill was the end of the runway. It wasn't. You still had about 3000 feet of runway left, going down the hill, so there was no need to try to screech to a stop on the hilltop and blow out your tires, as many pilots before you had done.

On their way from Nandi to the town of Lautoka, where B-24 crews often went window-shopping in stores owned by Indians, they passed thriving fields of pineapple and sugarcane. It was customary for enlisted men to raid pineapple patches, but one crew's sergeants, who also reached Viti Levu on the twenty-fifth, got their hands on two watermelons. Allred's crew was the first to leave Viti Levu on the morning of the twenty-sixth. The watermelon raiders were still asleep, so their watermelons left Nandi on 210. Allred's enlisted men ate them on the flight from the Fijis to Plaines des Gaïacs, in New Caledonia, a French possession. Lack of rank devised its own privileges.

There were military personnel stationed on all the islands on the way to Australia. On the twenty-sixth, some of the officers based at Plaines des Gaïacs invited Allred and his officers to go swimming in a clear stream halfway across the island. The enlisted men ate and watched a movie. John Campbell, Allred's nose gunner, kept a terse diary of his wartime years. Campbell was given to grousing about food. His comments on what he ate in Honolulu and on Canton Island are unprintable. In his judgment, Viti Levu was "better than Canton but it wasn't like home." New Caledonia met with his approval. "Good chow here" was his verdict.

David Becker was a diarist with a specific complaint. After watching *Lives of a Bengal Lancer,* a film he had first seen back home in 1935, he told the GI running the projector at Plaines des Gaïacs that he had just seen the same film on Canton Island and on Viti Levu. "Hell, you're the one carrying it," the projectionist explained. The GIs were grateful that the B-24s flew in different movies every day, although they would have preferred a supply of Wacs or nurses. One soldier told Becker he hadn't seen a woman in ten months.

The legs of the journey became shorter. It had taken Allred five hours and forty-five minutes to fly from Nandi to Plaines des Gaïacs. On January 27, he flew from New Caledonia to Amberley Field in four hours and forty-five minutes. The men were glad that their island-hopping was temporarily over. "When I saw Australia's east coast come into view, it was nice to know there was a whole continent behind it," Lee Shelton says.

It was raining when Allred landed at Amberley Field. The rain didn't let up, so the crew members were stranded for a couple of days, as they had been a continent ago, at Fairfield. They were paid for the first time in a week. Their January 12 orders from Topeka to "Overseas Destination" had specified that they would receive a flat per-diem rate for travel—but no payment for mileage. They went into the nearby town of Ipswich and spent some of their pay on steak and beer. Ipswich struck them as an anachronism. The clothes were the style that had been worn back home fifteen years earlier, the cars were of similar vintage, and by six-thirty everyone had turned out the lights and gone to bed. The residents of Ipswich were unfriendly to Americans; the B-24 crew suspected that too many GIs had already passed through, so they tended to stay out at Amberley Field until there was a break in the weather.

On January 30, Allred flew to Townsville, a seaport north of Brisbane, in four and a half hours. Since he first flew, at Hicks Field in October 1942, he had flown a grand total of 638.25 hours—more than most of the men with whom he had crossed the Pacific. Between Fairfield-Suisun and Townsville, he had logged forty-nine hours and forty minutes of flying time. Bauder covered the same route in the same number of days in forty-seven hours and fifty minutes, but it took many other B-24 pilots more time, and some were delayed along the way. Becker's engineer neglected to tighten the caps on the plane's gas tanks at Hickam, so Becker missed the 11:00 A.M. takeoff deadline for Canton Island and was ordered to fly to Christmas Island, which was closer to Hawaii. The men stationed on Christmas had the unforeseen pleasure of watching *Lives of a Bengal Lancer*. One pilot hit a guy wire on Canton Island as he was taxiing to a revetment, clipped part of a wingtip, and had to lay over while it was fixed. The crew to which Larry Wulf, another Toggle Joe, had been assigned had a magneto go out on an engine as the plane was about to leave Canton, and spent half a day working on it. Bob Dent came down with flu on Viti Levu. A doctor who examined him there would not permit him to fly for twenty-four hours.

The B-24s that the pilots had signed for at the depot in Topeka had to be left at the depot in Townsville, and the pilots were sorry; some had hoped to fly their missions in those planes. Upon arriving in the Pacific theater, Allred and his crew were assigned to the Fifth Air Force's 22nd Bombardment Group and were ordered to proceed to the Fifth Bomber Command's Replacement Center, near Charters Towers, 60 miles southwest of Townsville. They and the crews of two other B-24s left Townsville for Charters Towers by train on the afternoon of January 31. The train was the most notable anachronism they saw in Australia. It wasn't like something remembered from their childhoods; it was like something they had seen in Hollywood movies of the Old West. The seats were wooden benches in separate coaches; to go from one coach to the next, one had to get off the train, which chugged along a narrow-gauge track, making frequent stops. The scenery was scrubby. To break the ride's monotony, a few men fired their .45s at termite hills. Others got off and walked, for exercise. When they thought they had had enough exercise, they waited for the train to catch up and climbed back on. As the train pulled into Charters Towers, five hours after leaving Townsville, night was falling. The men drew cots and slept in an open-air hangar. The next day, Allred and his crew were assigned to one of the 22nd Bombardment Group's four squadrons, the 19th, and moved into tents.

January 1944 was a turning point in the history of the 22nd Bombardment Group: it was the month when the 22nd began converting from a medium to a heavy bombardment group. On January 11, men from its 19th Squadron (who had been flying two-engine B-26s) and men from its 33rd Squadron (who had been flying B-25s) were taken out of combat and sent to Charters Towers to train in B-24s. One man who trained in B-24s in Charters Towers was Adolph Leirer, of whom David Becker might have said that his career in the Army Air Corps was like everyone else's—only more different.

Leirer, Class of 43-E, had graduated from Multi-Engine Advanced Flying School in Colorado on May 20, 1943. On May 23, he flew a B-25 for three hours. Those hundred and eighty minutes aloft transformed him into "a qualified B-25 copilot." On May 27, he was given a ten-day leave; on the sixth day of the leave, he was recalled to Colorado and ordered to proceed by rail to Hamilton Field, California, "for further movement by air transportation to overseas destination (temperate climate)." To Leirer, a resident of Alaska, "temperate" eliminated Alaska and the Aleutians and the need for winter uniforms (he shipped his woollies to his brother), and California eliminated Europe, because European-theater replacements were sent east or southeast for transatlantic transportation.

In late June, Leirer and twenty-four other instant B-25 copilots were put on an LB-30, a cargo version of a B-24. One fellow-passenger had been given sealed orders for all twenty-five, which were not to be opened until an hour after takeoff. The destination orders were less precise than the ones Allred received seven months later: they read simply "Amberley Field." One man went forward to the flight deck to ask the crew where Amberley Field was. Leirer was pleased to find out that he was going to Australia. He had read about Brisbane in grade school, and its year-round balmy temperature sounded appealing. He had no idea what he would be doing there. In June 1943 he had never heard of New Guinea. Second World War dispatches were purposely vague, with datelines that read "Somewhere in the South Pacific." There were no seats in the plane, and the men sat or lay down on mail sacks and on the plywood floor covering the bomb bay. Whether the plane was flown by night or by day, they traveled in darkness; there were no windows in the passenger section of the bomb bay—just a knothole in the plywood floor, which the men took turns looking out of. The bomb-bay doors had been left open a bit to allow gas fumes to escape if there should be leakage from the wing tanks or from the fuel lines that snaked through the bomb bay.

The 22nd Bombardment Group was proud of its string of "firsts." In March 1942 it had been the first fully equipped group to fly as a unit from Hawaii to Australia, and two weeks later it had become the first to use B-26s in combat. Like all the early bomb groups in the Southwest Pacific, the 22nd entered combat against overwhelming odds. Its B-26s gave a good account of themselves, but the group lost so many planes in action in the second half of 1942 and received so few replacements and spare parts that in January 1943 it had to be removed from action—part of the group for six months, the rest of it for nine.

In March 1943, while the 22nd was out of commission, General George C. Kenney flew to Washington to plead for more planes for the fledgling Fifth Air Force he commanded. In early 1943, he had a total of five hundred and thirty-seven aircraft, including bombers, fighters, and transports; the number kept going downhill, and on any given day about two hundred planes were grounded, getting bullet holes patched or shot-up engines replaced. The Army and the Army Air Forces gave priority to Europe. Even when Kenney suggested that the Southwest Pacific be allotted 10 percent of the aircraft production, and the rest of the war the remainder, the answer was no. He did leave Washington with a pledge from General Henry H. (Hap) Arnold, Commanding General of the Army Air Forces, that he would get five hundred more aircraft by the end of 1943, including a considerable number of B-25 Mitchells.

When the 22nd Bombardment Group's battle-scarred B-26s were sent to Townsville in January 1943, word came from the depot that only enough of them could be reconditioned to equip one squadron. The B-26, which was officially named the Marauder, had stubby wings and was often called the Flying Prostitute (because it seemed to have no visible means of support). The crews of the 19th Squadron liked the B-26—the Marauder was a "hot" plane, with exceptionally powerful engines to give it swift takeoff and landing speeds—and voted unanimously to stick with the depot rehabilitations. The three other squadrons of the 22nd—the 2nd, the 33rd, and the 408th—were outfitted with some of the B-25 Mitchells that Kenney had gained from Arnold, and were taught to fly them with the help of some of the B-25-combat-crew replacements.

Shortly after Adolph Leirer's aerial odyssey to Australia, he was assigned to the 19th Squadron and was taught to fly B-26s. The 19th had been allowed to strip away the olive-drab paint from its B-26s and take them down to their natural metal finish. This not only made them hundreds of pounds lighter, and thus about 15 miles an hour faster, but also gave the 22nd, in the words of one of its historians, another distinction: "First squadron with all silver planes . . . the original 'Silver Fleet.'" After a few lessons in the Marauder, Leirer started flying combat missions in July 1943 as a B-26 copilot. "I'm thankful I learned to fly B-26s overseas rather than stateside," Leirer says. "MacDill Field, near Tampa, Florida, was a B-26 training field. Back in '43, there was a saying 'One a day in Tampa Bay.' Our maintenance overseas started out as a baling-wire-and-pair-of-pliers operation, but as spare parts and the equipment to install them became available and the mechanics became experienced it was superior to maintenance at home. Between July 1943 and January 1944 the Silver Fleet lost only three planes, and just one of these was a casualty of enemy action."

On January 2, 1944, Kenney was back in General Arnold's office, begging for more airplanes. Again, he was told that the war in Europe had first priority, but he was also told that as good luck would have it, the European theater preferred the B-17 Flying Fortress to the B-24 Liberator, and that B-24 production was in excess of European requirements. Arnold agreed to let Kenney turn his 22nd Bombardment Group into a heavy one: its B-26s were to be honorably discharged, its B-25s would be transferred to other medium groups that were short of planes. Within a few days of Kenney's conversation with Arnold, B-24Js were on their way to Australia. Some of the planes went to the three heavy bombardment groups already in the Southwest Pacific—the 90th, the 43rd, and the 380th—which needed replacements for their war-weary B-24Ds. The rest of the planes were assigned to the 22nd, which soon achieved another "first"—it became the first group in the United States Army Air Forces ever to fly B-26s, B-25s, and B-24s successively in combat.

Europe's preference for Boeing's B-17 was understandable. The B-17 flew higher than the B-24 (German antiaircraft fire was far more formidable than Japanese ack-ack, and every thousand feet counted) and handled better at high altitude. The B-17 could also absorb a lot more battle damage and still come home, or, if necessary, it could be crash-landed or ditched in the sea with a greater chance of survival. Another reason Arnold could afford to be generous with B-24s was that the United States produced more of them than of any other plane in its history—a total of 18,481. (A total of 12,731 B-17s were manufactured.) The B-24's greater range was normally of no consequence in Europe—the distance from London to Berlin is 579 miles—though its "longer legs" did make it particularly suitable for the famous raid on August 1, 1943, from North Africa against the oil fields and refineries at Ploesti, Rumania. And, of course, they were often necessary for the long over-the-water distances in the Pacific theater.

On January 15, 1944, four days after flying his twenty-eighth B-26 mission, Leirer climbed into a B-24 for the first time. Between January 15 and February 29, he spent almost a hundred hours training on B-24s at Charters Towers. Leirer shot landings, practiced stalls, flew bombing and gunnery missions and formation, and became familiar with the B-24's radio compass and autopilot, just as many of the new members of the 19th had done at places like El Paso. David Becker and Larry Wulf were two of Allred's acquaintances who were assigned with him to the 19th Squadron. Lee Shelton went to the 33rd Squadron, Bob Dent to the 408th, and other pilots from Biggs to the 2nd. Still other Biggs crews were assigned to the 43rd, the 90th, or the 380th, which had been created as heavy bombardment groups.

The "new boys," as the 22nd's first B-24 crews from the United States were labeled, had hoped to start killing Japanese as soon as they reached Australia. Instead, as a result of the need for "old boys" like Leirer to go through transition for B-24s, the new arrivals found themselves killing mosquitoes and time. Between February 1 and February 25, Allred logged only twenty hours and twenty-five minutes in the air. For every hour he and his contemporaries flew, they played five hours of poker for pounds, shillings, and pence (once they had landed in Australia, they were paid in the currency of the realm) and watched four old movies starring Clark Gable and Lana Turner, William Powell and Myrna Loy, or George Brent and Brenda Marshall. Double features were shown every evening at open-air theaters on the base and in Charters Towers, 4 miles away.

The pilots got more than their customary six or seven hours of "sack time." Larry Wulf, according to his diary, often slept until 10:00 A.M., even though that gave the mosquitoes that got in under his net more of an opportunity to do a "buzz job" on him. It was an event worth recording if he got up at seven-thirty, in time for breakfast. Meals did not seem worth going to. The men developed an immediate distaste for mess-hall food—especially bully beef and mutton—and often bought hamburgers sold by the Red Cross. Atabrine gradually turned the skin a sickly yellow color that persisted as long as the drug was taken. David Becker entered the Army Air Forces in 1942 with white skin, weighing

209 pounds; he came home in 1945 with a chartreuse complexion, weighing 122.

Buses and trucks ran between the base and Charters Towers, an old gold-mining town with board sidewalks, where goats, horses, cows, and dogs wandered along the main street. The men scheduled their trips to town to coincide with "beer call" at one or another of the pubs. Each pub opened a keg of under-aged beer at a certain hour of the day and served beer until it ran out—generally in less than an hour. Most of the Americans didn't care for the flavor of the green beer, which was not improved by being served warm, but it was preferable to the local water, which was described as "having the color of chocolate soda without the taste." They drank quart bottles of Australian beer whenever they could get their hands on any. The flavor wasn't the sole reward: its high alcoholic content gave them the right kind of "buzz."

The Yanks had been told that water would be scarce in subtropical northern Australia; if the scarcity didn't fully register at first, it was because February was the height of the rainy season. They got wet in the open-air movie theaters, wet walking from the bus stops at the base to their tents, and wet inside their tents on particularly stormy nights. "Rain again. It's rained every damn day for two weeks," Becker wrote in his diary on February 19. "God I wish to hell it would go one day without raining." During a severe downpour, everything in Wulf's tent was soaked, including a schoolchild's exercise book he had bought in Charters Towers to use as a diary, although he had stored it in a briefcase.

Wulf attempted to fend off boredom by buying a bicycle, which he pedaled to and from town except when there was a severe storm. On one occasion, Becker went kangaroo hunting with another lieutenant; on another he rode as a passenger on a plane headed for Townsville. The thirty-minute flight compared favorably with the slow train's five hours. Despite Becker's resourcefulness, two typical diary entries read "Damn little doing today, just killed the day," and "This waiting around is no damn good. We'd be a helluva lot better crew if we'd come straight over from Biggs." Wulf and Becker also wrote countless letters home to the young women they were planning to marry as soon as they returned from the war. "One thing sure," Becker recorded in his diary, "I'll be a married man a week after I hit the states."

Any chance of getting in some flying made the men happy. Their few opportunities consisted of gunnery missions, compass swings, and formation practice. In the United States, the B-24 pilots had flown loose formation, but the old boys had flown their B-26s in combat in tight formation and planned to do the same with the B-24s. Tight formation was harder to fly but helped to keep one alive. The Japanese fighters were reluctant to risk penetrating the bombers' close ranks.

Allred and his acquaintances had been told soon after their arrival at Charters Towers that they would be going to their forward base in about a month. On February 20, 1944, he wrote to Howard that APO-713-Unit 1 would be his permanent address. APO 713-Unit 1 was Nadzab, an airbase about 20 miles inland from Lae, a town on the northeast coast of New Guinea.

The fact that the Allies had been able to retake Lae from the Japanese in September 1943 showed the progress they had made in the year and a half since the Japanese had first landed on New Guinea. Nine hours after the surprise attack on the United States fleet at Pearl Harbor on December 7, 1941, Japanese planes bombed Clark Field, near Manila. Within three days, Japanese forces made their first landing on Philippine soil, and occupied Bangkok and invaded the Gilbert Islands. The small American garrison on Guam surrendered on the tenth. The Japanese started into Burma on the eleventh, and by the sixteenth they had made their first landings on Borneo, in the Netherlands East Indies. Wake Island fell on December 23, Hong Kong surrendered on Christmas Day, and on January 23, 1942, the Japanese seized Kieta, on Bougainville, the largest island in the Solomons, and secured Rabaul, on New Britain, the island immediately east of New Guinea. Rabaul became Japan's major supply base for its entire operation in the Bismarck Sea, the Solomon Sea, and the New Guinea area. Britain's "impregnable fortress" of Singapore fell on February 15, and on February 27 the Japanese, under Admiral Takeo Takagi, destroyed an Allied fleet in the Battle of the Java Sea. On March 7, the Japanese seized Lae.

The island of New Guinea sprawls 1500 miles east to west, and lies across the Coral Sea north of Australia. Its eastern half, the Papuan Peninsula, known as Papua, was of great strategic value to both sides. At Papua's eastern tip lies Milne Bay, about 600 miles west of Guadalcanal. The villages of Buna and Gona are on the north side of the peninsula. Port Moresby, the capital, on the south side, was the key to stopping the Japanese. If Port Moresby fell, all New Guinea would fall, and the Japanese would not be satisfied until Australia had become part of the Greater East Asia Co-Prosperity Sphere.

When the United States entered the war, Port Moresby was a dusty trading post with one understrength Australian infantry battalion and two airstrips. Given the available resources, Australia was hard put to reinforce the area, but in May 1942 the Australians sent forward a second infantry battalion and began work to improve the airfield facilities. The Allies knew that the Japanese would soon make an all-out effort to seize Port Moresby. At the end of April, an invasion force sailed from Rabaul. Between May 4 and May 8, the United States Navy, under Admiral Chester Nimitz, turned back the Japanese in the Battle of the Coral Sea.

Undeterred by this failure—and by the smashing American naval air victory in the Battle of Midway during the first week of June—the Japanese next tried to take Port Moresby by land. On July 21 and 22, they put thousands of troops ashore at Buna and Gona, only a hundred miles from Port Moresby across the Owen Stanley Range, which William Manchester, in *American Caesar*, has described as Papua's most striking feature—"a razorback mountain range, stretching down the peninsula like the dorsal vertebrae of some prehistoric monster." By late July, the Japanese were moving along the narrow Kokoda Trail, which threads its way from Buna to Port Moresby, by way of the village of Kokoda, through some of the highest, wettest, and densest jungles in the world. They seized Kokoda, in the middle of the mountains, and fought their way to a ridgeline less than 30 miles from Port Moresby. There, on September 17, 1942, the Imperial Army was stopped by the Australians. That fall, while the Japanese were withdrawing to Buna, United States forces were in the process of winning the first of the major island battles of the Pacific, at Guadalcanal. The fighting around Buna, which lasted until January 22, 1943, officially ended the Papua campaign. The 22nd Bombardment Group received its first Distinguished Unit Citation for the air support it rendered during the six-month-long struggle.

Two months before the fall of Buna, the Allies began building an airbase on the Dobodura Plains, 9 miles southeast of the village. In July 1943 the 22nd's 19th Squadron moved there and went back into combat with its silvery B-26s. When one of Adolph Leirer's friends flew his first combat mission from Dobodura, on July 29, he and the others in the 19th were apparently not combat-ready—all their bombs missed the targets—and for three weeks the 19th Bomb Squadron became the 19th Practice Bombing Squadron: Dobodura was their MacDill Field. In early September, when the 19th was back in action, its targets included Lae, which had been the most active Japanese airbase in eastern New Guinea. On September 16, the Allies took Lae. Eleven days earlier, paratroopers had been dropped on Nadzab, with General Kenney and General MacArthur flying over the area in B-17s to watch the show.

On February 28, 1944, about eighteen B-24s from the 19th and 33rd Squadrons embarked for the new base at Nadzab, about 900 miles north of Charters Towers. The men had been told in a briefing that they would use the six-hour flight for additional training in formation flying. Most of the B-24s were carrying five or six ground personnel in addition to their own crews. The planes took off one by one in the morning under clear skies, circled the field until the last plane was airborne, and assembled into flights of three planes. Allred's plane dropped back shortly after takeoff, because of engine trouble, and landed in Townsville.

The other 19th Squadron B-24s went on. An hour and a half after passing Townsville, when they were between 10,000 and 12,000 feet over the Coral Sea, they saw an ominous-looking black frontal system directly ahead. Adolph Leirer was flying on the right wing of the lead aircraft. Its pilot kept boring straight ahead: he made no effort either to climb over the storm or to fly under it, and issued no call to the other planes to break formation. All of a sudden, it got very dark, the turbulence became greater, and the lead plane disappeared. Leirer had begun the standard breakaway—a 5° turn to the right—when the lead B-24 reappeared directly in front of him, also making a right turn. Leirer felt two violent shudders from the propeller wash of the other aircraft's right engines. To escape a collision, he pushed the nose of his B-24 down and made a hard left turn. He also had to be careful of the left wingman. The prop wash flipped his plane nearly upside down, and before he knew it he was descending at an airspeed of almost 300 miles an hour. His controls were very stiff, and by the time he was once again flying level he was at 5000 feet. Leirer asked his navigator for a heading back to Townsville. He wanted to have the plane checked before tackling another storm, and, besides, he had had enough for one day and figured he deserved to make beer call. After he landed, he reported to headquarters and overheard two pilots from the 33rd Squadron who had also turned back sending a message to Group Headquarters at Nadzab to say that they would "RON" (remain overnight) at Townsville. He asked them to include his name and the last three digits of his plane's serial number.

Larry Wulf and his pilot were flying on the right wing of an old boy, a first lieutenant, who was leading the second flight. The first lieutenant tried to climb over the weather, and Wulf and his pilot tried to follow him but ran into an ice storm and lost track of their leader. They went up 17,000 feet to attempt to get above the weather, and finally found a break in the clouds, determined their position, and headed for Nadzab. They flew up the east coast of New Guinea over Milne Bay to Lae, in order to skirt the Owen Stanleys, and then west into Nadzab. One of the bombers that left Charters Towers that morning, a B-24 from the 33rd Squadron, crashed into the Coral Sea an hour and ten minutes after taking off; all fifteen aboard were killed. Its pilot was an old boy; its copilot and some members of the crew were friends of Wulf's from Biggs Field.

Allred's engine trouble was taken care of quickly in Townsville. He took off again and encountered the bad weather that the original formation had met up with earlier. He decided to fly straight across New Guinea instead of around it, as Wulf had—the flight was shorter—and was soon enveloped in large cumulus clouds. Paul Harvey was nervous. "There are old pilots and there are bold pilots, but there are no old bold pilots" was a saying he had picked up at Charters Towers from men who had flown B-26s. Allred was too bold a pilot to suit Harvey, and Harvey told him to go up another couple of thousand feet. Allred pointed out on a map of New Guinea approximately where they were, and showed Harvey he was a thousand feet above the highest mountains in that part of the Owen Stanleys. Harvey said that the maps were incomplete and inaccurate— that the B-26 pilots had warned him that some peaks were higher than the maps indicated and that others weren't even on the maps. The B-26 pilots had discovered this when they were flying at an altitude that was presumably above the highest mapped mountains: they had suddenly seen higher peaks in front of them, and had had to climb steeply to get above them. Allred repeated that they were doing fine. It was the navigator's responsibility to attempt to convince the pilot of the necessity of climbing to a safe altitude, but Keith Holm was a soft-spoken man of twenty-three, and no match for Allred in a dispute, so Harvey persisted.

They had been flying blind in the clouds for quite a while, he argued, and they hadn't received an updated barometric-pressure reading since the Townsville sea-level setting of 29.92 had been put in the altimeter-setting window. If the plane had flown into a region of lower barometric pressure, the instrument would show the plane hundreds of feet higher than it actually was. Flying in clouds was perilous on an island whose national slogan, according to most American pilots who had flown there for any length of time, should have been "There's a rock in every cloud." After an angry exchange, Harvey prevailed. Allred climbed a couple of thousand feet. They made it safely into Nadzab that afternoon.

Leirer spent some time in Townsville and Charters Towers having repairs made to his plane and having his autopilot modified. (The loss of the plane that went down in the Coral Sea had been attributed to a defective autopilot.) On March 3, he set off again for Nadzab from Charters Towers, in another formation of 19th and 33rd Squadron planes. After the entire formation had flown three hours north, the flight leader determined that the weather farther north was bad, and all the planes returned to Charters Towers. Leirer finally got to Nadzab on March 5. The pilot who had been flying on the left wing of the lead B-24 on February 28 and had made it through that afternoon greeted Leirer with incredulity. Leirer's RON Townsville message had never reached Nadzab. "Hell, you were supposed to have gone down in the Coral Sea," the pilot said. "We had a wake for you last night." Leirer knew that the pilot was a drinking man, who would have had a wake if he'd suspected that an infantryman of his acquaintance had been killed in Europe. His bloodshot eyes attested to the fact that more beer had been consumed than tears shed and that the ceremony had gone on for several nights.

Nadzab was situated in the grassy Markham River Valley, about 20 miles northwest of Lae. The engineers flown into Nadzab in September 1943 had immediately gone to work improving its one dirt runway, and within three days they had selected a site for a second runway, cleared it of kunai grass, and leveled the ground so that the first C-47s filled with men and heavy machinery could land. Additional runways and taxiways were soon under construction, and in time those short-life, dry-weather runways were extended and improved. When the engineers left Nadzab in May 1944, it had approximately 50 miles of all-weather taxiways and six all-weather runways; three of the longest ones were surfaced with steel mat, to accommodate heavy bombers. In January 1944 the commanding officer of the 19th Squadron assigned his statistical officer, several other officers, and sixty enlisted ground personnel to move all the squadron's equipment from Dobodura to Nadzab and to set up a camp there while the airmen were going through transition training in Charters Towers. He promised the statistical officer a two-week leave in Sydney if the camp was ready when the air echelon arrived.

Virgil R. (Luke) Sewell, a B-24 pilot from Biggs who had been assigned to the 33rd Squadron of the 22nd Bombardment Group, flew from Charters Towers to Nadzab in a C-47 a week before Bob Allred made the flight. Sewell said recently:

> On February 21, 1944, when I looked out the window of that Gooney Bird I couldn't believe my eyes. I saw taxiways with hard stands to park airplanes curving every which way and half a dozen

long runways abuilding. There were hundreds of heavy bombers, medium bombers, light bombers, transports, spotters, and fighters—P-38s, P-39s, P-40s, and P-47s—as far as I could see. Three of the heavy bomb groups were there or were in the process of moving in—the 380th was still down near Darwin—and it seemed to me that most of the rest of Fifth Air Force was at Nadzab, too. The only disconcerting thing on the ground was a lot of fires. I was afraid they were the aftermath of a bombing raid, but they had just been set by some natives who were burning underbrush under the supervision of an Australian unit. The housing areas stretched from the hills that rimmed the northern side of the valley all the way south to the banks of the Markham River, which is where the 22nd B.G. was. The entire complex was twenty miles square. Nadzab was said to be the largest airfield complex in the world, and I believe it was, if you don't count England as all one airfield complex.

The 22nd's housing area, near the junction of the Erap and Markham Rivers, was divided into four sections, one per squadron. Each squadron's turf was further divided into officers' and enlisted men's living quarters. Officers slept four to a 16-by-16-foot pyramidal tent, and enlisted men six to a tent. Officers and men had separate but equal showers and latrines. (No one in the 22nd Bombardment Group ever saw an indoor toilet in New Guinea. In Port Moresby, General MacArthur lived in a rambling bungalow with fine furniture, wide verandas, colorful tropical trees, and a latrine.) Between the 19th Squadron's officers' quarters and the enlisted men's stood a few thatched shacks—an administration shack, a communications shack, a shack used as a dispensary—and some more substantial buildings. One of these was a kitchen with an officers' mess hall on one side, an enlisted men's mess hall on the other. "The enlisted men thought we ate better, but we got the same food," Leirer recalls. "The only difference was that they got their food slopped into their mess kits, and officers served themselves on plates." The statistical officer remembers that his last chore as construction superintendent was hammering the galvanized-iron roof on the mess halls, on February 27; on the twenty-eighth, the CO agreed that he'd earned his leave.

When the 19th Squadron's crews reached Nadzab, on and

after February 28, they were given tents and permission to pitch them on any vacant "street and lot." Before Larry Wulf went to sleep on the twenty-eighth, he and his tentmates had cleared out tall grass and tree stumps still on their lot, set up their cots, and hung up their mosquito netting. The next morning, their first priority was to put some distance between themselves and Nadzab's ants, by raising the tent off the ground. They learned that money was useless for getting logs converted into two-by-fours or acquiring any ready-sawed wood. They had to deal for such things. The most valuable medium of exchange at Nadzab was liquor, and many air crews had opportunely brought some over from the United States or bought some in Australia. Wulf rode 15 miles to a sawmill in a truck with a sergeant who had been "around the islands" for two years. By March 2, he and his tentmates had traded sufficient whiskey with its Aussie proprietor to get the makings of a tent platform. "All this exercise has kind of pooped us out," Wulf wrote in his diary that night. "We've been working like beavers on our hut and we aren't used to all this exercise. We're used to laying on the sack and drinking beer."

By March 3, after Allred, Harvey, Holm, and Clark had also acquired black-market lumber for their tent floor, their wheeling and dealing was interrupted. The CO of the 19th Squadron needed men to go to the Fifth Bomber Command's Replacement Center, at Port Moresby, for a month to teach some Australians how to fly B-24s. He gave Allred, his three officers, his engineer, his radio operator, and his nose gunner the assignment. Allred's contemporaries have no idea why he and his men were chosen for the thirty days of detached duty, but they believe that it was another decision inspired by the alphabet: his surname began with A. In addition, they surmise, it might have been because he was among the early 19th Squadron arrivals at Nadzab (David Becker didn't get there until March 5), and because he had as many hours in B-24s as any of the pilots in the squadron—404.5 by February 28.

It had now been almost two years since Allred took his Army Air Forces entry examination and seventeen months since he first flew a Primary trainer. His January hopes of starting combat had faded in February; they would now be deferred another month. He and his crew were disappointed, because they knew that the 22nd would soon be in combat with its B-24s. They were assured they would be given extra missions, so that they could catch up with the other crews after they returned from Port Moresby, and not be delayed in getting back to the States. The original requirement of fifty missions to go home had already been modified once and would be modified again. The new boys were told in March 1944 that they would have to fly three hundred hours in combat before they could see the Golden Gate again. In December 1944, when many of them had completed their three hundred hours, the system was changed. A hundred points were needed to go home. Each man received one point for every five combat hours and additional points for such experiences as being hit with antiaircraft fire or being intercepted by fighters.

On March 4, Allred and six members of his crew went on a transport to Port Moresby. Once in Port Moresby, Horace James, the radio operator, was temporarily assigned to another crew. The men were given a tent at Jackson's Airdrome, the site of the Replacement Center. In March, the Replacement Center was being used not only to train Australians but also to give further instruction to new-in-country B-25 crews, and the 2nd and 408th Squadrons of the 22nd, who had flown their last combat missions on January 30, were going through transition training for B-24s there.

The weather in Nadzab at the beginning of March was agreeable: hot sunny days, cool nights. In Port Moresby, it rained steadily, and the verdict of Allred's nose gunner, John Campbell, on what still mattered most to him was "Chow lousy." Allred and his crew were not called upon to train Australians during their first week at Jackson's. They were idle except on a day they flew back to Nadzab to see if they had any mail. No mail had reached them at Charters Towers, and little or none at Nadzab by the fourth. Campbell was "proud" to receive several letters from Trena, his eighteen-year-old bride. (They had married on November 20, 1943, toward the end of combat-crew training at Biggs.) The Army postal service had failed Keith Holm. After finishing a breakfast in bed of apples, K-ration cheese, and coffee on March 13, he wrote to his brother Wallace from Port Moresby that he hadn't received a single letter in two months— not since the day before he left Topeka. Except for the dearth of mail, he had few complaints. He liked Nadzab ("The eating is the best I've done since I left the States," he wrote), he was looking forward to returning there to work on the tent, and he and the crew were prepared to pay for home improvements. ("You can buy anything over here for a bottle or two of liquor or beer. We have a case of 48 bottles in our fox hole for use when we get back North.") As for Port Moresby, he wrote, "So far we've done nothing except lay in our bunks and play poker at sixpence and shillings. We still have two weeks or so to sweat out here before we go North again."

Shortly after Keith Holm wrote to his brother, Allred and his crew were given some Aussies to train. General Kenney, on his second trip to Washington, in January 1944, not only acquired surplus B-24s for the 22nd Bombardment Group and his other American heavy bomb groups but also got Arnold to agree to send him enough B-24s, starting in May, for seven Royal Australian Air Force squadrons he wanted to organize. That would allow Kenney to take the 380th Bombardment Group out of Darwin, from which it was bombing targets in the Netherlands East Indies, and move it north to increase the punch of the Fifth Air Force. The Australian squadrons would be based in Darwin and would take over the missions that the American B-24 squadrons based there were then performing. Kenney offered to train the prospective Australian B-24 crews, using Fifth Air Force facilities, crews, and war-weary B-24Ds, which would be relegated to places like the Replacement Center by his heavy bomb groups when they took receipt of the B-24Js. After a "thirty-day conversion course" at Jackson's, the Australian crews were to spend two months with the 380th.

The men whom Allred and his crew helped to train had returned from completing tours of duty in England. They had been attached to the Royal Air Force and had flown four-engine Lancasters. Within a day of flying B-24Ds with the Aussies, the American instructors realized that the Australian students, as Paul Harvey put it, could "fly the pants off us in the air." Their only trouble with the B-24 was getting it back on the ground.

Lancasters were conventional tail-wheeled bombers, like B-17s. The B-24 was the first American heavy bomber with tricycle landing gear—two main landing wheels under the wings and a small wheel under the nose. The pilot had to come in with the nose higher when he was landing a B-24, because if the nose wheel hit first the strut supporting it could break off; it wasn't as strong as the main landing gear.

"It was frightening to land with the Aussies," Harvey recalls. "Even after the wheels were on the ground, they had a problem with the B-24's brakes. They were used to planes that had a hand lever on the control wheel. When pressure was applied, it went to each brake equally. The B-24 had toe brakes mounted on the top of each rudder pedal. You could apply more or less pressure to the right or left toe brake as necessary for both turning and braking."

The Americans admired the Aussies' conscientiousness. One night, after the heavens had opened up, a young lieutenant told Harvey he was going to the revetment where the plane they had flown that day was parked, to make sure that the Norden bomb-sight in the nose had been covered. Harvey pointed out that if it hadn't been covered it would already be wet. The young man went to the plane anyway, and returned saying, "Thank God it was covered, sir." Jim Pitts, Allred's engineer, was partial to the Aussies' accent and vocabulary. He had learned to order "stike and igges" in Charters Towers when he wanted steak and eggs. At Jackson's, he found out that the translation of "airscrews" was "propellers," and that when a student asked "Is the undercarriage lowered and secured?" his question was "Is the landing gear down and locked?"

On March 18, Allred, Harvey, Holm, and Pitts ferried thirteen or fourteen Australian airmen from Port Moresby to a field near Darwin. Allred let the senior ranking Australian fly the plane, with Harvey flying copilot. The Australian was so keen to pilot the B-24 that he flew all six hours manually. The Americans, for whom the novelty of B-24s had worn off long since, would have had it on autopilot most of the way. "As we were landing at a field near Darwin, a mob of wallabies bounced across the runway," Harvey recalls. "That excited the Aussie pilot. Then, as we were taxiing, some more wallabies leaped in front of us. The Aussie was going too fast and, in the excitement, he hit the left toe brake too hard, causing the plane to veer to the left. I hit the brakes, but it was too late. The left main landing gear went off the taxiway into the soft ground, sinking down to the axle. The two left props gave the grass a good cutting job. It took several large tractors and wreckers with winches to pull the plane back onto the hard taxiway."

Allred, Harvey, Holm, and Pitts returned to Port Moresby on the twentieth. Jim Pitts had felt ill on the eighteenth. As soon as the plane landed at Jackson's, he went to see a doctor at a service squadron. He was taken by ambulance to an Army hospital in Port Moresby, where his ailment was diagnosed as spinal meningitis. He was put into semi-isolation. Allred, Holm, and Campbell visited him in the hospital on the twenty-first and talked to him through a screen. Pitts remained in the hospital until the end of April.

Wednesday, March 22, 1944, was a free day for Allred and his crew. There were no Australians to train. He asked the officer in charge of the Replacement Center if he might take a B-24 up to Nadzab that morning and bring it back in the afternoon. With at least another week left in Port Moresby, Allred, Holm, Harvey, Clark, and Campbell wanted to check the mail. They also wanted to draw A-2 flying jackets, which they had heard were being issued at Nadzab. In March 1944 there were always large numbers of men in Port Moresby who had to go to Nadzab— men who had been to Australia on leave and were hitchhiking back to rejoin their units, and members of replacement crews who needed rides to their new units. The interior of a B-24 was far better suited to carrying bombs (the purpose for which it was designed) than carrying passengers, even if it had been converted to a transport—as Adolph Leirer learned on his June '43 flight across the Pacific. An unconverted B-24, which lacked a wooden floor, would, however, accommodate about twenty-three men who were prepared to be uncomfortable. About seven could squeeze on the flight deck behind the pilot and copilot. Another seven could stand on the narrow catwalk between the front and rear bulkheads of the bomb bay; the bomb-bay doors were too flimsy to sit on. Another seven could sit with their backs up against the rear bomb-bay bulkhead. Some pilots regarded the catwalk as too dangerous a place for passengers and so would cram more men on the flight deck and against the rear bomb-bay bulkhead.

On the morning of March 22, at least thirty men piled onto the B-24 that Allred had been given to fly. The plane was so crowded that he suggested to Clark and Campbell that they go down into the nose. It wasn't considered safe for men to be in the nose of a B-24 at takeoff: in the event of a collapse of a nose wheel or a crash on takeoff the chances of survival were poor. In 1944, on missions, the nose gunner and the bombardier usually stayed on the flight deck until the bomber was airborne; in the early months in the Southwest Pacific, they often had to be in the nose when the plane was taxiing, because American aircraft were apt to be attacked by Japanese fighters immediately after takeoff.

Around ten o'clock, a jeep pulled up to the B-24 while it was still at the flight line. There was a B-25 at Jackson's with a brand-new-in-country crew aboard bound for Nadzab. The man in the jeep asked Harvey, on behalf of an officer at the Replacement Center who knew he was a qualified B-25 pilot with a little experience flying in New Guinea, if he would be willing to fly as copilot on the B-25. Harvey agreed, and was driven to the B-25. The B-25's copilot, who had never flown a four-engine plane, got into the jeep, boarded the B-24, and sat down in the right seat. It wasn't considered sensible to have a man who was unfamiliar with a B-24 as its copilot—if one or two of the engines failed he wouldn't know how to feather the props, and if the pilot became incapacitated he wouldn't be familiar with the plane's landing characteristics and proper landing procedures— but in New Guinea little flying was done by the book. "Most of it was done by guess and by God," David Becker says. There were few rules, and even those few were frequently broken. One bomber pilot remembers flying with his squadron's cook as co-pilot.

Most B-24 pilots would have been equally unwilling to take off in a B-24 without a B-24 engineer aboard, to check that the gear was down, to attend to the generators when changing power, and to transfer fuel. Although a pilot would expect to fly the 190

miles between Port Moresby and Nadzab on the fuel in his main
tanks, a fuel transfer might become necessary. A minimum crew
of four was deemed adequate on a B-24 ferrying mission—a
qualified B-24 pilot, copilot, navigator, and engineer.

The B-24 was parked closer to the runway than the B-25.
Allred taxied to the turnabout, revved up his engines, checked
his propellers, magnetos, and controls, and found that one engine wasn't working properly. He pulled aside. The B-25 pilot
with whom Harvey was flying passed the B-24, taxied to the
runway, lined up, went through the checkout routines, applied
full power, took off, and landed in Nadzab forty-five minutes
later.

Allred taxied back to the flight line, where he and Holm,
Clark, Campbell, the B-25 copilot, and the passengers disem-
barked. While the plane was being worked on, the men went to
eat lunch. It was 2:00 P.M. when Allred was ready to take off
again. Clark and Campbell decided to stay in Port Moresby and
let Allred and Holm bring back their mail and their A-2 jackets.
Clark reminded Allred that his size was 40 long. At 2:37 P.M.,
Allred lifted off from a steel-mat runway at Jackson's Drome.

Paul Harvey wasn't surprised that Bob Allred didn't show up in
Nadzab on the twenty-second; he assumed he had been delayed
at Jackson's overnight by the engine trouble. When Allred still
hadn't reached Nadzab by the afternoon of the twenty-third,
Harvey went to base operations and asked if Allred had taken
off from Port Moresby. Nadzab made contact with Jackson's and
was informed that he had—on the afternoon of the twenty-
second.

On the twenty-fourth, Paul Harvey flew back to Port Moresby.
All he could find out was that Allred's B-24 had not been seen or
heard from after takeoff. On March 25, after the plane was
officially reported missing, the Army Air Forces went about preparing the requisite Missing Air Crew Report, which was typed
up on March 28. The Missing Air Crew Report gave the aircraft's type and model (B-24D), its serial number (42-41081), the
serial numbers of its engines, the weapons installed in it (ten .50-
caliber Browning machine guns), the type of mission (administrative cross-country flight), the number of persons aboard (a

crew of three and eighteen passengers), and their names, ranks, and serial numbers. (It was subsequently determined that a nineteenth passenger—Lieutenant Harvey E. Landrum—had boarded the plane; his name was added to the Missing Air Crew Report in late July.) No. 41081's report was more confusing than most, probably because two planes had been involved. A paragraph added to the report on July 20, 1944, read:

> Original loading list as compiled by the pilot, showed thirty (30) passengers. The pilot was scheduled to take off in the morning but due to engine trouble, took off in the afternoon, another aircraft (B-24D—42-41081) being taken. As indicated by attached statements, there were thirty-six (36) men originally scheduled to board aircraft. As list showed thirty (30), the pilot apparently promised the extra six (6) transportation without so indicating on the loading list. This possibly applies to 2nd Lieut. Landrum.

The report indicated that the route suggested to Bob Allred on the afternoon of the twenty-second was to go southeast down the coast at a compass heading of a 135° to a well-known landmark, Hood Point. It would take a B-24 about twenty minutes to reach Hood Point, and when it got there it would be at an altitude of 10,000 feet. (A B-24's climbing speed was approximately 150 miles per hour, and it climbed at approximately 500 feet per minute.) According to the recommended route, Allred was then to proceed over the Owen Stanleys to Dobodura. If he continued to climb, he would be well above 10,200-foot Mt. Obree, which was 40 miles from Hood Point and was the highest peak on a direct course to Dobodura; indeed, if he wished, he could be above 17,000 feet—high enough to clear any peak in the range and allow for the treacherous downdrafts prevailing in the mountains. At 13,255 feet, Mt. Victoria is the highest peak in the Owen Stanleys. From Dobodura (for which he had been given a favorable 2:00 P.M. weather forecast), Allred could proceed over low hills along the coast to Nadzab, where the 2:00 P.M. weather was also favorable. It was assumed that Allred had flown that route, and on March 27 a pilot from the Replacement Center conducted a special search for the plane between Jackson's, Hood Point, and Dobodura, "with no sightings made." A second plane was scheduled to search "the supposed route" on the twenty-eighth.

On March 24, two pilots from the 19th Squadron and part of one pilot's crew had been sent from Nadzab to the Replacement Center at Port Moresby on detached duty for a month to train Australians. On the twenty-ninth, Harvey, Clark, and Campbell received travel orders to return to Nadzab by March 31. By the thirty-first, Larry Wulf had built a clothes cupboard, a writing desk, a chair, a fireplace, and some steps for his "house," and had fixed up a rock walk leading to it. Although his house was a tent, it eventually had almost as many amenities as a thatched hut that Luke Sewell had built for himself with wood liberated from the 33rd Squadron's sawmill one night between February 21 and February 28 when his gunners were assigned to guard it. On March 10, the 19th Squadron had flown its first B-24 mission. By the thirty-first, Larry Wulf had flown half a dozen missions. He had bombed Japanese targets like Wewak and Hollandia, had been fired on by Japanese fighters, and, as a result of a series of mechanical problems that his plane experienced shortly after takeoff on March 26, had come as close to being killed in the war as he hoped he ever would.

After Bob Allred vanished, Paul Harvey began to fly as first pilot. On April 3, 1944, he flew his initial mission, with Clark as bombardier and with the first of a series of copilots and navigators. The enlisted men in Allred's crew, including Pitts, after he got out of the hospital, flew most of their missions with Harvey. In January 1944 the 22nd Bomb Group had become known as the Red Raiders: their new group commander, Colonel Richard W. Robinson, was a redhead, and so were others on his crew. Harvey continued to wear his leather jacket. "I wore a Red Raider patch with our Viking logo on the right side," Harvey says. "I wore my Toggle Joe patch on the left side, over my heart, where many men wore a large Fifth Air Force patch. My middle name is elephant." Larry Wulf didn't wear his leather jacket in New Guinea, and it disappeared. "The Toggle Joes were temporary victims of circumstances, and I got on with fighting the war and trying to survive," Wulf says.

*　　*　　*

In mid-January 1944, after Bob Allred left Topeka to go overseas, Juanita drove Mollie and Henry's car to Des Moines. Helen Bauder, Doris Holm, and Paul Harvey's wife, Betty, kept her company as far as Omaha, where the Bauders lived. Doris had met Keith while he was stationed in Everett, Washington, her hometown, and she was going to stay with his parents in Kimball, Nebraska, his hometown. Betty Harvey was from Scottsbluff, Nebraska. Her parents owned a jewelry store there, and she was planning to work for them. After dropping off her three passengers (Doris and Betty took trains to Kimball and Scottsbluff from Omaha), Juanita drove on to Des Moines. It was the first time she had been alone on a highway, and she felt as frightened as she had when she took her first solitary train ride to San Antonio, in September 1942. Since then, Juanita's life had been disrupted by Bob's frequent changes of station, but it was only now, when he was heading overseas, that she realized what it meant to be a pilot's wife. There was a war on; no one expected the war to end for another year or two; she wouldn't be seeing Bob anytime soon. Still, many women she knew were in similar situations or worse. Her sister-in-law Emily's husband, Carl, was a Seabee, shifting from one island to another in the South Pacific. Bill, the husband of Emily's daughter Dorothy, was also in the Navy, on a ship in the South Pacific. The husband of Emily's daughter Margaret had been a B-17 navigator, had been shot down over Schweinfurt, Germany, on August 17, 1943, and was in a prison camp on the Oder River. When Juanita returned to Des Moines in January 1944, Emily was sharing her house with her youngest daughter, Betty, and with Dorothy, Margaret, and Margaret's newborn baby. Juanita went back to work for Judge Meyer, rented out the house on Diehl Avenue, and moved in with her parents.

On the morning of Saturday, April 1, 1944, there was a knock on the door of the St.Johns' house. Monte St.John and Juanita were at work in the courthouse. When Jessie St.John opened the door, she saw a boyish-looking Western Union messenger on the front porch. He was holding a two-star telegram addressed to Mrs. Juanita Allred. Messengers were forbidden to leave two-star telegrams in people's mailboxes (the two stars stamped on them by Western Union signified that they dealt with an emergency or a death), and were instructed to hand them only to the addressees, after warning them of the nature of their contents. Jessie St.John talked the inexperienced messenger into giving her the telegram. As soon as he had left, she opened it and read:

THE SECRETARY OF WAR DESIRES ME TO EXPRESS HIS DEEP REGRET THAT YOUR HUSBAND SECOND LIEUTENANT ROBERT E. ALLRED HAS BEEN REPORTED MISSING SINCE TWENTY-TWO MARCH OVER NEW GUINEA PERIOD LETTER FOLLOWS

Mrs. St.John telephoned her husband, in the auditor's office, and read him the telegram, which was signed by an Acting Adjutant General. Monte St.John worked on the second floor of the courthouse, Juanita on the fourth. He walked up the two flights of stairs, broke the news to her, and said he would take her home. On the way, they stopped at the Allreds' house. Mollie had an everything-will-turn-out-all-right attitude about life— her children believe that it helped her survive her early married years—and Bob had been in and out of scrapes most of his life. He had always landed on his feet, Mollie assured Juanita, and he would on this occasion, too.

Juanita was shocked and puzzled. The last letter she had received from Bob had been written on March 17. He wasn't even flying combat missions then—he was training Australians. She had the home addresses and telephone numbers of the families of the nine men in Bob's crew and the work phone numbers of some of the married men's wives. She called Trena Campbell at work, in Port Hueneme, California, and read her the telegram. Trena hadn't received one. She ran home and found a letter from John telling her that Bob and Keith were missing.

A week later, the letter heralded by the telegram followed:

The term "missing" is used only to indicate that the whereabouts or status of an individual is not immediately known. It is not intended to convey the impression that the case is closed. . . . Experience has shown that many persons reported missing are subsequently reported as returned to duty or being hospitalized for injuries. . . . I will again communicate with you at the expiration of three months.

The letter held out hope, but it was vague, and three months was a long time. Juanita wrote to the Adjutant General's Office to request additional information. Her letter was forwarded to the commanding officer of the 22nd Bomb Group's 19th Squadron at Nadzab. In early June, the CO answered Juanita's letter. Nothing whatever was known of the plane after takeoff, and an intensive search for it had been fruitless. After he spelled out some of the hazards of flying in New Guinea she almost wished she had settled for hopeful vagueness:

> It is necessary to cross high mountain ranges on practically every flight made on the island. Thick jungle growth goes right up to the tops of the peaks and entire squadrons could completely disappear under this foliage. No matter how thorough the search is, the possibility of locating the plane is rather remote. We have had numerous other instances of like nature and no word has come concerning those crews or airplanes. The weather and terrain account for more airplanes than combat flying.

In July Juanita received a letter telling her that Bob's plane hadn't been seen or heard from "after it left its base, at 2:35 P.M." Enclosed with the letter was a list of the twenty-one men who were on the plane and the names and addresses of their next of kin. Juanita, an optimist by nature, still hoped that good news would be forthcoming before the Office of the Adjutant General dispatched its next form letter, three months hence. All through 1944, she worked six days a week; taught Sunday school, as she had been doing since 1935; continued to join in Allred family gatherings; and remained an active member of Beta Nu, a businesswomen's sorority she had pledged in 1936. The sorority had dinner parties, theater parties, slumber parties, and formal and informal dances. Evening meetings with refreshments and games were held in members' homes. In 1944 Juanita and a girl friend whose husband was in the military saved up and took a trip to Chicago "to put a dent in the blahs." They treated themselves to a room at the Palmer House, heard Hildegarde sing, shopped at Marshall Field, and met Ollie Clark's fiancée, Bianca.

The joy of the excursion to Chicago was dispelled in the latter half of 1944 by extensive correspondence with the Army about Bob Allred's belongings. Paul Harvey had packed up the clothes and personal effects that Bob and Keith had in their tents in Port Moresby and Nadzab, and had turned them over to the squadron CO. In the fall, Juanita received two cartons and two envelopes containing some clothes, a camera, three identification cards, and a leather briefcase filled with papers documenting Bob Allred's career in the Army Air Forces. There were special orders and personnel orders, reporting-in forms and instrument-flight-check forms, and Bob's Form 5s—monthly records of all his flying hours between October 1942 and March 1944. Each time an officer in the Kansas City Quartermaster Depot sent her any of her husband's personal effects, he also wrote to say:

> My action in transmitting this property does not, of itself, vest title in you. The items are forwarded in order that you may act as gratuitous bailee in caring for them, pending the return of the owner. In the event he later is reported a casualty, and I sincerely hope he never is, it will be necessary that the property be turned over to the person or persons legally entitled to receive it.

In Bob's letter of March 17, he had said that many of his and the crew's belongings were to follow them to New Guinea by ship. In November, Juanita received his footlocker. When she opened it, on her parents' porch, it smelled musty. She took out a few things—a manicure kit, an electric iron, some photographs—and then spread mildewed trousers, shirts, socks, handkerchiefs, and shoes on the porch. She called an Army post in Fort Des Moines, and someone there offered to fetch the clothes and shoes and dispose of them.

The Adjutant General's Office wrote Juanita on March 23, 1945, that Bob's case had been carefully reviewed and that he was being continued in the status of missing. Juanita was thereby continued in a status of limbo. From time to time, she got to feeling sorry for herself. I'm going to buy myself something from Bob, and when he gets home I'm going to show it to him, she remembers thinking, and she bought herself a suit, a matching hat, and a $40 piece of costume jewelry. "You'd have thought

I'd spent a million dollars on that pin, and it was a lot of money then," she says. "One birthday, I really splurged, and bought myself a ring with an opal, my birthstone."

In 1945 Juanita moved back to the house on Diehl Avenue. Emily's husband and two sons-in-law and all the other men she knew who had been in the service returned safely, and she was thankful, but it was difficult to see other couples reunited while she was still alone. "I was able to keep a stiff upper lip at work and at social gatherings with relatives and married couples," she says. "It was when I came home and closed the door behind me on a quiet house, a house it was harder and harder to believe that Bob would ever return to, that I felt so lost. The things I had to do that I hadn't had to do before—setting and emptying mousetraps, stoking the furnace—also tended to bring on moments of self-pity and tears."

Juanita heard again from the Adjutant General's Office in January 1946. Since March 22, 1944, the War Department had "entertained the hope" that Lieutenant Robert E. Allred, 0-679012, Air Corps, "survived" and that "information would be revealed dispelling the uncertainty surrounding his absence," an Acting Adjutant General wrote. No trace had been found of the B-24 on which he had been a crew member after its departure from Jackson's Drome, Port Moresby, on an administrative cross-country flight to Nadzab. "Since no information has been received which would support a presumption of his continued survival," the letter went on, "the War Department must now terminate your husband's absence by a presumptive finding of death." A presumptive date of death for the purpose of termination of pay and allowances, settlement of accounts, and payments of a "death gratuity" had been set as January 26, 1946.

For the next few months, Juanita was engaged in correspondence resulting from the financial repercussions of the War Department's decision. As the beneficiary of Bob's $10,000 National Service Life Insurance policy, Juanita had a choice of accepting $55 a month for twenty years or $36.80 a month for the rest of her life. She chose the latter. She also started to draw a $50-a-month pension from the Veterans Administration, which would be discontinued if she remarried. When Juanita

wrote to Railway Express applying for Bob's benefits, she received a check for $270.83—4 percent of his earnings of
$6,770.77 during his years with the company—and a letter from
the company's general agent saying he had anticipated being
able to use Bob in the company's legal department after his
graduation from Drake. On May 14, she got a check for
$3,317.35 for "pay and allowances due decedent at presumptive
date of death." The Acting Adjutant General had concluded his
letter of January 1946 by saying that he trusted "that the ending
of a long period of uncertainty may give at least some small
measure of consolation. . . . May Providence grant a measure of
relief from the anguish and anxiety you have experienced during these many months."

Providence did not oblige. In late 1945 and early 1946,
searches by United States Army and Australian Graves Registration teams were conducted in New Guinea. Similar teams
searched in other countries where planes had gone down and
had yet to be recovered, and in 1946 newspapers and magazines
printed stories about these searches. On May 14, 1946, Juanita
wrote the first of a number of letters to the authors of the articles
and to the searchers they named about the possibility of Bob's
being alive if he had survived the crash and about the likelihood
of his plane's being found if he hadn't. The replies were dis-
couraging. The most informative letter came from a colonel who
was searching for planes that had gone down in South America.
"I am a pilot myself and have been flying for some fifteen years,"
the colonel wrote. "I spend many hours over the jungles, savan-
nahs and mountains of this part of the world and I know that the
chances of locating a crash in the jungle are virtually nonexistent
unless one has previous knowledge of its location. An airplane
going into the trees makes a very small gash in a limitless sea of
green. Even this gash soon heals and grows over with new
growth here in the tropics and since there are many thousands
of square miles of uninhabited jungles and mountains, it is
doubtful if these crashes will ever be found."

On July 3, 1946, Juanita wrote to Howard and his wife and to
Hazel and Margaret and their husbands, and sent them pho-
tocopies of letters she had recently received, among them the
colonel's, which she had already shown to Louise and Emily, the

only members of Bob's immediate family still living in Des Moines. She acknowledged that handling the copious correspondence resulting from the War Department's letter of January 26 had worn her out physically and emotionally in January, February, and March; she had become inactive in Beta Nu; she had given up teaching Sunday school for almost six months but had just taken her class back. Juanita had kept in touch with Mollie and Henry after they moved to California in 1945. Once, when they had driven to Des Moines to visit, she had helped them drive back to California. When Juanita wrote to her in-laws in July, she reported that Mollie had asked her if she was satisfied that Bob would not return. Juanita's answer had been that she didn't think she would ever stop wondering and speculating but that her periods of definite belief that Bob was alive and would be returning were growing farther apart with the passage of time. "However," she added, "one can't complete all the forms and answer all the questions I have had to answer, receive mail as 'Mrs. Juanita A. Allred, widow,' and checks every month made out to 'Mrs. Juanita A. Allred, unremarried widow of Robert E. Allred,' without its having an effect—and not a happy one, I might add." She said she realized that she couldn't continue to think "I'll wait to decide that until Bob gets back," and that she would have to rely on herself. "I'm beginning to know that I'm on my own," she wrote.

The last letter Juanita wrote to the Army in regard to Bob's whereabouts was dated November 25, 1946. She asked if there were any unidentified men from the South Pacific theater of action in government hospitals. A colonel in the Office of the Surgeon General in Washington replied promptly: There were no unidentified patients in military hospitals. Patients who were suspected of suffering from amnesia or were otherwise unidentified were fingerprinted. The Adjutant General's Office had a record of the fingerprints of all Army personnel. In November Juanita bought an illuminated chancel cross for the wall of her church; it was dedicated in a Sunday-morning church service. Underneath the cross is a brass plate engraved TO THE GLORY OF GOD AND IN MEMORY OF ROBERT E. ALLRED—WORLD WAR II.

*   *   *

Juanita's sister, Marilyn, and Marilyn's husband, Jerome, asked her to go with them to the Ice Follies in November 1946. A day or two before the performance, Marilyn telephoned Juanita to ask whether she objected if a friend of Jerome's came along. "It makes me no mind," Juanita said. At the ice show, the seating arrangement was Juanita-Marilyn-Jerome-Alvin Beck, Lincoln High Class of 1940, who was home on leave from overseas service with the Coast Guard prior to his discharge.

"Alvin and I didn't do much talking that night, but there was a mutual feeling of 'hitting it off,'" Juanita says. "Alvin called the following week to ask me out, and from then on we dated steadily." Until November 1946 the only man Juanita had gone out with in almost three years was a cousin she had scarcely seen since childhood. She still pinned Bob's wings to her blouses and sweaters, and she still wore her engagement ring and wedding band. Sometime in 1947 she stopped wearing them. In the fall of 1947, Alvin proposed, and Juanita accepted. She felt ambivalent about marrying "a younger man." (Juanita is six years older than Alvin.) She expressed concern that she might be perceived as disloyal to Bob by remarrying "too soon." Mollie wrote her a letter saying that she approved of the remarriage—especially to Alvin (whom she knew, because he had briefly dated Emily's daughter Dorothy in high school)—and that the age difference was immaterial. Mollie reminded Juanita that she herself was two years older than Henry.

Juanita and Alvin were married in Fort Des Moines Presbyterian Church on February 14, 1948, in a morning ceremony, with just their immediate families present, including Emily and Louise and their husbands. Marilyn was Juanita's matron of honor; Jerome stood up for Alvin. After a brief wedding trip to visit one of Alvin's six sisters, the Becks settled down in the house on Diehl Avenue. The last official communication that "Mrs. Juanita Allred" received from the Office of the Adjutant General was dated March 24, 1949, and said, "The records of the Department of the Army are being amended to show that Lieutenant Allred was killed on 22 March 1944, when his plane crashed in New Guinea, between Port Moresby and Nadzab."

Alvin was hired by the Des Moines Fire Department in April 1947. In the late forties, firemen were required to live within the city limits, and Fort Des Moines was still outside those limits. In 1949, Monte St.John helped Alvin build a house within the city, and in February 1951 Juanita and Alvin moved into it, with their eight-month-old son, Arlen. A second son, Leslie, was born in 1953. Juanita had given up her job at the courthouse at the end of 1948. In 1965 she went back to work as a secretary to the director and the board of a nonprofit, nondenominational private organization that provides services to children and to families in trouble. Alvin retired from the Fire Department, as a captain, in 1977. Juanita gave up her job in 1980. In 1981, the Becks took square-dancing lessons. Square dancing became their favorite pastime.

When the Becks left the Diehl Avenue house, Juanita threw out every letter Bob had ever written her—she felt she had to make that break with the past—but she still wore a pendant that Alvin had made for her using the small diamonds in the engagement and wedding rings Bob had put on her finger. She kept Bob's briefcase with the Army Air Forces documents, his manicure kit and iron (which she had given him), and photographs dating back to the plays in which they had appeared. She also kept a letter that the six enlisted men who had been in his crew had mailed to her on May 1, 1944. "We have no doubt that if Lt. Allred is alive that he will get back," the men had written. "He just wasn't the type to give up and he could always handle any situation that arose. . . . There wasn't a better pilot or officer in the Air Corps. We were all proud to be under his command."

The families of the twenty-one other men on the B-24 that took off on March 22, 1944, from Port Moresby and never made it to Nadzab got telegrams and follow-up letters from Acting Adjutants General similar to those that were sent to Juanita Allred. A few days after receiving a two-star telegram, Maria Geis, the wife of Second Lieutenant Raymond J. Geis, Jr., who was the B-25 copilot who had traded places with Paul Harvey, received a letter that her husband had written on March 21, 1944, the day before his twenty-first birthday. The letter's March 24 postmark and its contents were reassuring. Ray had been having fun—even when pilot training got tough he had written lighthearted poems about Army Air Corps life. He looked forward to seeing his father, a Seabee stationed in New Guinea, for the first time in over a year. He hoped that the grass skirt, the pennants, and the money he had sent from Hawaii had reached Maria. "Just think, Honey, tomorrow I will be a man," he wrote. "My my and here I am out where I can't even get a case of Scotch to celebrate. Hard luck but anyway we'll make up for it when I get back home again. I guess you know that's not so far away. . . . Be a good little girl and don't worry about me. This is more like playing Boy Scout than anything else." Ray's letter convinced Maria that the telegram was a terrible mistake, and she told the Army she refused to believe its contents. When the telegram proved to be accurate, the fact that Ray had been lost on his twenty-first birthday was particularly painful.

Ten of the passengers on 41081 had something in common with Ray Geis: they were headed for the 345th Bombardment Group (medium). In March 1943 the newly formed 345th had had orders to go to England with its B-25s, but as a result of General Kenney's first plane-begging trip to Washington it was diverted to the Southwest Pacific. The 345th went into combat in June 1943. By February 1944 the first of the original aircrews had finished their prescribed missions and were homeward bound. Geis, Staff Sergeant Thomas J. Carpenter, Jr. (an engineer-gunner), and Staff Sergeant William M. Shrake (a radio operator–gunner) were new replacements. Four members of one B-25 crew were on 41081—Second Lieutenant Emory C. Young (pilot), Second Lieutenant Melvin F. Walker (copilot), Staff Sergeant Robert C. Thompson (radio operator–gunner), and Sergeant Charles Samples, Jr. (engineer-gunner). B-25s had crews of either five or six men. A number of the crews crossed the Pacific together, and a number of the crews split up in California, with some flying new B-25s to Australia and some going to Hawaii by ship and on to Australia by transport plane, as Sergeant James A. Miller (gunner), another member of Young's crew, had done. On March 22, 1944, Samples was carrying a set of Miller's dog tags that Miller had lost in the States. Four members of a second B-25 crew—Second Lieutenant Charles R. Steiner (pilot), Second Lieutenant Stanley G. Gross (bombardier), Staff Sergeant John J. Staseowski (radio operator–gunner), and Sergeant Clint P. Butler (engineer-gunner)—were also aboard.

Eight men were on 41081 because they had been to Sydney, seven of them on furlough. They had traveled on transports to Port Moresby and were there on March 22 trying to catch rides back to their bases in or near Nadzab. One of the hitchhikers, Corporal Joseph B. Mettam, was an armorer with the 345th Bombardment Group, and five were in the ordinary Army. First Sergeant Harold Atkins, First Sergeant Weldon W. Frazier, and Staff Sergeant Frank Ginter were serving in New Guinea with small antiaircraft units. Technician Fourth Grade Joseph E. Kachorek, Jr., was a medic with a field hospital, and Private First Class Carlin E. Loop a medic assigned to an aircraft-warning battalion. Ground personnel in the Army Air Forces like Mettam had much less chance of rotating home than the aircrews did. Generally, Army enlisted men were also overseas for the duration of the war and got fewer furloughs than aircrews. Though they were not exposed to the hazards of combat flying, their life was more tedious.

In February 1942 Frank Ginter had sailed from San Francisco (where he had been quartered at a dog track) for Australia. Two and a half weeks later, the ship sailed into Brisbane, where his unit set up camp at a racetrack. Since early 1942, he had been helping to protect airstrips in northern Australia and New Guinea. In the fall of 1943, he got a letter from his brother Joe, who was working as a tool-and-die maker at an aircraft factory back home in Buffalo. When Joe wrote that Frank was better off, because of the rationing back home, Frank decided that it was time to sound off about Army life from Gusap, a fighter base near Nadzab, where his unit was stationed.

Did you ever try eating rice and sardines three times a day for three months? Try it sometime for breakfast, I'll bet you won't go for seconds . . . it makes me burn every time I read about people back home complaining about rationing and the hours they have to work. How about the hours we put in and what about our pay? Twenty-four hours a day we're on the go and no days off. Every time the moon is up, we have to spend half the night waiting for all hell to break loose. It's no fun getting out of bed at 2:30 or 3 in the morning and standing in a slit trench or fox hole, especially if it's raining and 9 times out of 10 [it is]. How would you like to wear a full uniform at all times and not be able to shed your shirt because of being bit and getting malaria and the temperature up around 115 degrees or 120 degrees? . . . How would you like going to bed every night at 8 or 9 o'clock or sit up and look at the same faces you have been looking at for the last 3 years and argue about everything? Silly little things that sometimes lead to a battle royal. Every day it's the same old routine and we more than welcome Tojo whenever he appears. Every time we shoot our guns and the raid is over, it gives us new arguing material. . . . Right now we've got a lull, but the moon will soon be bright enough to start night raids. That's really fun, the sky looks like a movie premiere with all the lights and the fourth of July effect. What a barrage, large guns going off overhead and the concussion enough to knock one on his hinder. . . . We're over here doing our best, and making in one month what the average man back home is knocking out in one week. . . . Compared with the people back home we're paupers. In a couple of months we'll have [had] two years of this . . . and no relief in sight. . . . Don't get angry just because I flew off the beam, really it's not too bad after the first 2 years.

The only officer on 41081 among the seven men returning from leave was Second Lieutenant Harvey E. Landrum, a P-39 pilot with the 82nd Reconnaissance Squadron. Between his arrival in New Guinea, early in December 1943, and March 8, 1944, Landrum had flown fifty-one missions; fighter pilots flew shorter, more frequent missions than bomber pilots.

The eighth passenger returning from Sydney, where he had been hospitalized for two weeks because of an infection, was Stanley C. Lawrence. Staff Sergeant Lawrence, a gunner, had been flying combat missions in B-25s with the 38th Bomb Group for over a year. On December 1, 1942, six planes from his squadron bombed a Japanese convoy over the Bismarck Sea, near New Britain. The bombers were intercepted by twelve Japanese fighters, which concentrated on making head-on strafing passes at the leading flight of three bombers. All three bombers maintained the attack and scored at least one direct hit on a destroyer but were damaged by the Zeros' guns. One B-25 burst into flames and crashed, and one was so badly damaged that it was forced to cease bomb runs. With the Zeros still attacking, Lawrence's pilot elected to reduce speed in order to protect the crippled airplane, and led the flight back to the base. The pilot was awarded the Distinguished Flying Cross; the rest of the crew received Air Medals for meritorious achievement. In the fall of 1943 (putting in for awards and writing up citations takes time), Lawrence's hometown paper published a photograph of General Kenney pinning the Air Medal on Lawrence, and quoted the citation. Only a few months later, the newspaper reported that Lawrence was missing in action.

Captain Charles R. Barnard, 0-734785, a bombardier with the 43rd Bombardment Group, was the twenty-second man on 41081. Between July 1943 and January 1944 Barnard and his crew had completed their missions, as had another crew, on which the bombardier was Phil Barber, 0-734784, a roommate of Barnard's from their days in Bombardiers' school, which accounted for the closeness of their serial numbers. Barnard and Barber had been promoted to first lieutenant in November 1943. Both men were married and became fathers while they were overseas; Barnard's daughter was born in September, Barber's in October. Barber was eager to see his baby and left New Guinea as soon as he was eligible to go home. Barnard was a highly regarded bombardier who had been awarded a Distinguished Flying Cross for a mission on which his B-24 had been hit and its navigator killed. He had been recommended for promotion to captain by the 43rd Bombardment Group but had to agree to spend three more months overseas in his new rank to secure promotion. The 43rd had told him he would get his captaincy without having to fly another mission. Barber's pilot and copilot had also advised him to stay on, because he wouldn't have a chance to make captain in the States—it was a pilots' war. Barnard got his promotion, a leave in Australia, and an assignment to the Replacement Center in Port Moresby. On February 29, 1944, he wrote to his sister that he hoped to leave New Guinea within six weeks. On March 22, he was en route from the Replacement Center at Jackson's to 43rd Bomb Group headquarters, in Nadzab, to pick up his orders to go home.

Between April 1944 and January 1946 the eight other wives of the men on 41081 were subjected to a series of disheartening experiences like the ones that Juanita Allred endured. As "gratuitous bailees," they took receipt of musty, unsavable clothes, and the months of uncertainty took a toll on them. "If I'd received a telegram in April 1944 telling me Keith Holm had been killed in action, it would have been easier," Doris says. "Certain death is something you have to face up to, but when someone you love is declared missing you hope against hope, and that is a terrible thing. It takes a long time before you force yourself to decide that you must start over and go on with your life." Between 1946 and 1958, all but one of the wives remarried.

A mother will keep hoping long after it is unreasonable to hope. Years after their daughters-in-law had remarried, most of the mothers of the men on 41081 continued to harbor fantasies that their sons were alive and perhaps living happily in the jungle with native women. After Charles Samples, Jr., was declared missing, his mother sent a fruitcake to his last address. When the box in which she had shipped it came back empty, she regarded that as proof that the cake had reached her son. She kept writing to Charles, and gave the letters to her younger son, Donald. He never told his mother that he didn't mail them.

Stanley Gross was Jewish. Some people of Jewish faith follow the custom of remembering a deceased relative by giving a child a name beginning with the same initial as one of the relative's names. In April 1945 Stanley's sister Perle had a daughter and wanted to name her Stacy. Bertha Gross, Stanley's mother, wouldn't hear of it. She didn't believe that her son was gone for good. Perle named her daughter Marilyn. Bertha Gross was the mother of eight children. Two of her daughters died after Stanley's disappearance. She accepted their deaths because of the finality. Until her own death, in 1975, whenever Mrs. Gross spoke of Stanley she said simply, "He's gone." Where he had gone she didn't say. The former wives and the brothers and sisters gradually became resigned to never knowing any more about the fate of the plane and the twenty-two men on it than they did in 1944.

On April 30, 1982, Juanita Beck spotted a headline in the Des Moines *Tribune* which read, WWII PLANE REMAINS FOUND IN ISLAND JUNGLE. Enough of the details given in the accompanying Associated Press story about a B-24 that had just been found in Papua New Guinea by a team from the United States Army's Central Identification Laboratory in Hawaii matched the information she had received from the Army in the 1940s to persuade her that the CIL team had recovered Bob's plane. That same day, Howard Allred, a vice-president and general counsel of a large insurance company in Oklahoma, read a similar version of the AP story in the Tulsa *Tribune* and reached the same conclusion. Over the years, the Becks had remained close to the Allreds. Juanita is "Aunt Juanita" to Emily's daughter Betty, and Alvin is "Uncle Alvin" to Betty's children. Juanita got in touch with the Directorate of Casualty and Memorial Affairs in Alexandria, Virginia, which presided over the CIL in 1982. In May she learned that the plane was Bob's and that she would be informed "if and when the identification processing was complete."

Emily assumed that Bob would be identified, and called Juanita to ask how she felt about burying him in Des Moines. Juanita said that neither she nor her father—Monte St.John was then an alert eighty-nine-year-old, who recalled with joy the houses he had built with his sons-in-law ("two mighty fine boys")—placed great value on visiting cemeteries. Twice a year, Alvin, Juanita, and Mr. St.John decorated the graves of Jessie St.John (who died in 1971), Alvin's parents, and several other relatives buried in Des Moines. Emily then proposed, as an alternative, burying Bob in Whittier, California, where Mollie (who died in 1953), Henry (who died in 1962), and Hazel and Margaret and their husbands were buried. Juanita and Louise were unenthusiastic about that suggestion. Bob had no connection with California, and no relatives who had known him lived there. Howard had been to Hawaii several times, had seen Punchbowl, the National Memorial Cemetery of the Pacific, and thought it would be appropriate to have Bob buried along with thirteen thousand other men who had lost their lives in the South Pacific during the Second World War. Juanita, Louise, and Emily concurred.

The initial shock experienced by the families of the men on 41081, whether they had read the AP story, or learned of the recovery of the plane in January 1983 after Tadao Furue had identified all twenty-two remains, was followed by relief. "It was a relief to learn that Charles hadn't suffered," Donald Samples observed after studying the photographs of the crash site, the skeletal diagrams, an Anthropological Narrative that Furue had written, and other material that the CIL had compiled. "No one walked away from that crash. No one was taken prisoner by the Japanese."

To newspapers and television stations in the towns and cities where the families of the men on 41081 lived, the plane's recovery was a "human-interest" feature. Reporters descended on the brothers and sisters and former wives, Middle Americans who had had little or no previous experience with the press. They found many of the reporters either "pushy" or inaccurate, or both. After reading one story in the Des Moines *Register,* which stated initially that Juanita's first marriage had occurred in 1938 and then that she had married Bob Allred two years after his high-school graduation, in 1934, she asked the writer (who had also made other mistakes) why he didn't learn to add.

A national weekly magazine whose pages are customarily devoted to celebrities—actors, movie stars, rock-and-roll singers, sports stars, and royalty—decided to run four pages of photographs and text about 41081. Juanita Beck was one of the relatives who consented to an interview. She brought some of Bob's school records down from her attic and fetched his briefcase from a basement storage closet to show the magazine's representative, a young woman. When the reporter learned that Bob had played football in high school, she asked what position he had played.

"Line, I think," Juanita answered.

"Gee, I seem to know more about my boyfriend than you know about your former husband," the reporter commented.

"Would you after thirty-nine years?" Juanita inquired.

The reporters had come into the lives of families who were preoccupied with making burial arrangements and were far more wrought up than the reporters realized. Most families had suppressed their grief during the period between 1944 and 1946. No disappearance is made final by a bureaucratic "presumptive finding of death." The families were doing their grieving thirty-nine years later. To Karl Shrake, it seemed as if his brother had died in 1983, and not in 1944. Maria Ulrich says,

"My life was shattered in 1944, and in 1983 it was shattered again after those many years of trying to forget." A couple of widows felt awkward talking to reporters in front of their second husbands, who showed resentment at all the unexpected attention being paid to their wives' first loves.

Looking at old photographs and letters and remembering things they didn't know they still remembered made many brothers and sisters sad. The young men on 41081 had grown up during the Depression and had not had a chance to enjoy much before their lives were snuffed out. At twenty-seven, Robert Allred was the fourth-oldest man on the plane, and the only one who had graduated from college. The families of most of the enlisted men made Henry and Mollie seem affluent. Carlin Loop and John Staseowski had had to drop out of high school and join the Civilian Conservation Corps. Clint Butler had dropped out of high school at fifteen, fibbed about his age, and enlisted in the service. Butler's fib was discovered, and he had to reenlist. Harold Atkins' father died in 1926, when Harold was five; his mother died of cancer in 1927, after making arrangements to place her nine children in foster homes. Atkins dropped out of high school, joined the CCC, and then enlisted in the Army; it was one of the best options a poor boy had at the time, and, like Weldon Frazier, he rose from private to first sergeant and planned to make the Army a career.

The newspapers printed photographs of the young men who had been lost and found, and in a number of cases their photographs were displayed at their funerals. "I was surprised to walk into the funeral home and see a photograph of Keith in uniform," Doris Holm Nelson says. "I looked at him, and I thought, 'There he is, forever young.' A group of his boyhood friends were in one pew. They were men in their sixties. Most of them were wearing bifocals or trifocals, and what hair they had left was gray. But if they had paunches and wrinkles, they also had children and grandchildren and length of days. I wondered what, if anything, went through their minds as they looked at Keith's photograph. I thought that none of them would have traded places with him. He didn't have a chance to live a life."

Among the hundreds of thousands of people who read the AP story about the B-24 wreckage discovered in Papua New Guinea in the spring of 1982 was a man named Joseph L. Bell. According to the AP story carried in Bell's local newspaper, the Idaho Falls *Post-Register,* "the pilot and/or the navigator at the time were from the 22nd Bomb Group," but a photograph that ran with the story showed the top two-thirds of the plane's crumpled right tail fin, which was embellished with a skull—part of the skull-and-crossed-bombs insignia of the 90th Bomb Group, the Jolly Rogers. Joe Bell had trained as a bombardier at Biggs Field in the summer and fall of 1943, had been assigned to the 22nd Bomb Group in January 1944 and knew that Allred and Holm had flown out of Port Moresby in March 1944 and had never reached Nadzab. Most of the bomb groups that were part of the Fifth Air Force during the Second World War, including the 22nd and the 90th, regularly publish newsletters that are mailed to the dues-paying men on their rosters. Bell, who was in the 22nd's 408th Squadron, sent the man who gets out the 22nd's newsletter a copy of the AP story, along with a note. "I believe it's possible that Lt. Allred's crew could have been one of those transferred to the 90th Bomb Group and orders so stating may not have been processed, which would account for the fact that a 22nd B.G. pilot was flying a 90th B.G. plane." The crash also came to the attention of the 345th Bombardment Group (the Air Apaches), the 43rd Bombardment Group (Ken's Men), and the 38th Bombardment Group (the Sun Setters).

The colonel who had written to Juanita Allred in 1946 to say that the chances of locating a crash in the jungle were virtually nonexistent unless one had previous knowledge of its location was not wrong. Had it not been for Bruce Hoy, it is almost certain that the remains of the twenty-two men on 41081 would still be lying on a ridge leading to Mt. Thumb. Bruce Hoy receives the 22nd Bomb Group's newsletter. When he read Joe Bell's letter in the June 1982 issue, he knew that Bell was mistaken. The CIL had Allred's and Holm's missing-in-action files with them in Papua New Guinea, and both men were still with the 22nd on the day of the crash, but what were they doing on a 90th Bombardment Group plane?

"Airplanes are my life," Hoy often says, without hyperbole. He is as deeply interested in a plane's life story as a Daughter of the American Revolution is in her family tree. As soon as he saw 41081's nose on the mountainside, he knew that the B-24 had flown with the 90th Bombardment Group's 320th Squadron. A pilot in the 320th had named his plane Moby Dick, after Melville's mythical white whale. One day in December 1943, after the pilot had become the 320th's CO, he found that the plane's nose had been painted. It had a white eye behind the bombardier's Plexiglas window, black eyelashes, a red mouth, and sharks' teeth. No one knew if the teeth reflected literary ignorance or artistic license. Soon most 320th planes sported identical nose decor, and the 320th became known as the Moby Dick Squadron.

After Hoy had 41081's right tail fin on his premises, he took a good look at what he believes is the only such example of Jolly Rogers artwork in any museum on earth. To his practiced eye, the numbers appeared odd. They had not been sprayed on in a factory—the *4* didn't have the telltale stencil breaks. Upon closer inspection, he saw that all the digits had been painted on by hand, the *2*, the *0*, and the *8* in stencil style—he could see the brush strokes. When he wiped the tail off with a rag, he saw the numbers 41127 underneath 41081. At some time during its career, 41081 had had right-tail-fin trouble and had received a right tail fin from another 90th Bombardment Group plane. (In a 90th Bombardment Group history, there was an undated photograph of 41127 flying high.) Planes were frequently cannibalized. Hoy had read of one bomber that contained bits and pieces from thirteen aircraft.

Consolidated Aircraft was the designer and major builder of the B-24, though four other companies also produced B-24s, including the Ford Motor Company's plant in Willow Run, Michigan; 41081 had rolled out of Consolidated's San Diego factory in April 1943. It cost the government $297,687. No. 41081 spent part of the summer in Texas—it was at Biggs Field, apparently being test-hopped, in July, a month before Bob Allred got there. It reached Australia in late August and was assigned to the Fifth Air Force in late September.

After consulting a few of hundreds of rolls of microfilm he had dealing with the history of the Fifth Air Force, Bruce Hoy knew that 41081 had flown missions on October 29, 1943, and December 14, 1943. He later learned from one of hundreds of American pen pals that it had also flown missions on January 18,

19, 23, and 25, 1944. (Expended rounds of ammunition were found at the crash site; they were presumably left over from the missions.) According to the Missing Air Crew Report, the plane's owner on March 22, 1944, was the Fifth Bomber Command. Hoy checked the 320th's weekly status-and-operations reports from January to March. Not a single 320th plane had been lost in combat during those two months, nor was there any mention of a B-24's being transferred from the 320th Squadron to the Fifth Bomber Command. Between March 5 and March 11, two B-24Ds were transferred out of the squadron. They did not go to a depot for repair or overhaul—they were simply transferred to another organization. Hoy believes that one of the two was 42-41081, and that it went to the Replacement Center. Because Hoy is such a precise man, he is exasperated by the imprecision of the Fifth Air Force's historical records. "For unknown reasons, most histories completely ignore the aircraft side of the story, and in a lot of cases aren't worth a crumpet," he says. "It is a terrible pity that no squadron in the 90th recorded full information concerning serial numbers on its weekly status-and-operations reports."

To Hoy, 41081 was not just a death ship. It had been a life ship that had carried men safely to and from targets like Vunakanau Airdrome, just southeast of Rabaul, and Pilelo Island, near Arawe, on the other end of New Britain. He suspected that it had a name as well as a number, and he was right. A crew that had flown 41081 fairly regularly in late 1943 and early 1944 was traced by means of the 90th Bombardment Group's newsletter. Its pilot was a man named Morgan F. Terry, and, in that era of the comic strip *Terry and the Pirates,* the crew members were called Terry's Pirates. The crew had named the plane, and the name, painted in yellow-brown block letters in a wavy line on the fuselage, was Weezie. Richard Grills, one of Weezie's gunners, remembers how the plane got its name. "Some plane engines purr, but this one's made a funny sound," Grills says. "They sort of wheezed, so we called our ship Weezie." A 320th Squadron mechanic remembers that one plane in his custody, The Eager Beaver, was popular, because it flew so well. Weezie, with its odd-sounding engines, was not popular. Still, when members of the crew read about the end to which Weezie had come, they said that the plane had never given them any trouble.

In May 1982 Juanita Beck wrote to a civilian in Casualty and Memorial Affairs to ask whether there would be an investigation regarding the cause of the crash. The answer she received was that an expert crash-site investigator at Norton Air Force Base in California had been called and had said that "due to the passage of time and the inaccessibility of the site, it would not be possible to determine the cause."

Bruce Hoy does not pretend to be an expert crash-site investigator, and wishes that one would be sent up to Mt. Thumb. Still, he thinks that "even a glorified desk jockey" can cast some light on the circumstances of the crash of 41081. In 1944, he says, nothing definite enough to be properly called a flight plan was given to a pilot, but Allred was given advice on the best possible course to follow on the afternoon of March 22. One thing is certain: Allred did not follow the course outlined on the Missing Air Crew Report. If he had flown 50 miles southeast to Hood Point, his plane could not have hit the side of Mt. Thumb—which is 40 miles northeast of Port Moresby—a few minutes after taking off from Jackson's. None of the many GI Elgin watches found at the crash site had a minute hand, but two had hour hands: the watches had stopped shortly before the hour hands reached the 3—perhaps seven or eight minutes before the hour. Allred had taken off at 2:37 P.M. If he had flown northeast at an approximate speed of 150 miles per hour, climbing at an approximate rate of 500 feet a minute for sixteen minutes (say, from 2:37 P.M. to 2:53 P.M.), Allred would have been about 40 miles from Port Moresby at an altitude of about 8400 feet.

Obviously, no pilot would purposely head for the side of an 11,000-foot mountain. Hoy suspects that Allred was heading for the most famous shortcut through the Owen Stanleys, the Kokoda Pass, which is only 14 miles from Mt. Thumb. Paul Harvey had flown through "the Gap"—as the Kokoda Pass was often called—on the B-25 on the morning of March 22; no other route would have put him in Nadzab only forty-five minutes after the plane took off from Port Moresby. Harvey had been told about the Kokoda Pass while he was at the Replacement Center; it is likely that Allred had, too. Perhaps Allred had forgotten that what is relatively safe on a clear morning is apt to be perilous in the afternoon, when the Owen Stanleys are almost always shrouded in clouds. As General Kenney wrote in his autobiography, in bad weather one "would have to go to 15,000 feet to play safe in clearing the range."

Bruce Hoy and the pilots who knew Bob Allred believe that he exercised his privilege as first pilot to disregard the suggested route, which was longer and safer. By midafternoon, he was probably in a hurry to get to Nadzab. Eighty-four hundred feet was an altitude commonly used to fly through the Gap. "The plane probably strayed off course," Hoy says. "At that altitude and at that time of day, Allred would almost certainly have been flying in clouds. He found a cloud with a rock in it."

The CO who had written to Juanita Allred in 1944 was accurate in saying that weather and terrain accounted for more airplanes than combat flying. Past events never respond fully to inquiry, but in 1985, when many more facts had been learned about 41081's last flight than were known in 1982, a Royal Australian Air Force historian in Canberra observed, "High ground, bad weather, overconfident and inexperienced young pilots. The mountains of New Guinea are littered with their aircraft."

While the 22nd Bombardment Group was stationed in Nadzab in 1944, each of its squadrons kept a junior officer in Australia to buy eggs and fresh produce and liquor and beer to supplement the dreary diet at Nadzab, where even Coca-Cola syrup was in short supply, and pancakes and marmalade were a relentless combination that made men cringe 40 years later. A "fat cat" (a war-weary plane) flew down periodically to fetch the provisions. Crews took the beer along on test hops: it cooled as well in a few hours at 12,000 feet as it would have in a refrigerator on the ground, and the men didn't have refrigerators on the ground.

On nonmission days, the officers played bridge and poker (Sewell's thatched hut had two card tables in round-the-clock use) and also softball, volleyball, and football, and built an officers' club. Occasionally, a "red alert" sounded, and they took refuge in slit trenches they had dug next to their tents. Missions were frequently called off because of bad weather, but between March or April and the end of July, most crews had flown between fifteen and twenty missions. By the end of July, there was little left of the Japanese Air Force on New Guinea. At the end of August, General MacArthur moved his headquarters to Hollandia, which had been the last major Japanese airbase on the island. Several weeks earlier, the 22nd had begun its move to Owi, one of the Schouten Islands, less than 900 miles from Mindanao, the southernmost island of the Philippines. The New Guinea campaign was over. From Owi's coral runways, the 22nd flew missions to the Celebes, bombed the oil fields at Balikpapan, Borneo (known as "the Ploesti of the Pacific"), and hit Mindanao. MacArthur's "I shall return" campaign to the Philippines was well under way.

The 22nd was supposed to move to Leyte in mid-November, but the move snafued. The metal runways that were laid on Leyte sank in the mud, and none of the 22nd's B-24s could take off from them, so the 22nd moved to Angaur, a small island in the Palaus. From Angaur, the group staged its first daylight raid on Clark Field, Luzon, and caught the Japanese unaware. The B-24s destroyed and damaged an estimated two hundred enemy planes in the air and on the ground.

Island-hopping continued apace. On January 21, 1945, the 22nd moved to Samar, in the Philippines. On February 1, David Becker flew his last mission—to Corregidor—which gave him 100.81 points and, on February 28, his going-home orders. He flew to San Francisco, arriving on Sunday, March 4; took the train to Terre Haute, arriving on Sunday the eleventh; and kept faith with his diary—he was married on Sunday, March 18.

Clark Field became the 22nd's base in March 1945. Its targets then included Formosa and Hong Kong, and, on March 21, Larry Wulf led the 19th Squadron on its first daylight raid on China. By the time the 22nd moved to Okinawa, back to Luzon, and back to Okinawa in May 1946, Luke Sewell was one of the last men from Biggs still with the 22nd. He was there by choice. Sewell had spent four years working in a lumberyard, rising from yardman to assistant manager, before receiving his "Greetings" card from the President, in 1941. He was eligible to go home in February 1945 and had the right to return to his job after the war, but he knew there would be a lot of men ahead of him for the manager's job. He departed for the United States in December 1946, when he couldn't get any more extensions overseas. By the time Sewell retired, in 1972, he had spent over thirty-one years in the Army and the Air Force. "Army Air Corps life just grew on me," he says. "I'd found a home."

Every August, the 22nd Bombardment Group holds a reunion. In 1985 the reunion was held in a hotel outside Washington, D.C., with three hundred and two men and their wives and guests in attendance. Among those who came to the reunion to attend the business meetings and the banquet, go on the sightseeing tours, and trade war stories over the free liquor served in the hospitality suite were Jane and Hy Webster (one of four couples from Biggs with whom Juanita has kept in touch since 1944); Adolph Leirer and his wife, Helen, whom he met on one leave to Sydney in 1944, dated on another leave in 1944, and married on a third trip to Sydney, to ferry a B-24 there for the RAAF, in 1945; Frances and Bob Dent (retired and raising cattle in Texas); Larry Wulf, a widower; Paul Harvey and his second wife, Rosina; Colonel and Mrs. Virgil R. Sewell and their son, daughter-in-law, and two grandsons; and Colonel and Mrs. Lee Shelton and Lieutenant Colonel and Mrs. Lee M. Shelton II.

Another man present who felt fortunate to be at the reunion was Bill Bounds. On March 22, 1944, First Lieutenant William H. Bounds, a navigator, was in Port Moresby trying to get back to Nadzab after a leave in Sydney. He got on Bob Allred's plane, didn't like its looks, and later—when an investigation was being conducted to determine whether Landrum had been on the plane—signed an affidavit saying he had got off because he didn't consider the aircraft safe.

Fred Moore, who served as an ordnance chief with the 345th Bombardment Group and attends its reunions, is another man who was briefly aboard 41081. "When I looked inside and saw that mass of humanity, I said no," he says. "I wasn't about to stand on a narrow catwalk, so I took my B-4 bag and left. I caught a ride around two-thirty with a plane from my squadron. The weather was terrible, so the pilot followed the coastline southeast all the way to Milne Bay and then turned north. As we approached Lae, the pilot was flying under the weather at about 150 feet. We could see native boats on the water. The flight took two hours—I remember we almost missed chow."

Ever since Oliver Clark got out of the nose of the B-24 that had engine trouble on the morning of March 22, 1944, and didn't get back on the plane in the afternoon, he has counted his blessings. So has John Robert Campbell. "Not getting on that plane was a gift of fate," Campbell says. "I guess my time hadn't come."

There were more people at Robert Allred's funeral on March 3, 1983, than Juanita Beck had anticipated the previous May, when she, Emily, Howard, and Louise decided as a family to have Bob buried in Punchbowl. Among the twenty-five men and women gathered under a metal canopy that had been set up near the grave were Alvin and Juanita; Emily and her husband; Howard and his wife; two of Howard's sons and their wives; Louise and one of her daughters; six friends from Iowa who were on vacation in Hawaii at the time; the only man on the 22nd Bombardment Group's roster who lives in Honolulu, and who was proud to represent the Red Raiders; and Tadao Furue and Leslie Stewart, from the CIL.

On a warm, breezy morning, with cardinals and helicopters flying overhead, the chaplain read the Twenty-third Psalm. He led the gathering in reciting the Lord's Prayer. He spoke of the grief that had been ended and the questions that had been answered "as we commit the remains of Robert to their resting place." Seven riflemen fired three volleys. A bugler played the heartache of Taps.

Juanita Beck tried to make arrangements with a florist in Honolulu to deliver flowers to her first husband's grave three times a year—on Bob's birthday, at Christmas, and on the anniversary of the crash—but the arrangements did not work out. Long before she gave up on the florist, in late 1984, and started using the services of Florists' Transworld Delivery, she learned that someone had succeeded where she had failed. A friend of Louise's took a trip to Hawaii in May 1983 and saw multicolored flowers at Bob Allred's grave. A year later, Paul Allred, nineteen, the oldest son of Howard's oldest son, Dr. Robert L. All-red, spent a semester studying at the University of Hawaii. On Sunday, May 27, 1984, the day before Memorial Day, he went to Punchbowl. As he approached his granduncle's grave, he saw a man standing in front of it gazing into the distance. In a flower container near the headstone was a bouquet of long-stemmed roses. Paul Allred waited until the man turned toward him, and then introduced himself, whereupon the man introduced himself. He was Tadao Furue.

Robert Allred was the first man Furue had identified at the CIL to be buried at the National Memorial Cemetery of the Pacific, and after the funeral service was over he had made a point of paying his respects to Robert Allred's family. Furue told Paul how much it had meant to him to meet Bob Allred's former wife, his sisters and brother, and his nephews, and now meant to him to meet his grandnephew. He said that he had brought twenty-two roses—one for each man on the plane.

Tadao Furue visits Bob Allred's grave at least twice a year. He keeps a gallon of water in the trunk of his car (if the radiator leaks he wants to be prepared to fill it) and also a roll of paper towels (he has used them to wipe his hands after tightening a battery cable and after changing a flat tire). On his visits, he always cleans the headstone and always brings flowers. No. 41081 had been Tadao Furue's most difficult and time-consuming case. As it happened, it had also taken him longer to piece together the remains of Robert Allred than those of any other man on the plane. Because Furue accepts sole responsibility for each identification he makes, he has a special feeling for Robert Allred. As the commander of the aircraft, Robert Allred had chosen the course. He bore the responsibility for the plane's meeting the mountain.

ACKNOWLEDGMENTS

ALTHOUGH IT MUST be apparent to every reader of this book that *A Missing Plane* could not have been written without the help of Bruce Hoy, Tadao Furue, and Juanita Beck, their help was so prodigiously and patiently given over a period of three years that I hope it does not seem redundant to express my formal gratitude to them here.

For Part I, I was fortunate to have had as collaborators Lt. Col. David C. Rosenberg, Sgt. David E. Kelly, Sgt. Jay Shawn Warner, Sgt. Richard B. Huston, Sgt. John J. Hennessy, George Washington Gardner, Charlie Obi, Peap Tomon, Beverly and Adrian Nisbet, Ambassador M. Virginia Schafer, Pastor Lester Lock, Pastor Chester Stanley, and Pastor L. S. Weber.

Among the generous contributors to Part II were Col. Joe Gleason, Lt. Col. William R. Flick, Lt. Col. Keith Schneider, Major Kenneth Shanabruch, Sgt. Douglas L. Howard, John Rogers, and Joe Ruggero; Lt. Col. Johnie E. Webb, Jr., Marla Mahoney, and Leslie Stewart; George L. Brooks, Ann Mills Griffiths, Kenneth A. Gronemeyer, Robert Springer, Earlyne Thomas, Dr. John P. Adams, Dr. J. Lawrence Angel, G. Robert Lange, D.D.S., and Prof. Charles P. Warren.

Relatives of each man on 42-41081, and friends of many of the men, shared their memories with me. I am indebted to Roland Atkins and Lyle Chotena; Nancy Linthicum, Lucille Jones, Dr. Amos Barnard, Philip W. Barber, James A. Meyer, and Col. Harry N. Young; Coy Butler, Vance Butler, Lois Mohler, and Betty Williams; Glenn Carpenter; Ida Frazier, W. C. Frazier, and Owen F. Dyer; Maria Ulrich; Andrew Ginter, Robert Ambrose, George Roth, Adelbert Fleischmann, and Dr. Thomas C. McDonough; Armand Gross, Perle Jacobs, and Milly Marcus; Doris Nelson and Wallace Holm; Edward and Rita Kaczorek; Celena Diamond, Mildred Tomlin, Dick Karr, Michael

Moffitt, and William E. Pictor; Cecelia and Myron Lawrence, Marvin J. Lawrence, and Col. Robert M. Renneisen; Larry Loop, Martha Stecklein, and Isabelle Reese; Charles Mettam, Clara Sturdivant, and Fred Moore; Donald Samples; Karl M. Shrake; Walter Rybski, Bernice Brewer, Mary Hollis, Carol Opalenik, Victoria Wilder, Chester T. Rybski, William A. Fritz, Leonard Konopacki, and August J. Pasquini; Velma Zimmerman and Doris Paris; Sue Fransko; Nancy Cape, Melvin R. Walker, Robert R. Baker, and Robert Johnson; Jack Young; James A. Miller, Harry C. Hilbert, and Wendell Bean. I offer special thanks to Emily Allred, Howard W. Allred, Louise Jacobs, Alvin Beck, Betty Flint, Dr. Noble Irving, Fremont St.John, Paul Allred, Sidney L. Adams, Arthur Clark, Robert M. Keefer, William L. Keefer, and the Reverend John E. McCaw.

The veterans of the Fifth Air Force have been more than good to me. Whenever I needed information about the 22nd Bombardment Group, Adolph Leirer and Jim Merritt referred me to a fellow Red Raider who had it. Thomas C. Fetter, my favorite Jolly Roger, was always willing to use the 90th Bombardment Group's newsletter on my behalf. Ken McClure of the 345th Bombardment Group faithfully tracked down Air Apaches for me.

I owe a great deal to David Becker, Joseph L. Bell, William H. Bounds, John R. Campbell, Oliver E. Clark, Carl Cole, Harry Dallas, Cliff De Mar, Robert E. Dent, John Dorfler, O. B. Finley, Paul Harvey, J. H. MacWilliam, James H. Pitts, William Rambin, William Robertson, Col. Virgil R. Sewell, Col. Lee M. Shelton, Jim Shipler, Henry T. Webster, and Lawrence E. Wulf of the 22nd Bomb Group; to Harry Azzopardi, John Budge, Carl D. Camp, Paul Gottke, Richard Grau, Richard Grills, Jack Holmes, Charles Karhan, Tom Keyworth, Edward J. Novak, Stanley Sajdak, James B. Stone, Morgan F. Terry, A. E. Tyra, and Wiley O. Woods, Jr., of the 90th Bomb Group; to William Bauder, Lloyd Boren, Robert H. Butler, Ray Holsey, and Jean A. Jack of the 43rd Bomb Group; to Edward Egan of the 345th Bomb Group; to Ken Darrow of the 38th Bomb Group; and to Col. Forrest Thompson of the 380th Bomb Group.

It is a pleasure to acknowledge the help so many of my colleagues at *The New Yorker* have given me: Laurie Witkin, Martin

Baron, Brendan Gill, and Barbara Solonche; Eleanor Gould, Elizabeth J. Macklin, Marcia Van Meter, Kate Egan, Mary Hawthorne, and Edward Stringham; Sheila McGrath, John O'Brien, Natasha Turi, Helen Stark, Edith Agar, and Linda Plantz; John M. Murphy, Bernard J. McAteer, William J. Fitzgerald, John Broderick, Patrick J. Keogh, Victor Webb, and Raphael Hernandez; Bruce Diones, Timothy Hoey, John Paribello, Edwin Rosario, and Felix Santos; Anne Neglia Caldarera, Patricia Goering, Rose Marano, Robert Gerin, and Randall Short. I gratefully acknowledge my debt to William Shawn, who encouraged me to undertake this project; to John Bennet for his exemplary editing; to Christopher A. Kenny for his careful checking; and to Peter Canby for his moral support and fine fact checking.

I am also thankful to Suzanne E. Thorin and Bruce Martin of the Research Facilities Office of the Library of Congress; and to Alan Williams, Melissa Carlson, Karen Mayer, Richard Nicholls, Gypsy da Silva, Sandro Renz, and Carol Catt of Putnam. No roll call of those who made this book possible would be complete without the names of Lt. Col. Ervan L. Amidon, Col. William T. Carter, John Fairey, Col. David Farnham, Robert J. Graves, Patti Domville Hall, J. B. Hampshire, William C. Heimdahl, Robert Lescher, Maria Losada, Robert McGuire, Robert Kendall Piper, Margo and Mark Shanley, Robert van der Linden, David C. Vaughter, and Col. Wilbur Weedin. Brian Senn set me down on Mt. Thumb one morning in his helicopter and circled above that limitless sea of green on another morning until he found me and brought me safely back to Port Moresby from the mountainside where, some thirty-nine years earlier, a plane had lost its way.

ABOUT THE AUTHOR

SUSAN SHEEHAN is the author of five books, most recently *Kate Quinton's Days* published in 1984. She has written articles primarily for *The New Yorker*, but also for *The New York Times* and other magazines. In 1983 she won the Pulitzer Prize for General Non-Fiction for *Is There No Place on Earth for Me?* She lives in Washington, D.C., with her husband, the writer Neil Sheehan, and their two daughters, Maria and Catherine.